Less Than Equals

Part 2

of

The Ambition & Destiny Series

By
VL McBeath

Less Than Equals
By VL McBeath

Editing services provided by Wendy Janes (www.WendyProof. co.uk) and Susan Buchanan (www.perfectproseservices.com)

Cover design by Michelle Abrahall (www.michelleabrahall.com)

ISBN: 978-0-9955708-4-9 (Kindle Edition)
978-0-9955708-5-6 (Paperback)

Main category – FICTION / Historical
Other category – FICTION / Sagas

First Edition

Explanatory Notes

Meal times

In the United Kingdom, as in many parts of the world, meal times are referred to by a variety of names. Based on traditional working-class practices in northern England in the nineteenth century, the following terms have been used in this book:

Breakfast: The meal eaten upon rising each morning.

Dinner: The meal eaten around midday. This may be a hot or cold meal depending on the day of the week and a person's occupation.

Tea: Not to be confused with the high tea of the aristocracy or the beverage of the same name, tea was the meal eaten at the end of the working day, typically around five or six o'clock. This could either be a hot or cold meal.

Money

In the nineteenth century, the currency in the United Kingdom was Pounds, Shillings and Pence.

- There were twenty shillings to each pound and twelve pence to a shilling.
- A crown and half crown were five shillings and two shillings and sixpence, respectively.
- A guinea was one pound, one shilling (i.e. twenty-one shillings).

For ease of reference, it can be assumed that at the time of the story £1 is equivalent to approximately £100 in 2018.

(Ref: https://www.bankofengland.co.uk/monetary-policy/inflation)

For further information on Victorian England visit:
https://valmcbeath.com/victorian-era-england-1837-1901/

Please note: This book is written in UK English
It is recommended that *Less Than Equals* is read after Part 1: *Hooks & Eyes*

To Emma and Sarah
Never underestimate how far we've come

Previous Books
in
The Ambition & Destiny Series

A Short Story Prequel: ***Condemned by Fate***

Part 1: ***Hooks & Eyes***

Get a copy of *Condemned by Fate* for FREE.

Sign up to a no-spam newsletter with further information and exclusive content about the series.

Details can be found at:

https://valmcbeath.com

The Jackson and Wetherby Family Tree

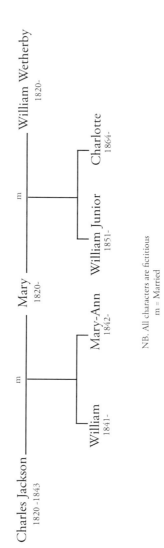

Charles Jackson
1820 -1843

Mary
1820-

William Wetherby
1820-

m

m

William
1841-

Mary-Ann
1842-

William Junior
1851-

Charlotte
1864-

NB. All characters are fictitious
m = Married

Chapter 1

Birmingham, Warwickshire, England. October 1865

WILLIAM LEANED FORWARD AND KISSED the cheek his mother offered him. After the bickering of the last few months, it was performed more out of duty than affection, but it was done now. He was free to go. He straightened up and climbed into the carriage that waited for him as the coachman stood to one side. With a final glance at the tear-stained face of his mother, he eased himself into his seat, placing his hat on his knee.

As the carriage moved away, his new employer Mr Watkins welcomed him. William had known him for almost eight years and usually his manner was formal, but today he smiled as he offered William his hand. William returned the gesture, extending his greeting to Mrs Watkins who sat opposite her husband, but it was a cursory gesture. All he wanted to do was focus on the young woman sitting opposite him. It was two years since he had last seen her and being so close to her now aroused feelings he hadn't experienced before. She looked beautiful with a pale blue bonnet that framed the ringlets around her face and set off her blue-grey eyes, eyes that danced mischievously when she smiled at him. William's heart pounded as he imagined them being alone together, but as his eyes left her face to appreciate the contours of her dress, Mr Watkins broke the silence.

"We've found an excellent property in Handsworth, Mr Jackson, I trust you'll be comfortable."

William jumped at the sound of his name and turned to listen to Mr Watkins.

"It's larger than the houses around Summer Lane. It has two reception rooms and a scullery downstairs. Then there are two bedrooms on the first floor and a further two on the top floor. You'll be in a room at the top. A domestic servant will be in the other."

"Thank you, that sounds marvellous." He turned back to face Miss Watkins, but Mr Watkins continued.

"That's not the best part though. It has a back garden with stabling, and once we're settled, I'm going to purchase my own carriage."

William let out a gasp. "Did you tell Mr Wetherby? I remember when I was a small boy he told me he would have his own carriage one day. He hasn't managed it yet but if anything gets him to move to Handsworth that will be it."

Mr Watkins laughed. "No, I didn't tell your stepfather. I didn't tell him I'd bought the house either. That will give him something to think about. You've reminded me though, I've agreed with him that I'll take some housekeeping money from your wages. I hope that's what you expected."

"I'd no idea what to expect, but it doesn't surprise me. Mr Wetherby likes to organise everything." William turned and gazed out of the window. Wasn't that one of the reasons he was leaving? Even Mr Watkins had been forced to delay his move to Handsworth by six months until Mr Wetherby had found a replacement for William. Why it had taken so long, William didn't know, but he was free now. He just needed to make the most of it.

When they arrived at the property, William thought Mr Watkins had done it a disservice such was its appearance compared to the houses in Birmingham. It was still part of a terrace, constructed of red brick, but it was much larger than he'd expected and it stood on a wide tree-lined street. To the left of the front door was a bay window topped with ornate arches, covered by a roof of lead. On the first floor, a window sat above the bay with a second positioned above the front door. A dormer window on the second floor finished the design.

William let out a whistle. "You've bought this?"

"Impressive, isn't it?" Mr Watkins said. "We should be comfortable here. Now, let's get the bags and we can go inside."

Mrs Watkins, a short, plump woman in her mid-forties, led the way to the front door where they were greeted by Ruby, the maid. Once inside, William stood open-mouthed. He had never been inside a house like this before. The hallway was spacious with doors leading to the front parlour, the back living room and, at the end of the passage, a scullery. Partway down the hall, opposite the door to the back room, stairs led to the first floor.

William and Mr Watkins took the bags to the bedrooms, where the furniture had already been delivered and set in place. When they returned downstairs, Mrs Watkins had ordered tea and was arranging some personal property around the living room. Miss Watkins perched on one end of the couch watching her.

"I like it here," she said. "It's much better than the house in Birmingham. We must go for a walk to see the neighbourhood."

"I don't think I have the energy." Mrs Watkins looked exhausted after walking around the living room. "It's been a busy day and we need to unpack. We'll have to wait until tomorrow."

"Must we? I need to stretch my legs after sitting in that carriage. If you're too tired, perhaps Mr Jackson could accompany me?" Miss Watkins flicked her eyes towards William.

Mr Watkins studied the clock on the mantelpiece. "Haven't you got things to do? I, for one, would like a cup of tea and I'm sure Mr Jackson would too."

William noticed Miss Watkins's shoulders drop. "Actually, I'd like to go for a walk," he said. "It's still light and I don't have much to unpack. If Miss Watkins needs a chaperone, I'd be happy to go with her."

Mr Watkins didn't have time to respond before his niece jumped up, a smile lighting her face.

"Shall we go now before it gets too late?"

Mr Watkins hesitated. "Very well, but don't go far and be back before dark. Tea will be on the table at five o'clock."

William and Miss Watkins were out of the house within minutes. The air smelt sweet after the smoke of Birmingham and they both took a deep breath before they closed the front door and turned left down Grosvenor Road.

"Do you enjoy walking, Mr Jackson?" Miss Watkins asked as they set off.

"I do, especially when I have company. Thank you for inviting me. Do you have any idea where we're going?"

"No, I've never been to Handsworth before. I just wanted to get out of the house and have some time to myself. It's like I'm never alone."

William's smile faded. "I hope I'm not intruding."

"Don't be silly; I was hoping you'd come with me." Miss Watkins smiled and linked her arm through his. "I thought it was about time we got to know each other."

"Well, I'm glad you did." William returned her smile.

"What made you come to Handsworth?" Miss Watkins asked.

"It was a good opportunity and as much as I like Mr Wetherby, I needed to get away from him. He wasn't happy about it to start with but once your uncle agreed to delay the move by six months he mellowed."

"Your mother didn't look very pleased when she waved you off this morning."

William sighed. "She wasn't. I told her I was moving at the end of last year and she's barely spoken to me since. I wish we'd been able to move sooner; the last few months have been unbearable."

"Do you think she'll get over it?"

"She will in time, but if she thinks I'm going back and apologising she can think again. She acts as if I'm still a child and doesn't let me do anything unless Mr Wetherby agrees to it."

"What do you want to do?"

"Years ago, when I was about ten years old, Mr Wetherby took me to the Great Exhibition in London." William smiled at the memory. "I remember it as if it were yesterday. The first time we went was probably the best day of my life. The Crystal Palace was a magnificent building made of metal and glass and I remember saying to Mr Wetherby that one day I'd like to make something special."

"And is that still what you want?" Miss Watkins ran her hand down his arm.

"It sounds silly when all I do is make tools, or hooks and eyes, but yes. I love working with metal. When I asked Mr Wetherby if I could, he said anything was possible as long as I wanted it enough. *Just believe in yourself and work hard*, he said. The problem is, it's not easy when you work for Mr Wetherby."

"So why did you do your apprenticeship with my uncle rather than doing the work you wanted?"

"It was either making hooks and eyes with Mr Wetherby or working for your uncle. I didn't have any other choice."

Miss Watkins thought for a moment. "Does that mean you'll leave one day?"

William shrugged. "I don't know. It may be too late now, but at least I haven't got Mr Wetherby telling me everything I have to do. I just want to be able to make my own decisions."

"You can do more than I'll ever be able to." Miss Watkins let out a sigh. "Even for something as simple as going for a walk I have to ask permission and have a chaperone. Have you any idea how hard it is being a woman? I often wish I were a man so I could do what I want."

William stopped and studied her. "You can't say that."

"Why not? Why is it wrong for me to want to be my own person when it's acceptable for you to want the same?"

"Because men and women are different. We have

different roles. Women are special; we need to take care of you."

"And that's why I wish I were a man. I don't want to be looked after; I want to have the freedom you have."

William was lost for words. "I'm glad you're not a man," he said eventually. "I like you as you are."

"Was that a compliment?" Miss Watkins cocked her head at him and smiled.

William rolled his eyes at her. "You know it was."

"Well … thank you. I'm sorry if you don't like the way I feel, but I can't abide the unfairness."

"It's not unfair. We just have our own roles."

"You wouldn't say that if you swapped places with me for a week. You'd be begging to have your old freedoms back."

William's pace slowed. "How long have you felt like this?"

"Ever since I realised what my life would become. Did you know my uncle couldn't understand why I wanted to carry on at school? When I complained, he sent me away to a school *for ladies* to learn how to behave. I've had it drilled into me from everyone I've ever known that I'm a woman and the most I can expect from life is to get a husband, a good one if I'm lucky, and look after his children."

"Don't you want to get married and have children?"

Miss Watkins stopped. "I'm sorry … again. I'm not giving you a good impression of me, am I? When we left the house, I was excited because we were going to be alone together, but in the last five minutes I've probably made you wish you'd never come to Handsworth."

"No you haven't." William gazed into her doleful eyes

as he subconsciously ran his fingers through her short, blonde ringlets. "I like you, but … I don't know what to say. Women aren't supposed to learn or be left alone."

Miss Watkins turned away and blinked back the tears welling up in her eyes. "I'm sorry, I've misjudged you. Can you take me home and forget we had this conversation?"

William turned her to face him. "You intrigue me, Miss Watkins, and I don't want to forget it. I know how I am when I'm with Mr Wetherby and so perhaps I can begin to understand … if you'll let me."

Miss Watkins smiled. "You won't be shocked or think me strange?"

William's heart was pounding. "I can't guarantee that, but I'll try to understand. It can be our secret."

Chapter 2

MARY SAT IN THE LIVING room, staring into the fire. There were chores to do, but since William had moved to Handsworth, they seemed unimportant. He hadn't written to her in almost a month, despite the fact she wrote to him several times a week. It was as if he'd forgotten about her. As the fire burned down, she sighed and stood up to add more coal. She would be on her own this afternoon. Her eldest daughter, Mary-Ann, now lived in the back house with her Aunt Alice, Mary's twin sister, and she didn't see her as often as she liked. She would call in the afternoons if she were free, but today she was visiting her friend Mrs Harris.

Mary looked down into the pram of her youngest daughter, Charlotte, and considered how generous the Lord had been to grant her another child at such a late stage in her life. At the moment, Charlotte was the only reason she got out of bed in the morning. She pushed the pram out onto the street before she walked into the court for some water.

As she returned to the house, she saw her sister-in-law, Sarah-Ann, walking towards her. Although she was her late husband's sister, Sarah-Ann bore no resemblance to her beloved Charles. Instead of his dark brown hair, she was fair, and her eyes were dusky grey rather than being the deep brown of her brother's. Mary had often envied the way Sarah-Ann's eyes sparkled when she smiled, and on more than one occasion she'd caught Mr Wetherby staring into them for longer than was necessary. This morning, however, she'd lost her glow.

"My goodness," Mary said. "Are you all right? You're white." She ushered Sarah-Ann into the house and sat her in the nearest chair.

"I've felt better, but I'm not too bad today," Sarah-Ann said.

"Well, if this is one of your better days, I'm even more worried about you. Let me get you a drink. Do you want gin or tea?"

"Tea, I think. It'll warm me up."

"How long have you been like this?"

"A few weeks now, maybe longer. I've been quite sick, but I'm sure it'll pass."

"You don't know that. I'm going to ask Mr Wetherby to send for the doctor. You stay here."

Mary didn't visit the workshop often and saw the concern on Mr Wetherby's face as she walked in. He came straight to her. "Is Charlotte all right?"

"Yes, of course. I don't think it's anything serious, but it's Sarah-Ann. I've come to ask if you'll send one of the boys to fetch the doctor for her. She's at our house and looks dreadful; she says she's been ill for several weeks."

Mr Wetherby took a deep breath. "Has that fool of a husband not called a doctor?"

"It doesn't appear so."

"My boys shouldn't have to run around because of his negligence."

Mary noticed the colour rising in Mr Wetherby's cheeks as he rubbed his beard. "Please, it won't take them long."

"That's not the point. The man needs horsewhipping." Mr Wetherby turned away. "Sarah-Ann deserves better than him. You go and sit with her. I'll sort something out."

Half an hour later the doctor arrived and Mary showed him up to the bedroom where Sarah-Ann now rested. He'd been in the house about ten minutes when Mary heard a shriek and her name being called. She hurried upstairs and knocked on the door just as the doctor was letting himself out.

"Mary, it's happened again." The grin on Sarah-Ann's face was out of place against her sickly complexion. "I'm going to have a baby. Can you believe it? That's why I've not been well. The doctor thinks I'm about half-way through."

Mary returned her smile. "I thought you might be but didn't want to say anything in case I was wrong. Mr Flemming will be pleased."

Sarah-Ann's smile faded. "Yes …"

"You don't sound sure. I'd have thought after what happened last time … when you lost the baby."

"I must get home before he finishes work. He doesn't know I've called here today."

"You stay there and rest. I'll ask Mr Wetherby to get a carriage and he can escort you home."

Sarah-Ann froze. "No, please don't … I can easily pick up one on Summer Lane. I don't want to disturb him."

"You shouldn't be out on your own in your condition. What's the matter?"

"Nothing … but Mr Flemming will be worried. He blames himself for last time."

A puzzled expression crossed Mary's face. "Why would Mr Flemming feel guilty? He told me you'd slipped."

"Yes, I did, I'm sorry. I need to be going."

Mary could do nothing to change her mind and after Sarah-Ann had left, she sat down to consider what had happened to Sarah-Ann's first baby. She'd been told it was an accident, but she'd always had her suspicions about Mr Flemming. Now, with this second baby on the way she was more intrigued than ever, but she guessed she wasn't going to find out anything from Sarah-Ann.

❧

It was over an hour later when Mr Wetherby got home to find Mary sitting by the fire.

"What did the doctor say about Sarah-Ann?" he asked as he took off his hat and coat.

"She's expecting another baby, but something's not right." Mary gazed into the fire as she spoke.

Mr Wetherby stood with his mouth open, searching for the right question. "She's expecting another baby? What do you mean? Is there a problem?"

"No, nothing like that. She was happy when the doctor told her, but as soon as I mentioned Mr Flemming, she came over all peculiar. If you ask me, there's something funny about the way she lost the last baby. I don't think it was an accident."

Mr Wetherby's stomach churned and he took a deep breath, relieved that Mary had her back to him.

"Of course it was an accident."

"I think she's hiding something."

"Of course she isn't. You're imagining it."

"I'm not." Mary turned around to face him. "When I mentioned Mr Flemming this afternoon she went all quiet and said he felt guilty about what happened last time. Why would he feel guilty if it was an accident? If you ask me, I think he caused her to fall down the stairs. They probably had an argument and he pushed her."

"Now you're being silly." Mr Wetherby wiped his brow with a handkerchief and returned it to its pocket.

"I'm not saying he did it on purpose, it may have been an accident, but whichever way you look at it, I think it was his fault. I wonder what they were arguing about."

"You don't know they *were* arguing, now stop this."

"You saw the way he was when they were at our house the Christmas after it happened. I thought their marriage was over, the way he spoke to her."

Mr Wetherby took a deep breath and changed the subject. "What have you been doing all afternoon? You haven't put any tea on the table."

Mary looked around the room. "What time is it?"

Mr Wetherby took out his pocket watch. "Half past five. High time tea was ready. William Junior will be in shortly. What have you done with Charlotte?"

"Charlotte? I left her outside." Mary jumped to her feet. "Wasn't she there when you came in?"

"For the love of God, Mary, what are you thinking?" Mr Wetherby turned and headed for the door. "If anything's happened to her …"

Mr Wetherby stood by the front door, looking up and down the street. When there was no sign of her, he ran down the alley, into the court at the back of the house. His heart thumped as he looked from one side to the other, but there was no sign of her. He went to the laundry to see if she was there but when it was empty, he was at a loss for what to do. Running back to the alley, he was about to leave when a movement caught his eye. A pram was being pushed from one of the houses by a group of young girls barely tall enough to see over the handle.

"What are you doing with that pram?" Mr Wetherby yelled as he ran over to them. "You'd no right to move it."

"Mrs Wetherby said we could take her for a walk," the eldest said. "We told her we were coming here."

"Well, don't do it again." Mr Wetherby snatched the pram from them. "She's been out of her mind with worry."

Chapter 3

Handsworth, Staffordshire.

WILLIAM WIPED DOWN THE FILE he had finished and placed it in the nearby box before he turned his attention to the machine he was working on. The blackness of the night through the window high in the wall above him suggested it was time to pack up. He needed to clean the machine thoroughly before he laid down his cloth and went to help Mr Watkins. He loved working with machines and metal, feeling the tools come to life under his fingers; it was much more satisfying than making those fiddly hooks and eyes.

Mr Watkins was a full head shorter than William, with receding brown hair and a neatly trimmed beard and moustache. As soon as he was ready, they would walk the short journey home, as they did every night, but tonight would be different. William wiped the palms of his hands on his trousers as he waited; starting a conversation like this was always the hardest part.

He'd been living in Handsworth for six weeks and had settled in well, but there was one problem. Except for the night they had arrived, he'd spent no time on his own with

Miss Watkins. It was clear they both wanted to be alone, and on several occasions had tried to arrange it, but always Mr or Mrs Watkins found a reason to be with them. William wondered if it was deliberate, and tonight he was going to confront Mr Watkins. Yes, it carried risks. He could end up losing his job, and his home, but if all else failed he could go back to Birmingham. As much as he didn't want that, he wanted to walk out with Miss Watkins, so it was a risk he was prepared to take.

He stood to one side while Mr Watkins locked up and the two of them set off towards Wellington Road. William swallowed down the lump that had formed in his throat.

"Mr Watkins, do you mind if I ask you a question?"

"Go ahead, my boy."

"It's about Miss Watkins. I was wondering … would you have any objections if I asked her to walk out with me?"

Mr Watkins said nothing for what felt like minutes and William thought he hadn't heard him. He was about to ask again when Mr Watkins spoke.

"Regarding you being a potential suitor for my niece, there's nothing I'd like more. If I'm honest, I initially hoped you'd end up together one day. The problem is, I worry that you've no idea what you'd be taking on."

"What do you mean? She's a lovely girl and we get on well, even though we haven't been on our own very often."

Mr Watkins kept his eyes fixed on the road ahead. "There's a reason for that. My niece can be rather … difficult, and now I've seen you together, I worry that you haven't got the temperament to handle her. She's prone to bouts of hysteria, and frankly, it's not pleasant."

"She told me you sent her to school and she's not like that anymore."

"She told you? You surprise me. I'd have thought she'd have kept the reasons for going to school to herself."

"It was on our first night here ... when we went for a walk."

"But how would you react if she reverted to type, especially if you were to marry her?"

"I can't say, given that I've not seen her like that, but I'm sure I could manage her. I won't take any nonsense."

Mr Watkins turned to face William. "But knowing she might change, would you still be willing to take her on? You could be with her a long time."

"I would. I've liked her since we first met in Birmingham and given our ages, I think it's time."

"Very well." Mr Watkins quickened his pace. "I'll speak to her beforehand and make sure she behaves. At least it will keep Mr Wetherby happy."

"Mr Wetherby? What's it got to do with him?"

"Nothing," Mr Watkins said. "Forget I mentioned him."

ৡৡ

The following Saturday, William and Miss Watkins took their first official walk together. They looked a picture of respectability as Miss Watkins, wearing a long grey cloak and matching bonnet, linked arms with William and let him lead her down Grosvenor Road. Mr Watkins watched them leave but once they were out of his sight, they both relaxed.

"I can't believe he said yes," Miss Watkins said, a smile

brightening her whole face. "Will you call me Harriet now? Miss Watkins sounds so stuffy."

William flinched. "Don't you think it's a bit soon for that?"

"Not when it's just the two of us. Please. You can still use my full title at home." Her eyes danced with mischief.

"If you insist," he said with a grin, "but tell me, what on earth you've done to upset your uncle? He nearly said no when I asked. He doesn't think I can control you."

Harriet's smile faded. "Ignore him. I've done nothing wrong. He doesn't understand that times are changing and wonders why I'm angry when he won't let me do things."

"What sort of things won't he let you do?"

Harriet stopped and turned to William. "Haven't you noticed? The latest one is reading. Every woman in the country is being encouraged to read, but not me."

"Why would he do that?"

"To his mind, women shouldn't read. Apparently, I'm a lady now, not a scholar, and you can't be both."

"You look every bit the lady to me." William squeezed her hand.

"That's beside the point." Harriet pulled away. "Reading is not going to make me any less of a lady. I don't care what he says."

"He's not the only one who says that."

"Well, they're all wrong and one day we'll show them. But can we change the subject? I don't want to argue with you."

William started walking again, unsure what constituted a safe topic.

"Look at you, anyway," she said after a minute. "You're

every bit the gentleman, tall and dark with a distinguished air about you."

"Are you trying to get round me?" He smiled as he spoke. "I can't take all the credit; a lot of it's down to Mr Wetherby. He's taken care of me since I was seven. Mother was struggling at the time and he changed our lives. Have you met him?"

"He called at the house in Birmingham once to talk to my uncle and made a point of speaking to me." Harriet shuddered. "It was like he was testing me, so I was on my best behaviour."

"I'm glad to hear it." William smiled at her.

"The only person I get angry with is my uncle; I don't have a problem with anyone else."

"I'll have to be careful I don't repeat his mistakes."

"You won't." Harriet smiled and the sparkle returned to her eyes. "I can tell that already. You don't mind me talking like this, do you? You make it so easy for me to be … me. You do understand, don't you?"

William laughed. "I won't even pretend to understand, but I know I enjoy being with you. As long as you behave as you should in public, I don't mind at all."

Harriet clapped her hands together. "Come on, let's walk to the woods. I don't like the idea that everyone could be watching us. I want us to be alone."

Chapter 4

Birmingham, Warwickshire.

MARY HELD UP THE KNITTING needle to check the length of the dress she was making. It may be long enough. Charlotte was growing so quickly she was constantly working on something for her. As she laid the piece on top of an older dress to check the size, there was a knock on the door.

"Come in," she called, without lifting her head from her work. A second later Mr Flemming opened the door

Mary straightened up and saw him remove his hat, revealing a head of neatly trimmed, light-brown hair. "Mr Flemming. What are you doing here?"

"Hello, Mrs Wetherby. I hope you don't mind me calling, but Sarah-Ann wanted me to tell you she's had the baby."

Mary's frown disappeared, and for the first time in months, she smiled. "Already? Well I'm glad you came. Congratulations. Did she have a boy?"

"No, a girl. We're going to call her Elizabeth."

"That's lovely. It must be a relief after last time. Sarah-Ann told me what happened." Mary cocked her head, waiting for a response.

"She told you?" Mr Flemming's eyes were wide. "I hope she said it was a terrible accident. As soon as she lost her balance I knew it had gone too far."

"What had gone too far?"

"The argument, but I was jealous, you see."

"You were jealous? Of what?"

Mr Flemming hesitated. "Did she tell you precisely what happened?"

Mary felt her cheeks reddening. "Well, she didn't tell me everything. Just that it was an accident ... but you couldn't have known what would happen."

Mr Flemming twisted his hat in his hands. "She didn't give you any details?"

Mary shook her head.

"I'd better go. Sarah-Ann will need me at home. I don't want anything happening to her."

"Send her my love ..." Mary shouted as Mr Flemming left, but when he didn't turn around, she closed the door and sat down. She should never have lied, but it was obvious they were trying to hide something. *What had Mr Flemming been jealous of?* Mary knew Sarah-Ann as well as anyone, and as far as she was concerned, Sarah-Ann had done nothing to provoke his envy. She stood and stared out of the window for several minutes before picking up her knitting. She would ask Mr Wetherby tonight; he might know.

Handsworth, England.

Harriet had been embroidering for over two hours and it was still only three o'clock. She put her work on the table and rested her head in her hands.

"What's the matter?" her aunt asked.

"I'm bored, that's what's the matter. Is life always going to be like this, merely sitting around waiting for callers or waiting for the men to come home of an evening? There must be something else we can do."

"What do you want to do? I can ask Ruby to fetch some wool if you'd rather knit."

Harriet stood up and went to the window. "You know, there's a whole world out there, places we're never going to see. Imagine what it would be like to travel to London or even further, to somewhere foreign. A lot of people go to other countries nowadays, to places where the sun always shines. Wouldn't you like to go and see somewhere different?"

"What do you want to go to a place like that for? Nobody needs to see the sun every day; it would be far too uncomfortable. I thought you'd got over these silly ideas. Birmingham is likely to be the furthest place we ever go."

"To travel back to Birmingham at the moment would be a treat. I haven't seen Miss Taylor or Miss Woodbridge since we moved up here, and there's only so much you can say to friends in a letter. Miss Taylor has recently accepted a marriage proposal from Mr Booth and she's so much to tell me. May I go and visit them soon?"

Her aunt bristled. "We'll have to ask your uncle; he won't let you go alone."

"Why do we always need permission? We could be there and back in the time he's at work; he'd never know. You could come with me; you still have friends in Birmingham."

"I have, but even if I go with you, we're not going without asking your uncle. What if there was a problem?

As it happens I'd like a trip to Birmingham myself and so I'll ask him tonight."

"Splendid." A smile lit up Harriet's face. "I'll write to both of them straight away and check when they're free."

"Your uncle hasn't agreed to anything yet so don't get ahead of yourself."

"I hope he wouldn't be mean enough to stop us going. Why would he? It's nothing to him."

It was turned six o'clock when Mr Watkins and William arrived home and sat down for tea. They ate without speaking and Mrs Watkins helped Ruby clear the table before she broached the subject of their trip to Birmingham.

"What do you want to go there for?" Mr Watkins said.

"It would only be for a visit," Mrs Watkins said. "Harriet hasn't seen Miss Taylor or Miss Woodbridge since we moved here and I have friends I'd like to see."

"Please, Uncle," Harriet said. "You've been back several times. Would you take us on your next visit?"

"I've no plans to go to Birmingham in the foreseeable future and you're not going without me."

Harriet was about to protest when William interrupted. "Mr Watkins, I've been here for over five months now and the only time I've seen my mother was at Christmas. Might you allow me to travel to Birmingham with the ladies so I can pay her a visit?"

"And miss a day's work?"

"I wondered if it might be an opportunity for me to discuss our plans for expansion with Mr Wetherby."

Mr Watkins sat motionless for a full minute before he spoke. "Perhaps it wouldn't be such a bad idea if you went. You're in a better position to talk to Mr Wetherby than I am and so I'll give my permission for you to escort Harriet to Birmingham. Once you've delivered her safely to the house of Miss Taylor you can pay Mr Wetherby a visit. I'll arrange a carriage to pick you up so my horse isn't standing around waiting for you. Shall we say next Wednesday at eight o'clock in the morning?"

"Yes, thank you." Miss Watkins squealed as she clapped her hands together.

"What about me?" Mrs Watkins said. "I'd hoped to travel to Birmingham as well."

"You can come with me next time I have business there."

"You said you don't know when that will be. I was looking forward to it."

"That's enough. Harriet will travel with Mr Jackson and you can wait until the next time I go."

As the evening wore on, Harriet couldn't keep the smile off her face. She had written to Miss Taylor and Miss Woodbridge to make arrangements for her visit. Admittedly she was only going to Birmingham but she would be travelling alone with William. What was her uncle thinking? She didn't know what had come over him, but whatever it was, she hoped it would happen more often.

As William left the back room to go to bed, Harriet made her excuses and followed him up the stairs.

"Can you believe he said yes?" she said in an excited whisper. "I can't."

William smiled. "Well don't do anything to change his mind. I want you on your best behaviour between now and next Wednesday."

"I'm always on my best behaviour. Besides, he won't change his mind now. I won't let him."

Chapter 5

Birmingham, Warwickshire.

THE CARRIAGE PULLED UP OUTSIDE the house at eight o'clock prompt and Harriet raced down the stairs.

"Are you ready?" she shouted as William finished breakfast. "We don't want to keep him waiting."

"I'm sure he won't mind for a minute." William smiled as he walked into the hall to collect his coat. "He hasn't knocked on the door yet."

"I don't care; I don't want to waste a moment."

"We'd better go then." William fastened his coat and picked up his hat before they said farewell to Mrs Watkins who was finishing breakfast.

"Isn't this thrilling?" Harriet said as William helped her into the carriage. "Just the two of us travelling together; I didn't think Uncle would allow it. I don't understand him at all. Sometimes he seems to be encouraging us, but at other times he's completely overprotective. Can you believe that ever since he agreed to this trip he's locked my bedroom door at night? Perhaps he's worried you'll pay me a visit in the middle of the night."

"I hope he doesn't think I'd do such a thing." William moved away from Harriet as she leaned in towards him. "I wouldn't dream of it while I lived in his house, or at any other time, come to think of it."

"It must be me he doesn't trust," she said with a giggle.

"What have you been saying?"

"Nothing." An expression of innocence rested on her face before the twinkle returned to her eyes. "Maybe, because we've been walking out for a while, he thinks we'll steal a night together. I have to confess, the thought did cross my mind."

"It didn't! Miss Watkins what are you saying …?"

"Don't call me that." She turned to face him and put her hand on his knee. "Miss Watkins makes it sound like you're angry with me."

"Miss Watkins … Harriet … you're supposed to be a respectable woman." William's face was scarlet. "Where did you get thoughts like that from?"

"Don't you think it would be fun?"

"No, I do not." William took her hand from his knee. "Your uncle would send me back to Birmingham if he found out. Then what would you do?"

"I wouldn't let you go."

"You wouldn't have any say in the matter. Please tell me you won't think such a thing again."

"I'm sorry." Harriet lowered her head, but studied him out of the corner of her eye. "I wouldn't really have done it; I just wanted to see your reaction."

William grunted and Harriet thought he was trying to hide a smile. After a break in the conversation he changed the subject. "How long do you want to stay at your friend's house?"

"As long as I can. I haven't seen them for such a long time; we've got a lot to catch up on. Why?"

"Your uncle hasn't arranged a carriage to take us home, and I wondered if you'd like to call on Mother. Mr Wetherby said she's invited me for tea and I don't want to upset her by saying no."

"I'd like that, but won't she mind me calling?"

"I'll visit her when I go to see Mr Wetherby. Give her some warning. She might be a bit cold with you when we arrive because I haven't told her we're walking out together, but give her a minute, and I'm sure she'll be fine. Promise you won't say anything you shouldn't?"

Harriet feigned shock at the suggestion. "How can you say that? You should know me well enough by now."

William laughed. "I don't think I'll ever know you well enough."

It was turned four o'clock when William collected Harriet and they made their way to Frankfort Street.

"I was beginning to think you'd forgotten about me." Harriet tightened her grip on his arm.

"I'm sorry, I was talking to Mr Wetherby and the time disappeared. It's been a worthwhile day though; your uncle should be pleased."

"Have you seen your mother?"

"I didn't have a chance, which means I'll be in her bad books before I arrive, never mind turning up with you."

"Nothing like putting a girl at ease." Harriet wondered if she'd been right to agree to the unexpected visit. "I hope she doesn't mind; I want her to like me."

"I'm sure she will when she meets you." William gave her the smile she loved. "I don't know how anyone could not like you."

❧

27

William was about to knock on the front door when it flew open and his mother swept him up in a tight embrace.

"Where have you been? I was expecting you hours ago. Let me look at you." Mary stepped back, holding William's hands, before she noticed Harriet standing behind him. She studied her and then turned back to William.

"Mother, I'd like to introduce Miss Watkins. I hope you don't mind if she joins us for tea. She's the real reason I came to Birmingham. Mr Watkins asked me to talk to Mr Wetherby while I was here."

"Good afternoon, Mrs Wetherby." Harriet gave a slight curtsy. "It's a pleasure to meet you. Mr Jackson talks very highly of you."

"Why didn't you tell me we'd have company?" Mary asked William once she'd put the smile back on her face. "I don't know that I've prepared enough to eat."

"I bet you've been baking all day and so I'm sure there's more than enough."

"I've been waiting for you for most of the afternoon so I haven't done much. Now come on in and tell me what you've been up to before everyone joins us."

Shortly after five o'clock, Mary-Ann and Aunt Alice came around from the back house. They had just settled down with a cup of tea when Mr Wetherby and William Junior arrived home.

"Miss Watkins, how nice to see you again," Mr Wetherby said as he removed his hat and coat. "I trust you've had a pleasant afternoon. I'm sorry I kept William for so long, but we had a lot to catch up on."

"Why didn't you tell me Miss Watkins was joining us?"

Mary asked her husband as she stood up to put more water over the fire.

"Don't blame Mr Wetherby, Mother," William said. "I thought you'd worry if you knew I was bringing a guest and I didn't want that." William didn't like lying to his mother but it was the easiest option. "I also wanted Miss Watkins to be with me when I told you we're walking out together."

Mary-Ann smiled at William but it took Mary several seconds to compose herself. "How long has this been going on? Why didn't you tell me sooner? You never write."

"I told you I was coming here, but you know writing letters isn't one of my strong points."

"That's no excuse …"

"May I write to you, Mrs Wetherby?" Harriet interrupted. "I enjoy letter writing and I'd tell you what William's doing. He doesn't tell me everything of course, but it would be a good reason for me to get to know him better."

"You know me well enough; there isn't much more to tell." William smiled at her.

"There's always more to learn and I can be very inquisitive." Harriet returned his smile before she turned back to Mary. "Would you be willing to correspond with me, Mrs Wetherby?"

"I would," Mary-Ann said. "If Mother doesn't want to, that is."

"No … I mean yes," Mary said. "Of course she must write to me about William."

"Perhaps I can write to both of you; I'd rather write than do embroidery."

William sighed at Harriet's honesty before Mr Wetherby interrupted.

"We'll be seeing more of you down here though, won't we? We need to stay in touch about the business."

"I hope so, but it'll be up to Mr Watkins to decide who comes to Birmingham," William said. "I'm hoping he'll allow Miss Watkins to visit her friends more regularly and he'll let me escort her. I'm sure you and Mother could come to Handsworth to visit us as well. The house Mr Watkins bought is fabulous and the air is so much cleaner."

"That would be lovely." For the first time since she'd seen Harriet, Mary smiled. "It's such a long time since I was last in Handsworth."

"Let me make it clear before you start thinking about it; we are not moving to Handsworth," Mr Wetherby said. "The business is in Birmingham and that's where we'll stay. Why else do you think William and Mr Watkins continue to come down here? If we go to visit, it will be just that, a visit."

Chapter 6

Handsworth, Staffordshire.

H ARRIET HAD LIVED WITH HER aunt and uncle for as long as she could remember. She was almost six years old when she learned they were not her real parents, but she hadn't minded. They were good to her and made her feel special. She had occasionally seen her mother and some of her younger brothers and sisters if her aunt and uncle called on them, but they didn't feel like her real family.

No one explained to her why, out of thirteen children, she was the one adopted by her aunt and uncle. She expected it was something to do with the death of her father, but she couldn't remember him. He was her uncle's eldest brother and she liked to imagine her father had asked him to take care of his favourite daughter once he was gone.

During her early years her uncle had been good to his word. He had cared for her as if she were his own and most importantly, he had sent her to school. Harriet loved school. When she first learned her numbers it was as if the puzzles that had been going around in her head were finally understood. She loved the patterns they made and the simplicity of them all, and she soon gained a reputation for excellence in arithmetic, but one day, without warning, it stopped. She was becoming a young lady, she was told, and ladies learned how to keep a house. As she was able to read and write, there was no need for her to continue at school.

Harriet wasn't an emotional person, but she had cried the day they made her stay at home. It was so unfair. Boys could carry on at school, so what harm would it do if she went to classes with them? Being at home made her feel as if she were suffocating. She didn't want to spend her days knitting or embroidering, or learning how to run a house. As she grew older, she began to argue with her aunt and uncle, to question them, and as a result the relationship with her uncle deteriorated. There were numerous occasions when her outbursts resulted in her feeling the back of his hand and gradually she withdrew into her own world. She would often sit and stare into the distance, playing with numbers in her head, doing the calculations she had learned at school. The only time she smiled was at Sunday school, but before long she was too old to go, and her despair grew.

They had been arguing for several years, when her uncle told her she was being sent away to school. Her heart soared and she imagined she would pick up where she had left off, but her joy was short-lived. She was to go to a school for young ladies, to learn the finer points of things like sewing and music. Her uncle told her in no uncertain terms that she was expected to return as a lady, ready to accept her place as a wife. There was to be no other future for her.

This time school was difficult. She was taught how to sew, embroider tray cloths, darn socks, knit baby clothes, crochet shawls; the list was endless, and when they weren't doing that they were being taught the history of music. It wasn't that she didn't like music, she did, just not the music they insisted she should listen to.

By the time she returned home the spirit had been knocked out of her. Her uncle accepted the praise heaped on him for 'curing' her, but nothing she did gave her any pleasure. Shortly after returning home, when she was feeling particularly sorry for herself, she met William again. She had seen him years earlier when he was apprenticed to her uncle and had been drawn to his dark wavy hair and deep brown eyes. In those early years she didn't think he had noticed her, but when it became apparent there was some attraction between them, she struggled to contain her excitement. There was something different about him. He was quiet, courteous and polite, but behind the facade she imagined there was someone else who wanted to break free. She often thought about him while she was sewing and imagined a life with him. When she first tested the water, she feared she had frightened him off, but once they got to know each other, she knew she was right about him.

As much as she liked him, however, he was infuriating. It had taken him almost two months to ask her uncle if they could walk out together despite the fact they had both wanted to. She needed to make sure he wasn't going to be so slow asking for her hand in marriage.

As they finished tea one evening, Mr Watkins announced he had invited Mr Wetherby and his family for dinner.

"I thought it was about time," he said. "They'll come next Sunday, straight after church."

"I bet you'll be glad to see your mother again," Harriet said to William. "It's such a long time since we saw them.

She's always asking after you in her letters and whether we're still walking out together. She wants to know if we have any plans for the future."

"She asks that?" A frown formed on William's face.

"Not in so many words, but I'm sure that's what she means."

"And what do you tell her?"

"I have nothing *to* tell her ... do I?" She looked directly into his eyes.

"Harriet," Mrs Watkins said, "I'd like some more tea. Go and ask Ruby to bring some in, please."

Harriet was about to object but thought better of it. With a final glance at William she got up and went out into the hallway.

The following day when they went for their stroll, Harriet linked her arm through William's, but he immediately pulled away. "What were you trying to achieve yesterday evening?"

Harriet kept her eyes on the path ahead. "What do you mean?"

"You know what I mean. What possessed you to talk about the future in front of your aunt and uncle?"

Harriet struggled to answer. Should she give the diplomatic answer or should she be honest? Knowing William liked her honesty she took a deep breath and opted for the truth.

"Do you remember when we first moved to Handsworth? We went for our first walk the night we arrived, but we weren't alone for months afterwards."

"Six weeks."

"And it took you all that time to ask my uncle's permission for us to walk out together."

"Yes." The hesitation in William's voice was unmistakable.

"Well, we've been walking out for over six months now and it strikes me you're happy to let things continue as they are."

"I am happy. I enjoy your company and we spend a lot of time together."

"But we're not really together, are we?"

"Of course we are; we're together now."

"That's not what I mean. In case you've forgotten, you're twenty-five years old. Most men of your age are married with a family and yet you show no desire to follow their lead. Don't you want to spend the rest of your life with me? I'm twenty-three myself and I don't want to stay with my uncle forever. I thought if I said something in front of them you might take me seriously."

William continued walking but said nothing. Eventually he stopped and took hold of her hands. "Of course I want to spend my life with you, I've thought of little else for months, but I want to do things properly."

"Just because you do something quickly doesn't mean you don't do it well."

"Maybe not in your head, but I like to take my time."

"You've had time."

William ran his fingers through his hair. "Not the time I need; now please can we say no more about this?"

Harriet bowed her head and said nothing.

"You have to let me do things my way. I love you and don't want anything spoiled."

"You do? Oh William, I love you too." Harriet bounced

on the spot before she raised herself up on her toes and kissed him on the cheek.

"You're going to get me in trouble," he said, before he took her in his arms and kissed her again, this time more slowly.

Chapter 7

MARY STOOD INSIDE THE CHURCH with William Junior and Charlotte waiting for Mr Watkins's carriage to take them to Handsworth. She hadn't expected Charlotte to be invited but for William Junior the trip was a necessity. He was officially apprenticed to his father and Mr Wetherby was keen for him to understand all aspects of the business. William Junior was less enthusiastic and didn't understand why he should have to work on a Sunday.

"The carriage is here." Mr Wetherby came back into church and bent down to pick up Charlotte. "Are you ready?"

"Of course we are." Mary turned around to check William Junior was with her.

Even though Mr Watkins had only invited them to Handsworth a week earlier, Mary had been looking forward to today for months. She had wanted to visit ever since William left Birmingham, and her curiosity had been heightened by her now regular correspondence with Miss Watkins. She was an eloquent writer and at Mary's request had described their house in detail. Mary longed to move back to Handsworth and she hoped this elegant house with its servant and stabling might be the thing to persuade Mr Wetherby.

As they arrived, Ruby opened the door and showed them to the front room. After the chill of the carriage, the heat from the fire overwhelmed them, but within a minute the door opened and William walked in.

"How good to see you all." He shook hands with Mr Wetherby and kissed his mother on the cheek. "Is Mary-Ann not with you?"

"I'm afraid not," Mary said. "She's had a chill all week and the doctor advised her to stay in bed. She was so disappointed. Now, let me see. What a wonderful room this is and what a splendid table." She turned and studied the room, taking in all its detail. The centrepiece was a rectangular table. It had been set for dinner with an exquisite china dinner service and candelabra at each end. Mr Wetherby was about to remind her they were not moving house when the door opened, and Mr Watkins walked in followed by his wife and niece.

After they'd made the introductions, Mrs Watkins seated everyone around the table before Ruby entered with a piece of beef, which she placed in front of Mr Watkins. She then brought in a tray of potatoes, carrots, swede and parsnips, all covered in gravy. Mr Watkins said grace, picked up the carving knife and ceremoniously sharpened it on a steel before turning his attention to the meat. Dinner was eaten in silence and once they had finished, Ruby cleared the table before placing an enormous steamed pudding in the centre of the table.

"That was delightful," Mr Wetherby said once his plate

was empty. "I don't think I shall need to eat again for a week."

Mrs Watkins put her hand to her chest and lowered her eyelids, delighting in the compliment.

"Can I get you some port, Mr Wetherby?" Mr Watkins asked. "The ladies can go into the back room but I have some work to discuss and I'm sure they don't want to listen."

Once they left the table, Harriet offered to show Mary the rest of the house; an opportunity she wasn't going to miss.

"The house is everything I expected and more," she said ten minutes later as she sat down in the back room. "Miss Watkins is such an excellent writer I already had a picture of it in my mind. The only thing I didn't appreciate was the size; it will make going back to Birmingham more dismal than usual."

"Apart from a few friends, I don't miss Birmingham at all," Mrs Watkins said. "My breathing is much better as well."

"I loved it when I lived here. My sister Susannah moved here a couple of years ago too. Only to a small cottage, nothing as grand as this, but I'd like to see more of her as well. Mr Wetherby won't hear of moving back though. He needs to be close to the workshop."

Mrs Watkins looked down at her dress as she straightened out the numerous layers. "I'd have thought he would be ready to move away from those small houses and purchase something more in keeping with his status."

"He's quite happy where we are. He owns half the houses on Frankfort Street and being a property owner gives him a lot of influence locally. Since he got the vote he regularly attends council meetings as well. He's very taken with politics at the moment and he wouldn't be able to do the same things in Handsworth. No, I'll have to bide my time; he'll move one day."

In the front room, the business discussion was coming to an end and the port was flowing freely.

"Another drink, Mr Wetherby?" Mr Watkins held the bottle high over the table.

"Most kind of you; I won't say no. Jolly good stuff you have. Do you come to Birmingham for it?"

"No, the inn-keeper gets it for me locally. Mr Jackson will you have some more?" Mr Watkins turned his attention to William.

"I won't, thank you," William said. "If you don't mind, I'd like to speak to Mr Wetherby on a personal matter before he leaves and I need a clear head."

"What is it, my lad?" Mr Wetherby laughed and patted him on the back. "Do you want to come back and work for me?"

William shifted in his seat. "No, nothing like that, I'm happy enough with Mr Watkins."

"What is it then?"

"Can we step into the hall for a moment?"

"And leave Mr Watkins on his own with William Junior? I don't think so. Come on, out with it, boy."

William's heart pounded as he struggled to find the right words. "It's about Miss Watkins …"

At this, Mr Watkins re-engaged with the conversation. "My niece? What about her?"

"Well, as you're aware, we've been walking out for some months now …"

"Has she been up to no good?" The smile fell from Mr Watkins's face. "Why didn't you tell me first?"

"No, not at all; quite the opposite, in fact. I actually wanted Mr Wetherby's blessing to ask you, Mr Watkins, if I may have her hand in marriage."

When he saw their expressions, William realised he had unwittingly asked them at precisely the right time. Mr Wetherby could hardly discredit the niece of his host, and the bottle of port was more than half-empty.

"My dear boy, what a splendid idea," Mr Wetherby said. "Your niece is a respectable girl is she not, Mr Watkins?"

"She is indeed, Mr Wetherby." Mr Watkins put his hand on his heart. "A lovely girl I've brought up as my own since the death of her father when she was not much older than your girl now."

"And would you be happy to accept as a son, my stepson, who I have brought up as my own since the death of his father when he was a small boy?"

"I should be delighted, sir." Mr Watkins reached for the bottle of port. "Let me refill the glasses; Mr Jackson and William Junior, you must have some too." A moment later he proposed a toast to William and Harriet.

William took a large gulp of his drink. "Thank you. I can't tell you how happy you've made me. Can I ask you to keep the news to yourself for a little longer? I'd like to delay asking Miss Watkins until Christmas."

"Why wait?" Mr Watkins said. "You can go and ask her now."

"No, please, there's something else I have to do first. Can you keep it to yourselves?"

Mr Wetherby chuckled to himself and within seconds he and Mr Watkins were giggling like schoolboys. Not knowing what he'd said, William turned to William Junior who shrugged but said nothing.

"Sshhhsh," Mr Watkins said.

Mr Wetherby put his finger to his lips, spilling some port as he did. "Sshhhsh," he slurred. "Don't tell."

"It's as well you're here," William whispered to William Junior. "Your father will need some assistance on the way home."

Chapter 8

Birmingham, Warwickshire.

DESPITE THE BEST EFFORTS OF the winter sun, the air was cold as William and Harriet took the carriage from Handsworth to Birmingham. William had a full day planned with Mr Wetherby, but he also had some personal business to attend to. As soon as they reached Birmingham he took Harriet to Miss Woodbridge's house and made his way to the Town Hall to meet his sister.

"Mary-Ann, over here," he shouted when he saw her waiting for him. "How lovely to see you. It's been too long."

"Don't I know it." She turned her cheek to receive his kiss. "Never mind that though, what is it you have to tell me?"

William took her arm and guided her across the square before he began. "You know I've been walking out with Miss Watkins. Well, I've decided it's time to propose marriage to her."

Mary-Ann stopped where she was and clapped her hands. "How exciting. What wonderful news."

"I know you write to her but I hope you get to know her better in person. She's like a breath of fresh air and such fun to be with … at least she is when it's just the two of us."

"I'm sure I will if she accepts your proposal. Is that why you wanted to see me?"

"Partly, but also because I need your help." William took her arm and they continued walking. "I plan to propose on Christmas morning and I want to give her a ring as a sign of our betrothal. The problem is, I've no idea what she'd like. Will you help me choose something?"

"I'd be delighted, if not a little envious. Do you have a shop in mind?"

"I thought we could go to Mr Flemming's place. Aunt Sarah-Ann always talks about the beautiful things he has and I want it to be beautiful. She deserves the best."

Dimples appeared on Mary-Ann's face as she smiled. "It's nice to keep it in the family, even if he was out of sorts last time we saw him. He might let you have one for a good price."

"I did hope that as well, but only so I can buy the best I can afford. I've been saving up for the last few months."

Five minutes later they approached the shop, and William opened the door, causing a bell to ring above it. At first there didn't appear to be anyone around, but within a minute Mr Flemming came out from the back room, his face looking unusually red.

"Mr and Miss Jackson," he said. "To what do I owe the pleasure?"

William explained that he wanted a ring and Mr Flemming showed them to the appropriate cases.

"We have some lovely ones at the moment. A lot of folks are going through hard times."

There were rings of all shapes and sizes, but it didn't take William long to find the one he liked. It was a thin gold band with five small blue stones arranged across the top, separated by smaller diamonds.

"Miss Watkins has such pretty blue eyes," he said, momentarily forgetting where he was. "This will set them off perfectly."

"You didn't need me," Mary-Ann said. "You made the decision all by yourself."

A pained expression crossed his face. "Do you think she'll like it though?"

"I'm sure she will, it's beautiful."

The price was more than William had budgeted for but with a bit of negotiation Mr Flemming agreed to lower the price as long as William paid the balance the next time he came to Birmingham.

As they left the shop, William remembered he hadn't asked Mr Flemming to keep the news to himself. He didn't want his aunt to find out and tell his mother; he needed to tell her himself. As he went back into the shop he was taken by surprise. A young woman was there who hadn't been there before.

"I'm sorry, I hope I'm not disturbing you," William said. "I didn't realise you had company."

"Have you forgotten something?" Mr Flemming said.

"I meant to ask you to keep my visit to yourself; I want the engagement to be a surprise." Mr Flemming looked to the woman and then back to William.

"Nobody will find out from me. Was that it?"

William confirmed he didn't want anything else and went back outside, a puzzled expression on his face.

"Is everything all right?" Mary-Ann asked.

"Yes, fine. He won't say anything." William said no

more, principally because he wasn't sure what there was to say. He put it to the back of his mind and offered his arm to Mary-Ann before they walked back to Frankfort Street.

By the time Christmas Eve arrived, Mary still had too much to do. She urgently needed more mince pies, she hadn't peeled the chestnuts and the Christmas decorations were still on the dining table. Usually she loved decorating the tree but this year her heart wasn't in it. It should be a family affair, but today she only had Mary-Ann helping her with the occasional input from Charlotte. At least William was joining them tomorrow.

Mary-Ann placed another tray of mince pies in the oven and turned her attention to the chestnuts.

"It's such a shame William has to work late tonight," Mary said. "I'd hoped Mr Watkins would let him catch the last carriage."

Mary-Ann glanced at her mother. "I think he'd like to see Miss Watkins in the morning."

"Whatever for? He sees her every other day; why can't tomorrow be an exception."

"I think he has a present he wants to give her. He's quite fond of her."

"A bit too fond for my liking."

Mary-Ann raised her eyebrow. "I thought you liked her?"

Mary sighed. "She's all right, but he could do better for himself. I still worry she's a bad influence on him. Her uncle didn't send her away to school for no reason."

Mary-Ann stopped her peeling. "I don't think it was

because she did anything wrong. William said it was because she wanted to carry on learning."

"But that's not usual, is it? Once a woman can read and write well enough to exchange letters or read the Bible that should be enough. Why couldn't he find a *normal* girl?"

Mary-Ann rolled her eyes. "She is normal. I liked her when we met."

"Maybe she is, but it'll still be nice to have William on his own tomorrow. I hope he can stay overnight. I'd hate it if he only stayed for a few hours."

Chapter 9

Handsworth, Staffordshire.

A S CHRISTMAS EVE TURNED INTO Christmas Day, William lay in bed, tossing and turning. He may have slept for a few hours, but if he had, he was still wide awake long before first light. He was strangely nervous about his proposal even though he was quite confident it would be accepted. He wanted it to be right and was annoyed he would have to leave his bride-to-be so soon afterwards. Lying in bed he listened to Ruby go downstairs, followed several minutes later by Mr Watkins. Suspecting it wouldn't be long before Mrs Watkins joined her husband, he decided now was the best time to have a word with him.

William had spoken to Mr Watkins about the proposal and was just finishing his second cup of tea when Harriet came downstairs. She burst into the room with a broad smile on her face and swished the skirt of her new dress around her legs. It was made of deep blue satin with a fitted bodice decorated with gems, giving way to a full skirt that fanned out behind her. As usual, she wore her hair tied back, with ringlets edging her face.

"Merry Christmas," she said, directing her conversation

at William. "Do you like my dress?" She did a full turn, holding a hand on her stomach to accentuate the flattened front of the skirt. William could do nothing but stare, unable to take his eyes off her.

"You look beautiful," he said after a moment. "Is the dress new?"

"Of course it's new." She laughed at William's puzzled expression. "Uncle bought it for me for Christmas."

"Very nice," her uncle said as he glanced up. "So it should be, the money it cost."

William continued to stare at her, momentarily forgetting what he needed to do next. A second later, he remembered. "Mr Watkins, will you excuse us for a moment?"

Mr Watkins nodded.

"What's going on?" Harriet said, her eyes wide. "Do you have a present for me? Shouldn't we wait?"

William said nothing but took her hand and led her into the front room, shutting the door behind them.

"Now I know something's up. Why hasn't Uncle said anything?"

William ignored her and focussed on the words he'd rehearsed. "Miss Watkins, can I say something for a minute?" He held up his hand. "We've been walking out for over a year now and in that time I have come to truly love you."

"I love you too." Her eyes danced with delight but she remained still.

"Not only are you beautiful, but you make me happy." He stopped and got down on one knee. "Would you do me the honour of being my wife?"

Harriet's smile brightened her whole face. "Of course I will, and what a marvellous day to propose marriage."

"That's not all." William stood up and reached over to the gifts beneath the Christmas tree. He picked up the smallest package. "I hope you like it."

Harriet unwrapped the box and opened the lid.

"It's beautiful," she whispered as William took the ring and placed it onto her third finger. "And it fits perfectly."

"The sapphires are almost the same colour as your dress; I couldn't have planned it better if I'd tried." They both laughed before William took her in his arms and kissed her tenderly. "I don't want this moment to end," he said. "You've made me the happiest man alive."

"Not as happy as you've made me." Harriet gazed into his eyes. "We don't have to go into the back room yet. Just another couple of minutes."

They remained in the front room for as long as they dared, before they rejoined Harriet's uncle. Her aunt had arrived downstairs while they'd been gone, and when Harriet showed them her ring, Mr Watkins suggested an early sherry to propose a toast. One sherry quickly turned to two and before he knew it, William had to rush down the road, hoping the carriage hadn't left without him.

William reached the house on Frankfort Street as the rest of the family arrived home from church. He kissed his mother before he wished her and Aunt Alice a Merry Christmas. He then hugged Mary-Ann and gave her a knowing smile. Once inside, Mr Wetherby poured them all a glass of gin punch. William took a large mouthful before he called the room to order.

"Can I interrupt you for a minute?" he said. "I have an announcement to make. This morning before I left Handsworth I made a proposal of marriage to Miss Watkins and I'm delighted to say she accepted. We'll be married sometime next year."

Mary-Ann grinned at him. "I knew she'd say yes … congratulations!"

Mr Wetherby stood up and shook his stepson by the hand. "I'm delighted to hear it. This will bring two important families together; I couldn't have chosen better for you."

William smiled as he turned to Mary to gauge her reaction.

"Aren't you happy for me, Mother?"

"Unlike others in the room, I'm surprised, that's all." She looked at the clock on the mantelpiece. "I can't talk now; the dinner will be ready."

William emptied his glass and allowed Mr Wetherby to replenish it. He didn't want to argue today, but his mother looked mad at him. *Stay calm. You're only here for another few hours.*

Once dinner was finished and the table cleared, William was unable to keep his eyes from the clock.

"Mother, what time do you think Aunt Sarah-Ann will join us?"

"Not long now; she should be here by five o'clock. Why do you ask?"

William took a deep breath. "I need to catch the six o'clock carriage; I'm working in the morning."

Mary's face glowed bright red. "Couldn't Mr Watkins have given you the morning off? You wouldn't be living up there if it wasn't for him."

Mr Wetherby stood up and walked to the sideboard. "I have a rather good bottle of port here, a gift of the season from Mr Grimshaw. Mary, let me pour the first glass for you."

The pure blue of Mary's eyes appeared icy cold as she glared at William. "Why not, it can't make me feel any worse than I do."

"Mother, please be happy for me. I thought you liked Miss Watkins."

"I may be getting used to her, but I worry she'll bring you trouble."

"Here, drink this." Mr Wetherby handed her the port. "None of us know our futures so you can't say that. William's a grown man; he has to make his own decisions. I remember you had doubts about me once upon a time, but we're doing rather well now."

Mary took a sip of port. "You're right, I'm sorry; just give me time to get used to it."

Mr Wetherby had just sat down when the door opened and Sarah-Ann walked in carrying Elizabeth; Mr Flemming was close behind.

"Merry Christmas," Mary said, cheering up at the sight of them. "It's been too long since you were last here."

"Two years to the day." Mr Flemming's eyes narrowed to slits as he stared at Mr Wetherby.

"The less said about that, the better," Mary said. "Will you both have a glass of port?"

"I'll have one, but none for her."

Mr Wetherby glanced at Sarah-Ann. "I'm sure she's capable of deciding for herself."

"Don't tell me how to look after my wife; you stay away from her."

"I'm fine, honestly." Sarah-Ann gave Mr Wetherby a weak smile.

William watched the exchange but had no idea what was going on. He thought back to the Christmas two years earlier and realised little had changed. Mr Flemming and Mr Wetherby still disliked each other and poor Aunt Sarah-Ann was in the middle of it. Knowing he needed to leave within the hour, he took the chance to break up the conversation.

"I'm glad you're here," he said to his aunt who was now preoccupied with her daughter. "I wanted to tell you my news before I left."

Sarah-Ann's face lit up. "Don't tell me you've made a marriage proposal to Miss Watkins."

"I have, and what's more, she accepted." A grin spread across William's face. "We'll be married next year."

"Congratulations."

"So she accepted, did she?" Mr Flemming forced his eyes away from Mr Wetherby.

"Did you know about it?" Sarah-Ann asked.

"He came into the shop to buy a ring the other week, him and Miss Jackson here."

William thought his mother was going to cry.

"Why didn't you tell me?" Sarah-Ann said.

"He asked me not to; he wanted it kept a secret."

"More of a surprise than a secret." William took a deep breath to calm the thumping of his heart.

"Did you meet the new assistant?" Sarah-Ann said. "I haven't met her yet, but I believe she's got a lot of experience."

William hesitated; the young woman he'd seen in the shop didn't look experienced.

"She wasn't there," Mr Flemming said without hesitating. "She'd gone out … I was on my own."

"Was that the young girl who was in the shop when I popped back?" William asked.

Sarah-Ann looked to William and then to her husband, opened her mouth to say something but closed it again.

"I don't think so," Mr Flemming said without flinching. "She must have been a customer."

William left Frankfort Street earlier than he needed to. He had never been so glad to be going back to Handsworth and not only because he was keen to get back to Miss Watkins. Within minutes of his aunt and Mr Flemming arriving, the tension had become intolerable. He realised it was partly his fault. He would make amends with his mother when he could, but there was more to it than that. There was something going on with Mr Flemming, although he couldn't work out what it was. Harriet always delighted in gossip, and he couldn't wait to tell her everything when they were next alone. It would keep her thinking for weeks.

Back in Handsworth, the Watkins family were waiting for him. There was an empty seat by the fire and a glass of port alongside it. Harriet sat to his left and he smiled at her as he leaned back in the chair. He was now more comfortable with this family than he was with his own.

Chapter 10

A S SPRING ARRIVED AND THEY made their way to church for morning prayer, the scent of blossom on the trees brought a smile to Harriet's lips. The cold dark days of winter were almost over. She linked her arm through William's as they walked along Upper Grosvenor Street before they took the path leading directly to St Mary's. Her aunt and uncle walked behind them, but a glance over her shoulder confirmed they were far enough away for her to talk freely.

"What do you do when you go to work all day?" she asked William.

"You know what I do; I make tools."

"No, but what do you actually do? How do you work? Do you have your own machine or do you have to share with everyone else? I've no idea how you spend your days and that can't be right."

"You shouldn't be worrying about such things. I spend my days on several different machines if you must know, but it's a man's workplace; hot, dirty and noisy, nothing for you to concern yourself with."

"Why are men so dismissive of women who show an interest in their work? I don't want to work there but I'd like to see inside the workshop, just once, so I can see what you do each day. How can I understand your moods of an evening if I don't know anything about what you do?"

William smiled at her. "You're always so inquisitive. Why can't you be content with what you have? I doubt your aunt has ever been to the workshop and yet I don't suppose she thinks any less of your uncle as a result."

"And my aunt is happy to sit and knit or embroider every afternoon. I need more to fill my days; I want to understand."

"Once we're married and you have baby William you'll have plenty to fill your days. You won't be worried about where I work as long as I bring home the money."

"But I don't want my life to be a constant cycle of having babies."

William turned to her, his mouth gaping.

"Don't look at me like that," she teased. "Of course we'll have children, God willing, but I need to do more. I want to read, to carry on learning. Once we're married, will you let me read?"

"I've never given it any thought, to be honest with you. Mother reads occasionally, often the Bible or Mrs Beeton's book. Sometimes she reads magazines about caring for the home. I don't understand why your uncle won't let you read that sort of thing."

"I do read the Bible, but there's only so much you can take at a time, and I'm not interested in household chores. I had them drilled into me for two years when I was at school. I'd rather read novels or learn about what's going on in the world. Is that so wrong?"

"I don't know. I don't want to upset your uncle as soon

as we're married, but I want you to be happy. Let me think about it."

A smile returned to Harriet's face. "If you want to make me happy, does that mean you'll show me around the workshop one day?"

"No, it does not! Your uncle would have my guts for garters if he saw you there."

Harriet's eyes sparkled. "We'd better make sure he doesn't see me then."

With hindsight William should have seen it coming, but his mind didn't work the same way as Harriet's. He thought she'd forgotten about visiting the workshop but clearly she hadn't. Two weeks later he found himself standing outside his place of work with Harriet by his side. Her uncle had been in Birmingham all day and when they left home for their walk Harriet suggested they go in the opposite direction for a change. Before he realised where he was he found himself walking down Church Lane in the vicinity of the workshop.

"Uncle's workshop's around here, isn't it?" Harriet asked as if the idea had just occurred to her. "Which one is it?"

"It's further down on the left, behind the wall."

"I've never been to this part of Handsworth before; we don't usually walk this way. While we're here, could I go inside?"

"I don't have the keys with me; I left them on the sideboard for your uncle when he gets home."

"Silly me, I didn't realise you left them there on purpose. I put them in your jacket pocket so you didn't lose them."

William patted his pocket and felt the keys beneath his fingers. "Are you sure that's why they're there? I think you knew exactly what you were doing."

"I don't know what you mean." Harriet turned her head but William caught a glimpse of her smile.

"Whether you do or not, we can't go into an enclosed building; anyone could see us."

"We can leave the door open. If anyone asks you can say you left something behind and you've come to collect it. Besides, you said it was behind a wall, so nobody should see us."

William stopped and turned her by the shoulders to face him. "Have you been planning this all day?"

"No! I'm not that slow. I thought of it last night as soon as Uncle said he wouldn't be around. Please, William, a quick look and I'll be happy."

How could he stay angry with her? "Only if you promise to be quick. I'll stand outside and you can walk to the door of the workshop as long as you don't go in."

Harriet stepped through the door William held open for her. He kept it open while she walked down the short corridor and stopped by the door to the workshop. The room wasn't big but it was full of machines, too full if she was being honest and they weren't small either. In fact, the room was packed and she wondered how six men could work in such overcrowded conditions. She stepped into the room to get a better sense of the space. Admittedly her skirt was wide, but in places there was barely enough room to walk between the machines, let alone work.

"Harriet, where are you going?" William called. "Come back here, and for heaven's sake don't touch anything."

Ignoring William, Harriet continued to walk around the workshop. She'd reached the far wall before he caught up with her.

"Do you have all these machines running at once?" she asked.

"Of course we do. Now come back here; it's time we left."

"And when these wheels turn do they drive the parts that shape the metal?"

"Yes, why?"

"Where do you work?"

William put his hand to his forehead. "It depends what I'm doing. I use all the machines although I often stand at the workbench over there." He pointed to a workbench on the left-hand wall situated beneath a row of high windows.

"I don't like it, William. It's too dangerous; there's no room for you to move. It would only take one slip and you'd lose an arm."

"I told you it's no place for a woman. It's a man's environment and we don't have a problem with it. Now come back here. If you're not careful you'll catch your skirt. Look, it touches the machines on both sides of the aisle." William shook his head. "I shouldn't have brought you."

"You didn't bring me, I brought us and I'm glad I did. It must be worse when all the machines are switched on. The noise and all the steam must be terrible."

"Come here." He took hold of her hand. She could tell he was intending to pull her past him, but instead she stopped directly in front of him and pressed herself to him, trapping him between two machines.

"You will be careful, won't you?" She ran her hands up his chest and gazed into his deep brown eyes. "I want you … just as you are." She put her arms around his neck and pulled his face towards hers before pressing her lips to his. William responded momentarily before he pulled away.

"Harriet, stop this. What are you trying to do to me? This is all wrong and your behaviour is completely inappropriate."

Harriet let her bottom lip drop. "We're not doing anything wrong; we're about to be married."

"We shouldn't be here, let alone doing this, now get out of here." He pushed her towards the door as he fumbled for his keys. "Why do you do this to me? Look at me, my hands are shaking."

He locked the door before he took hold of the top of her arm and walked her back to the footpath. The strength of his grip hurt her arm, but she daren't complain.

"What are you frightened of? Nobody would have seen us."

"That's beside the point. What were you planning on doing in there? Women don't behave like that, not respectable ones anyway."

Harriet had to run to keep up with him. "I'm sorry, please don't be angry with me. I thought you'd like it."

"There's a time and a place for things like that and the workshop five minutes ago was neither. What if your dress had got caught on the machines? Anything could have happened. Don't you realise your uncle has the power to send me back to Birmingham whenever he chooses. Do you want that? Because I don't. Until I have my own workshop, we do what your uncle and Mr Wetherby tell us to and you're going to have to get used to it."

Chapter 11

THE BACK ROOM OF THE house on Grosvenor Street was cool, despite the sun blazing from a bright blue sky. Even at the height of summer, the sun didn't reach the back of the house, but Harriet's cheeks still burned. She sat at the dining table staring at the wall ahead, her fists clenched in front of her. She should have been in Birmingham today. It had all been arranged. She'd been up early and should have taken the eight o'clock carriage with William to spend the morning with her friends before visiting Mrs Wetherby. She'd been looking forward to it, particularly as her friend Miss Woodbridge had recently married Mr Kent and she wanted to know *all* the details. She had been ready to go, wearing one of her new-style dresses, but when she tried to leave her bedroom, the door was locked. There was no clock in her room, but she could tell from the voices downstairs that if someone didn't open the door soon, she would miss the carriage. She banged on the door, asking to be let out, but it was only after William had left that she heard the key in the door. As the door opened, her uncle marched into her room and struck her across the face with the back of his hand.

"Don't you ever talk to me like that again or it'll be

more than my hand you feel," he shouted. "Your aunt will keep an eye on you between now and the wedding and if you're not careful I'll be cancelling it." He stormed back out as quickly as he arrived, slamming the door behind him.

Harriet blinked back the tears. Her face was sore and warm to the touch and she took her face cloth and soaked it in water before holding it to her cheek. At least there was no blood.

The trouble had started the previous evening. She had come home with William to find the house empty. It was a thrill to think they had the place to themselves. Harriet picked up the newspaper and sat in her uncle's chair, impersonating his pompous mannerisms. Before long she had tears running down her cheeks from laughing. William was enjoying himself as much as she was and as she paused for breath he bent over and kissed her. Because of the noise they'd been making, neither of them had heard the front door open, nor had they seen her aunt and uncle walk into the back room. It was only as William straightened up they became aware of Mr Watkins glaring at them. William jumped to attention, while she had thrown the newspaper onto the table as if it was about to burn her.

"What on earth's going on here?" Mr Watkins asked.

"Nothing," William said. "We were only having a bit of fun."

"Fun? It didn't look like fun to me, and what was she doing with the newspaper?"

"I do have a name," Harriet said.

Her uncle glared at her. "And is this what you've

learned from the newspaper, to talk out of line and show no respect? I always said encouraging women to read would lead to this sort of behaviour. Well, let me tell you, it's not going to happen in my house."

Harriet stood up to face him. "What's wrong with reading the newspaper? A lot of women read them. There are some papers with pages specifically for us. Why does it concern you so much? What are you frightened of?"

"That's enough," her uncle said. "Get up those stairs and out of my sight."

Harriet stared at him, determined not to back down, but the scowl on her uncle's face left no room for argument. Her resolve faltered and as tears started to sting her eyes, she swept past him and out of the room.

❧

Mr Watkins followed her upstairs and William heard him lock her door before he returned to the back room.

"What was going on when we walked in?" he asked William.

"Nothing, sir. Harriet was just reading the newspaper to me."

"I wasn't talking about the newspaper, I meant what you were doing to her? Do you think that's an acceptable way to behave?"

"It was only a kiss."

"Only a kiss? You're not married yet; imagine the disgrace you could bring to us."

William saw the veins jutting out of Mr Watkins's neck and bowed his head. "I'm sorry, sir, it won't happen again."

"You're damn right it won't. You will not be left alone

with her until after you're married. Do I make myself clear? I don't want to see her with the newspaper again either. Don't you realise that's where she gets her ideas from? I told you before you started walking out together, she needs a tight rein, but all you do is encourage her. If you allow her to become involved in anything other than raising your children and keeping a tidy house, you're storing up trouble for yourself. If I hadn't kept her in check over these last few years, heaven knows what she'd be like now."

"I'm sorry, we didn't mean to upset you. I won't let it happen again."

"I'm afraid after what I've seen tonight, that's not enough. She's still my responsibility and to teach her a lesson, she'll be confined to the house until you're married. Either Mrs Watkins or I can keep an eye on her around the clock. You can go to Birmingham by yourself tomorrow and explain to everyone that she's not well."

William's face turned white. "It's a month until the wedding, you can't keep her indoors for so long. Will you still allow me to walk out with her of an evening? She needs to take the air."

"I've told you, you're not spending any time on your own with her until after the wedding and that means going out for walks. A month indoors is the least she deserves; if she needs air she can go into the back yard."

William's heart was pounding. "I don't mean to question you, but is this the best way to deal with her?"

"I know my niece better than you, Mr Jackson, and I'll deal with her as I see fit. Now, I suggest you go upstairs yourself before you say something you shouldn't. I'm in two minds about whether I should permit this marriage at all."

William's eyes bulged in their sockets. "You can't cancel the wedding."

"I most certainly can, and if I have another word from you, I will."

It was years since William had been sent to his room, but he wasn't sorry to go. He had no desire to spend any more time with Mr Watkins and was thankful he would be away from the workshop tomorrow. Mr Watkins had lost all sense of proportion and William knew he was making a mistake with Harriet. He wanted to go to her but with the door being locked he went to his own room where he prayed the next month would pass quickly.

The following morning, once it was clear she was not going to Birmingham, Harriet remained in her bedroom not wanting to leave while the mark on her face still smarted. By midday, when she thought she was about to suffocate, she selected a grey bonnet that would shield her face and went downstairs to prepare for a walk. As soon as she reached the bottom step, her aunt stopped her.

"You can take that off." She nodded at the bonnet. "I've been given instructions not to let you out the house until your wedding day."

"My wedding day! Why? Because I picked up the newspaper. You do realise this is 1867. What's the matter with him?"

"That's enough. You won't speak to your uncle as you did last night and I won't have you speaking to me like that either. You live in your uncle's house and you'll abide by his rules. Now take your bonnet off and come and do some embroidering; you need to remember your place."

Harriet stood and stared after her aunt, her hands shaking as she held them together, intertwining her fingers. *How dare they?* She wasn't a child anymore; she was twenty-four years old and about to be married.

"Get in here now." Her aunt stood by the door, her hands on her hips. "And you can snap out of that mood too. I'm not sitting with you all afternoon when you've got a face like that."

She'd been forced to embroider for over two hours and as soon as her aunt went out to the privy Harriet threw her work onto the table and slammed her fists down. Once she belonged to William they couldn't treat her like this. She would sit and read the paper all day long if she wanted. To spite her uncle she would take an interest in business and follow the dealings of local companies. She would learn what they did and how they worked, and she'd tell William what she had read … while he sat and listened. If she had a daughter of her own, she would make sure she had the best education and she would delight in it.

As her thoughts gathered pace, she realised it would be better if they didn't have to live with her aunt and uncle at all. She would persuade William to rent a house of his own; then she really could do what she wanted. She would talk to him about opening his own workshop too. If her uncle and Mr Wetherby could start their own businesses when they were young, William could too. He was as good as them and she would help. Then she wouldn't have to see her uncle at all. What a pleasure it would be to encourage William to be his own man, to help him set up his own business and let them know she was behind it all. If her uncle thought she was going to sit back and take his brutality, he could think again.

Chapter 12

Birmingham, Warwickshire.

WHEN HARRIET TRAVELLED WITH HIM, William rarely noticed the carriage ride, unless the driver hit an unusually large pothole, but today the journey was tedious. He stared through the window, watching the landscape change, until he smelt the bitterness of the breweries and he knew he was nearly there. As soon as he reached Birmingham he called on Harriet's friend, Mrs Kent, before he visited on his mother. He hadn't spoken to her for a couple of months and given the events of the previous evening he needed to talk to her.

Mary was tidying away her baking utensils when he arrived but with one look at him she sat him by the fire and made a pot of tea. As they waited for the tea to brew, William rested his head on the back of the chair and looked his mother in the eye.

"I'm sorry for the way I've behaved over the last couple of years," he said. "You don't deserve it."

"What's brought this on?"

"I've realised how important you are to me. I'm sorry I grew so distant. Will you forgive me?"

Mary smiled. "Of course I will. Has this got anything to do with Miss Watkins? You're not having second thoughts about the wedding, are you?"

"It is to do with Harriet, but I'm not having second thoughts. In fact, if I could bring the wedding forward to tomorrow I would."

Mary raised her eyebrow. "What's happened?"

"To tell you the truth, I don't know. Are you happy with your life, looking after Charlotte and taking care of the house?"

"Of course I am. I count myself fortunate to have a young daughter at my age and a house to take care of. If it wasn't for Mr Wetherby goodness knows where we'd be."

"Have you ever wanted to do anything else?"

Mary stood up to pour the tea. "You forget that I did other things before I met Mr Wetherby. When I had to look after the three of us I sold my knitting, then I worked for Mr Wetherby making hooks and eyes. That was before Aunt Lucy set me up in business."

William thought for a moment. "Did you enjoy it?"

"Not all of it, and not making the hooks and eyes, if I'm honest." Mary frowned at the thought of it. "I was happy in the short time I was with Aunt Lucy. I had some responsibility there."

"So why did you leave?"

Mary shrugged. "Because Mr Wetherby asked me to marry him. It was as simple as that."

"And you didn't mind giving up a job you liked?"

"I thought we'd have a better future with Mr Wetherby and it meant I could spend more time with you and Mary-Ann. What's this about?"

William hesitated. "Is it wrong, do you think, for a woman to want to learn about business?"

"Miss Watkins, you mean?" Mary handed William his tea and sat down again.

"She's so dissatisfied with her life. She wants to do so much but her uncle refuses to let her even read the newspaper in case she gets ideas."

"I can tell by the way she writes she's more intelligent than most, which perhaps explains why she's frustrated. Once you have a child she'll change."

"Do you think so?"

"I do. She's still young and often it's the things we can't have that we want the most. If you let her read the newspaper once you're married she'll soon tire of it, but if you try to stop her she'll end up resenting you. She has to realise herself that understanding business won't make her happy and by then she'll have your baby." Mary paused to take a sip of tea.

"I hope you're right," William said. "I do think she wants what she can't have. I wish you knew her better."

"You forget, or perhaps you don't realise, she writes to me almost every day and so I do know her. Very well as it happens. How else do you think I keep up to date with what you're doing?"

William smiled. "I'd forgotten. Nevertheless, I wish you'd come and visit us again. Harriet would love to see you."

"And I'd like to see more of her. I admit I had my doubts about her when you first went to Handsworth, but since we've been corresponding, I've grown rather fond of her. You must bring her for tea later. Is she at her friend's house?"

The smile fell from William's lips. "No. She's not with me today."

"That's not like her."

William stood up and paced the room. "Her uncle won't let her come to Birmingham for the next few weeks. He caught her reading the newspaper and refuses to let her out of the house until the wedding."

Mary's brow furrowed as she considered William's words. "But that's ridiculous."

"I'm well aware of that. The man's an idiot, but what can I do? I've tried talking to him, but he won't budge."

"Is she all right?"

"Of course she's not all right." William ran his hand through his hair. "I haven't been able to talk to her properly, but she's furious. And rightly so. The worst part is, there's nothing I can do about it. Mr Watkins is still her guardian and for all intents and purposes, I'm nothing more than a lodger."

Mary stood up and took hold of his hands. "Of course you're more than a lodger. You must be able to do something."

William shook his head. "My biggest worry is she'll do something stupid and Mr Watkins will cancel the wedding. He's already threatened to, and if Harriet provokes him …"

"Let me write to Mrs Watkins. If I can visit them for the afternoon, I'll try and talk to Harriet for you."

Chapter 13

Handsworth, Staffordshire.

T HE SOUND OF HER AUNT'S knitting needles clicking together, hour after hour, was enough to make Harriet want to snatch them off her and snap them over her knee. She dropped her embroidery ring onto her lap and gazed out of the window. The sun was shining over the rooftops, bathing the far side of the yard, but she wouldn't feel its warmth; not if she stayed where she was. She hadn't been outside for over a week and she'd had enough.

"I'm going into the back yard for some air." She threw her work onto the table and stood up.

"Stay where you are," her aunt said. "I've got a visitor coming to see you and he'll be here anytime now."

"Who?" A smile put a spark in Harriet's eyes. "Nobody's written to tell me they're coming."

"Wait and see. I'm hoping he'll be able to talk some sense into you."

Harriet's shoulders fell. "It's not a social visit then. Who am I going to be subjected to?"

"You can drop that attitude before you start. If you

must know, I've invited the rector over to talk to you. You need to understand how hurtful you are."

Harriet threw her arms in the air. "Doesn't anybody think of my feelings? Every time there's a disagreement, it's always me who's in the wrong, never the person who upsets me."

"There you go again. You don't know when to stop."

"Well I'll keep my mouth shut, then I can't say anything wrong. You can talk to the rector if you like, but keep me out of it."

"He's here now." Her aunt stood up when she heard the knock on the door. "Don't you dare embarrass me."

A minute later the maid showed the rector into the back room.

"Good afternoon, Mrs Watkins," he said, stroking the back of the hand she offered him. "Thank you for inviting me. I always say that God moves in mysterious ways. I hope I can be of some assistance today."

"I hope so too, Rector. You don't know the strain we've been living with over the last week. I just pray that things can return to how they used to be."

"And we'll pray together, Mrs Watkins, later, but first I need to understand the child."

Child! She was twenty-four years old and about to be married. Harriet clenched her fists under her skirt and took a deep breath. He could think what he liked; she wasn't going to say a word to either of them.

The maid bringing in some tea interrupted their conversation. It was only after she had left, that the rector acknowledged her.

"Now, Miss Watkins, I believe you've been causing

some problems." The rector treated her as if she were a simpleton. When she didn't respond, he continued. "I hope you realise you've brought great distress to your aunt and uncle and shame upon yourself. Mr and Mrs Watkins have brought you up as their own since you were a small girl and yet you've shown no appreciation for what they've done. *Honour thy father and thy mother*, the Lord commands and in your case that applies to your aunt and uncle. May the Lord forgive you for disobeying him."

Harriet saw her aunt nodding as he spoke, using her handkerchief to wipe her eyes.

"Often children don't understand," the rector continued. "They take their families for granted, not knowing the sacrifices that have been made on their behalf ..."

Was this going to go on all afternoon? Harriet wondered. *It's like he's preaching a sermon.*

"For the Lord says *Let all bitterness, and wrath, and anger, and clamour, and evil speaking, be put away from you with all malice ...*"

Harriet stared at the wall ahead of her. What could she do? She refused to talk to the man, but if she did nothing he was likely to continue preaching at her for hours. As the rector spoke, an idea came into her mind and after a moment's thought she deliberately held her breath. It was easy to start with but within seconds her lungs screamed for air. Before long it became impossible to sit still and she squirmed in her seat. She managed to maintain her posture for over a minute but before long the room started to spin and she swayed in her seat. Her aunt noticed her eyes closing and interrupted the rector.

"Harriet, are you all right?" she said. "Speak to me. You don't look well."

Harriet was desperate to breathe, but she refused to give in to her body. She stood up to ease the pressure in her chest but as she did the room went black and she collapsed, prompting a bout of coughing.

"Harriet, what are you doing? Look at me." Her aunt slapped her face but Harriet lay where she was, her eyes closed.

"For God commanded, saying, *Honour thy father and mother, and he that curseth father or mother, let him die the death*," the rector continued.

"No, don't let her die, Rector, pray for her, please."

At least that's something, Harriet thought, she mustn't hate me that much.

After a minute of being prayed over, Harriet could take no more and opened her eyes. She immediately regretted it. Her aunt believed she had witnessed a miracle, which prompted further quotes from the Bible and the rector being invited to stay for another cup of tea.

It was a full two hours before he left and Harriet was exhausted. At least she had spent the whole time without saying a word, although she didn't think he had noticed. She'd never liked the man, but now she hated him. He had done nothing but pour scorn on her all afternoon and she was only thankful she hadn't listened to a word he'd said.

Chapter 14

Birmingham, Warwickshire.

MARY SETTLED HERSELF INTO THE carriage with Mr Wetherby, Alice and William Junior. It was the second time in two weeks she had been to Handsworth and she hoped this visit would be happier than her last. She had visited Harriet a fortnight earlier and was shocked at how thin and pale she had become. The sparkle had gone from her eyes, as had her energy, which was usually plentiful. Mrs Watkins had done most of the talking and Harriet had only spoken when Mrs Watkins left the room.

"Did William tell you they've imprisoned me here until I'm married?" she said as soon as they were alone.

"He said they'd stopped you from going out."

Tears welled up in Harriet's eyes. "They treat me like a child; even when I'm in the house I'm never left alone unless I'm locked in my bedroom. I've barely spoken to William for two weeks, although I know he's spoken to my uncle about being more lenient. The only concession they've made is for me to go to church to hear the banns being read … as if that was a treat. After I was forced to endure the rector talking about my morality for over two hours, he's the last person I want to see. May God forgive me but the man is so patronising he makes me want to scream."

"I'm sure they have their reasons."

"Only that they don't want me to be happy." Harriet blinked, causing the tears to run down her cheeks. "I haven't written to anyone recently because my aunt reads all my letters. Not that I've got much to say. She forces me to sit and embroider every day and I swear once I'm married I will never pick up a needle again."

Mary leaned forward and took hold of Harriet's hands. "You need to calm down. Take some deep breaths for me. It won't be for much longer, but you mustn't do anything silly. The wedding's only two weeks away and once you're married you'll forget about all this. Try and stay calm until then. Promise me."

Harriet wiped her tears on the sleeve of her dress and nodded.

"Once you're married, you can visit us in Birmingham if you'd like to."

"Of course I'd like to."

"I ought to warn you, the place is becoming more intolerable by the month."

"I don't care how bad it is; it can't be any worse than being here. The next two weeks are going to be like torture. If I had to live like this for any longer, I think I should die."

"Don't talk like that and please be careful. You don't want to upset your uncle any further."

Harriet was about to answer when Mrs Watkins came back into the room. She immediately fell silent, refusing to utter another word. When Mary spoke to her she would shrug her shoulders or nod her head. Her aunt ignored her and acted as if she wasn't in the room. Mary hoped things hadn't got worse since her last visit.

When they arrived in Handsworth, the Wetherbys went straight to the church. They were joined by most of Mary's first husband's family, except Sarah-Ann who had sent word that she couldn't join them, and Richard, Charles's brother. With no explanations forthcoming, Mary supposed Sarah-Ann must be ill, but worried about Richard and his family. It was most unlike them to miss a family gathering.

She surveyed the congregation and waved to her sister-in-law, Martha, as William walked towards her.

"I'm so glad you're here." He bent down to kiss her cheek and took her elbow ushering her to one side. "I'm concerned about Harriet. Could you spend some time with her after the wedding? I've never seen her so unhappy. She's barely spoken a word for the last month and I'm worried she's made herself ill."

"Of course I'll spend some time with her. I've been worried myself since I visited, but I suspect she'll be back to her usual self today."

"I hope you're right."

"I'm sure I am. Today is the last day of what she would call her imprisonment and the day her uncle gives her away. She's been looking forward to it for a long time and I think you'll see the woman you love again."

William wasn't convinced. "These last few weeks have been torture for all of us. I think Mr Watkins underestimated the impact his curfew would have on the whole household, but he was too stubborn to admit it. Goodness knows what's going on now with the two of them alone at the house."

"Stop worrying; everything will be fine. Come on, we'd better take our places; she'll be here soon."

Harriet stood by the window in the front room and waved at Mary-Ann and Charlotte as they climbed into the carriage that would take them to church. They were so excited to be part of her day and she forced herself to smile until she was sure they could no longer see her. How she wished she was travelling with them. At least her uncle had bought them bridesmaid dresses and allowed them to come to the house to get ready. She supposed that was something.

As she watched her uncle help her aunt into the carriage, a tear fell onto her cheek. Neither of them had spoken to her this morning and even now, they didn't turn around to acknowledge her. Today should be the happiest day of her life, but just like everything else, her uncle had spoiled it. The last hour should have been special; she should have had her family and friends with her to celebrate, but instead they had all been asked to go to the church. No pre-wedding toasts, no smiles, no gasps of wonder when she appeared in a beautiful new dress. She didn't even have a new dress.

She watched her uncle return to the house, where he went into the back room, doubtless to have several glasses of whisky. How she wished she could simply walk out of the front door and take herself to church. Freedom was so close, and yet she still needed him to release her.

Five minutes later he stood by the door waiting for her.

She couldn't look at him. She didn't want to be near him, but as she walked into the hall and picked up her bouquet, he took hold of the top of her arm and squeezed it tightly.

"There are people outside waiting for you, so you'd better put a smile on your face."

Harriet pulled her arm from his grasp but said nothing. She would smile when she had something to smile about.

The ride to church only took a couple of minutes, but the silence in the carriage made it feel like hours. She had to get out before her tears started again. As soon as the carriage came to a halt, she opened the door herself, tentatively climbed down the steps and made her own way to the building. It gave her a minute to wipe her eyes on the back of her hand.

As the organist struck the first note, she reluctantly linked arms with her uncle and put on her best smile. William turned to face her and it was all she could do to stop herself running down the aisle into his arms. She had to be strong. If she let down her guard, the tears would return and William couldn't see her crying. Not now.

Mercifully, the wedding ceremony was short, and once it was over she and William returned to the waiting carriage for the journey back to Grosvenor Street.

"Come here," William said as he climbed into the carriage and put his arm around her shoulders. "Everything's going to be all right now."

As the carriage pulled away, Harriet buried her head into his chest and sobbed. "Promise you won't leave me."

"Of course I won't leave you. I don't ever want to be without you again." He lifted her chin and wiped her eyes with his handkerchief. "I don't want any more tears either. This is the happiest day of my life and I want you to be happy too. You're mine now and I won't let anything happen to you."

Harriet smiled and clung to him as if her life depended on it. "I am happy, really I am. I just wish we didn't have to go through this performance with the wedding breakfast."

"Stop worrying. I'll make sure we sit with Mary-Ann and Mother and as far away from your uncle as possible. Everything will be fine. I promise."

For the first time that day, Harriet relaxed. "I do love you, you know."

"Not as much as I love you."

By the following morning, the smile on Harriet's face was there because she was happy again. She had spent the night in William's arms and her uncle could do her no more harm. Not only that, she had William to herself for three full days before he went back to work, and she was going to make the most of it. They stayed in bed for longer than usual but as soon as they had taken breakfast, they left the house, arm in arm, on their way to the woods.

"It's such a relief to be out of the house again," Harriet said. "I still can't believe we're married."

William smiled and patted her hand. "You can believe it. I feel like the luckiest man alive this morning."

The smile widened across her lips. "Can we live differently now I don't have to do what my uncle tells me?"

William frowned. "We do still live in his house and so we can't upset him."

"Do we have to stay in that house? Can't we find a place of our own?"

"I'm sure there's no need for that."

"Why not? Most people live in a house of their own once they're married. I don't want to be with my aunt and uncle forever."

"It won't be forever." William patted her hand. "What would you do all day if you were in a house of your own. If we stay where we are, you'll have your aunt for company and we don't have to worry about running the house. You need to concentrate on having a baby and looking after it."

Tears welled up in Harriet's eyes. "I thought you understood me. You know that's not what I want. Why can't things be different now we're married?"

"Because they don't need to be. Your uncle knows you're my responsibility now; he won't treat you as he did before the wedding. Trust me; it'll be for the best."

Harriet blinked the tears down her cheeks and wiped them with the back of her hand. "I want it to be just the two of us."

"We have our own room and I'll buy a couple of chairs so we can be on our own whenever we want."

That was not what she meant, but Harriet didn't want to argue on the first day they were married. "Will you let me read? The newspaper ... or perhaps some magazines. Please don't force me to embroider every afternoon."

William kissed her hand. "Why does it matter to you so much? Do you want to read just to annoy your uncle?"

"Not at all. I wish it didn't upset him, but I get bored. It's all right for you. You're out all day and have people to talk to about things that matter. I've so many questions running through my mind about how things work, about what life is like outside Handsworth and Birmingham, about the empire, but I've nobody to talk to. When you're at home, I'm not allowed to join in. If I could read the newspaper at least it would satisfy my curiosity."

"You can talk to me. When we go out, we can pick a different topic each evening. Will that help?"

Harriet sighed. "Only if you let me read the newspaper so I know what to talk about?"

"I suppose so, but please don't flaunt it in front of your uncle."

"How about some magazines, something I can read in public?"

"Why don't you ask my mother what she reads? I'm sure they'll be fine …"

Harriet shot him a warning glance.

"Don't look at me like that; what's wrong with asking Mother?"

Harriet took a deep breath to control her voice. "She hasn't got the same interests as me. I'd like to read something like *Belgravia*. They serialise novels, amongst other things."

William gasped. "I don't think so. I've heard some rather unsavoury comments about it."

"It's not that bad," Harriet said. "Mrs Kent reads it and says it's great fun."

"Well, Mrs Kent can keep it to herself. I'm not letting your uncle see you with that."

"What about *Cornhill*? It's reputable enough and they print novels in there as well."

William thought for a moment. "Yes, that should be acceptable. I'll get a copy for us to read together to see what we think. Reading one of the novels out loud in the evening would be a good way to show your uncle they needn't lead to your moral decline."

"Are you always going to tell me everything I can do?" Harriet stuck out her bottom lip.

"I'm doing it for your own good. We shouldn't deliberately upset your uncle."

"You've just said he has no right to tell me what to do anymore."

William sighed. "Maybe not, but let's take it slowly, shall we?"

Harriet's shoulders slumped. "Will you be able to bring me a copy by tomorrow?"

"It'll be next week now; will that do you?"

"Yes … thank you," she said, trying, but failing, to hide her disappointment. It was a start, she supposed, but she was going to have to use all her charms if she was going to persuade William to find a house of their own.

Chapter 15

Handsworth, Staffordshire.

THE FRONT DOOR OPENED SILENTLY but closed with a bang that made Harriet jump from her chair. She moved to the mirror to check her hair before she turned and stood in front of the fireplace, waiting for William to join her. It was almost three weeks since the wedding and this morning they had had their first argument. She held her breath as the door to the back room opened.

"You're early," she said forcing a smile to her lips.

"Only by five minutes. I had to leave work early to pick this up." He waved a copy of *Cornhill* at her. "Are you happy now?"

Harriet rushed towards him and threw her arms around his neck. "Thank you, you don't know how much this means." She pulled away and took the magazine from him. "I'm sorry I shouted this morning, but I was getting desperate. I now have something to do other than knitting or embroidering."

"I thought you'd started to read the newspaper."

"I have, but I'm fed up with my aunt staring at me whenever I pick it up. I've started taking it upstairs, but she still comments when I come back down. In a few more weeks it will be cold in the bedrooms and she won't let me light a fire up there during the day." Harriet flicked through the pages, her eyes widening with each article. "Besides, this is much more interesting than the newspaper. Look there's something here about travelling around Spain. Wouldn't you love to go there one day?"

"Not particularly."

Bewilderment crossed her face. "No? Why not? It would be like going to a different world."

"I'm happy with the world I have."

Harriet shook her head. There was no point arguing. "Well, what about the novels? There are two serialised at the same time; I hope they're not too far into the stories."

William took the magazine from her and studied the rest of the contents. "Since when has game poaching been of any interest to you?"

"Since now." Harriet snatched the magazine back from him and sat down. "Don't make fun of me; can't you see this will open the door to another world? One that's passing us by."

"One that we need know nothing about."

"Where's your sense of adventure? I can see I'm going to have to work on it."

William rolled his eyes and smiled. "I think the sooner you have a baby the better."

Harriet stopped flicking through the magazine and looked up. "Having a baby won't make me any less interested in the outside world. Besides, what if I can't have any?"

William stared at her.

"Don't look so surprised. Not all women can have children."

"Is that what you want? To be seen as an incomplete woman?"

"I'm just saying it's a possibility and if we have no children, we'll have to find other things to do."

"Now you're being ridiculous. Of course we'll have a family. I don't want to hear any more of this. It's about time you went and fetched the tea."

It took less than three days for Harriet to read *Cornhill* from cover to cover, but no sooner had she finished than she read it again; this time more slowly. She longed to visit the places they described in Spain and tried to conjure up images of the picturesque mountain ranges and seaside villages as she read. Her longing wasn't helped when she read about the benefits of taking a holiday. Apparently recreation was good for you, but how she would persuade anyone to travel with her to Spain she had no idea.

She was about to start an article on the subject of time when the maid interrupted to give her a letter. It was from Mary, and Harriet's heart leapt as she read. Maybe she would get her holiday after all.

As they retired to bed that evening, Harriet took the letter from her dress and showed it to William.

"Your mother's asked if I'd like to stay with them for a few days. Can I go … please?"

"What's brought this on?"

"I told you she'd asked me to visit once we were married."

"I thought you'd only go for the day."

"I read an article in *Cornhill* saying it was beneficial to have a change of air; it's supposed to relax and refresh you. I mentioned it to her in a letter and she must have remembered. Of course I'd like to go with you and preferably further than Birmingham, but for now Birmingham is the best offer I've had."

William laughed. "The air in Birmingham won't do you much good."

"It's the change that's important; a change of routine and of diet, meeting new people, that's what does you good. Please say I can go."

William sighed and moved towards her. "I'll miss you if you go, but I suppose it can't do any harm if you're with Mother. I'll speak to your uncle tomorrow and arrange how to get you there and back. Now, come here." He took her in his arms and kissed her neck. "If you're going to go, let me make the most of you while you're here."

∽∾

Birmingham, Warwickshire.

Four weeks later, William and Harriet travelled to Birmingham. They were cold as they made their way up Summer Lane and the smell of pea and ham soup as they walked into the living room made them realise how hungry they were. The table was set for seven and within five minutes they were sitting down with bowls of steaming soup in front of them and a loaf of bread in the centre of the table. Harriet sat between William and Mary-Ann, and for the first time in months she enjoyed the company. It was so different to being at home and, with the exception of Mr Wetherby, so much more informal.

"What do you have planned while Harriet's here?" Mr Wetherby asked Mary once they had finished eating.

"Just a few visits, nothing unusual. Martha's invited us to her house on Tuesday and we'll visit Sarah-Ann. I've still not seen her since she sent her apologies for the wedding."

"You'd better go when Mr Flemming's at work." William Junior laughed into his hand. "They don't want a repeat of Christmas, do they, Father?"

Mary was about to scold him but Mr Wetherby stopped her.

"I'm sure he'll be at work so there's no need to worry."

Harriet hadn't spent much time with William Junior but following this exchange she paid more attention to him. He seemed to think he was better than everyone else and if there was an opportunity to belittle anyone he would, always looking to his father for approval. When his aunt Alice and Mary-Ann left to go to the back house, he couldn't resist mocking the fact they didn't have a man to head the house. On occasion Mary raised an eyebrow to him but in typical fashion he dismissed her. Nobody else seemed to think his behaviour strange and Harriet said nothing until she was alone with William.

"Do you think your brother sees himself as better than the rest of us?" she asked as she climbed into bed.

"It's just the way he is, although he was worse than usual tonight," William said.

"Mr Wetherby does indulge him though, don't you think?"

William shrugged. "He is his son. I'm sure if I had a son, I'd indulge him too."

"Not like that I hope. Besides, you're like a son to him. Why does he treat you both so differently?"

"I've no idea," William sighed as he placed his trousers on the back of a chair. "I've got used to it and you'll have to as well. William Junior's always going to be his favourite. They even look alike with their fair hair and speckled eyes."

"Except William Junior's shorter and fatter. He must do nothing but eat."

"That's enough. Mother says he's still growing. Give him another few years and there'll be no difference between them."

"Doesn't your mother say anything to him?"

William climbed into bed beside her. "What is there to say? I'm grateful he took care of Mother when he did and he's generous to us all. Why would I complain?"

"Well, don't take anything for granted. William Junior's only sixteen. In my opinion, you need to keep an eye on him and make sure he doesn't exclude you from everything as he gets older."

Chapter 16

THE EDGE OF THE BED buckled as William sat down and leaned over Harriet.

"I need to go," he said as he brushed hair from her face and kissed her forehead.

Harriet rubbed her eyes and squinted at him in the dark. "What time is it?"

"Nearly six o'clock."

"Already? I wish you didn't have to go."

"So do I, but this is the holiday you wanted."

Harriet smiled. "You're good to me. I promise I'll make the most of it. Simply being away from Uncle for a week will do me the world of good."

"And getting to know Mary-Ann will too. She's been as excited about this week as you have."

"I'm looking forward to moving to the back house for the rest of the week. It will be interesting to live in a house with only women."

"As long as you don't like it too much." William kissed her again before he stood up. "I need to go now, but I'll be back on Saturday."

Once Harriet had washed and dressed, she breakfasted with Mary before she walked around to the back house.

Mary-Ann was waiting for her and Harriet sat down while her sister-in-law made a pot of tea. She hadn't noticed before how much Mary-Ann was like William. She had the same dark brown eyes and dark hair, which she wore plaited and twisted into a knot on the back of her head. She was an attractive girl, taller than Harriet and rounder; no doubt due to her mother's baking.

"I know I'm biased," Mary-Ann said once Harriet had settled in front of the fire, "but you're so lucky to have married my brother. If ever I get married, I should like it to be to someone like him."

"You're not wrong. I fell for him the first time I met him, but couldn't tell anyone. I was only thirteen at the time; my uncle would have been beside himself. *Girls of your age shouldn't be thinking about boys!*" Harriet laughed at her impersonation.

"I didn't think you'd known him for so long."

"I didn't know him well. He was my uncle's apprentice and so I saw him occasionally; there was something about him. It was a long time before we talked to each other, but it was worth the wait. Are you walking out with anyone?"

"No, and I don't know if I ever will. I don't meet many men and those I do are mostly married acquaintances of Mr Wetherby. When I go out it's to meet female friends. My best friend, Mrs Harris, has been married for five years. I'm sure she thinks there's something wrong with me."

"I'm sure she doesn't, but don't any of your friends have brothers?"

Mary-Ann thought for a moment. "No, they don't. Not that I know of anyway. Mother said she would ask Mr Wetherby to arrange some introductions, but nothing came of it. He doesn't have a lot of time for me; he only tolerates me because of Mother. Now I live here, I'm largely out of his way."

"That's terrible," Harriet said. "Why don't I speak to William and see if he knows anyone? You must come and visit us in Handsworth as well. William would like to see you and we can arrange some meetings for you."

"You don't need to; and please don't involve William. What will he think of me?"

"He won't think any the worse of you; he wants you to be happy."

ȣȣ

On Thursday, Harriet took a carriage with Mary, Mary-Ann and Charlotte to visit Sarah-Ann. They arrived shortly after Elizabeth had been put down for her afternoon nap, but Charlotte took no time waking her up, pawing over the baby until she started crying.

"I'm sorry." Mary gave Sarah-Ann an apologetic smile. "She hasn't seen Elizabeth for a while."

Sarah-Ann was in no mood for a spoiled three-year-old. "It's all right for you. You're not the one who'll have to deal with her later when Mr Flemming comes home. You can just go back to Mr Wetherby and forget about me."

Mary had never seen Sarah-Ann like that before. "Is everything all right?" she asked.

"Does it look as if everything's all right?" Sarah-Ann wiped her eyes on the sleeve of her dress. "It's hard enough looking after Mr Flemming every night without having an overtired child as well."

A puzzled expression formed on Harriet's face. "Why

does Mr Flemming need looking after? Surely you only need to give him his tea."

Sarah-Ann glared at Harriet.

"Perhaps there's more to it than that," Mary said. "Why don't you and Mary-Ann take Charlotte and Elizabeth to the park. It will help to tire them out."

Somewhat reluctantly, Harriet went with Mary-Ann. Once they were alone, Mary poured out two gins and pushed one across the table to Sarah-Ann.

"Are you going to tell me what this is about?"

Sarah-Ann took a mouthful of gin and stood up to go to the window. "He's started drinking."

"Who? Mr Flemming?" Mary said. "I thought he always went for a drink on his way home from work."

"Not like this. When Elizabeth was born he started staying out later and later; now he doesn't come home until they kick him out. By the time he arrives home he's drunk and if Elizabeth makes so much as a sound he takes it out on me."

Mary stared at Sarah-Ann open-mouthed. "What do you mean, he takes it out on you?"

Sarah-Ann opened the front of her dress and showed Mary the bruising across her chest. "There's more than that as well. I've been struggling to breathe this week, my ribs have been so sore."

Mary gasped and put her hand to her mouth. She knew ale made men violent, but she'd never seen it in real life before. A silence hung between them before she found her tongue. "Why?"

Sarah-Ann shrugged. "You tell me? He always wanted to be a father, but now he is, he hates it."

Mary shook her head and took a mouthful of gin. "He was so pleasant when we first met him. What happened?"

Sarah-Ann's face turned scarlet, but before she could turn to face the window, Mary saw her.

"You haven't done anything to deserve this, have you?"

Sarah-Ann shook her head. "Of course not."

"I would suggest Mr Flemming thinks you have."

Sarah-Ann didn't answer but buried her head in her hands, sobbing.

"Come here." Mary put her arms around Sarah-Ann and held her close. "You need to show him you love him; that way he'll want to come home."

As soon as Harriet and Mary-Ann returned, Mary turned them around and ushered them straight back out of the door. Elizabeth was asleep and with Sarah-Ann calmed, Mary didn't want either Harriet or Charlotte upsetting them.

"Is Aunt Sarah-Ann all right?" Mary-Ann asked once they were in the carriage.

"She'll be fine, nothing more than an argument with Mr Flemming." Mary stared out of the window. Lying always made her uncomfortable, despite her good intentions.

"She's not at all what I expected," Harriet said. "William's told me she argues a lot with Mr Flemming. He told me how nasty Mr Flemming was with her last Christmas. If I was her, I wouldn't put up with it."

Mary took a deep breath and turned to face her. "You of all people should know it's not easy to argue with the man of the house."

"Well, they shouldn't be allowed to get away with it. One day women are going to have to stand up for themselves and let men know we won't put up with it."

Mary smiled at Mary-Ann and shook her head before she turned to Harriet. "You know as well as I do, that's not going to happen."

"Well it jolly well should. I've had enough of being told what to do."

❧

The following Saturday, as she waited for William to collect her, Harriet sat with Mary and Mary-Ann.

"Thank you for letting me stay so long. The *Cornhill* article was right; I've enjoyed having a change."

"We've enjoyed having you," Mary said. "I bet William's missed you though."

"I'm sure he has, but I've not been much company recently. I was so miserable after what happened before the wedding. I'd hoped William would shake me out of it, but nothing's changed. Everything I want to do, William has to check with my uncle."

"I expect he's worried about you," Mary-Ann said. "He won't want you arguing with your uncle again, so he's being careful."

"You may be right, but I wish he'd stand up to my uncle and remind him I'm not his responsibility anymore."

"While you live under your uncle's roof, I'm afraid he'll still want some say over what you do," Mary said. "Have you thought about moving house?"

Harriet let out a sarcastic laugh. "There's nothing I'd like more, but William thinks we're better off where we are.

How we can be better off, I don't know. It was lovely staying in the back house with Mary-Ann and Aunt Alice for a few days. There was no one to tell us what to do and we weren't on tenterhooks in case we said something wrong."

"We are lucky Mr Wetherby pays for everything for us," Mary-Ann said. "I'd still like a husband though."

"I know you would, but be honest, why?"

"Because I want to be a mother. What's the point of being able to do what you want, if you don't have any children?"

Harriet stood up and walked to the window. Was she the only woman in the world who didn't want a house full of children? Every woman she knew was happy to surrender their identities to their husbands and lose control of their lives, if indeed they had control in the first place. Was there something wrong with her? What if her intelligence meant she couldn't have any children? Would that change anything? Maybe it would, but perhaps not in a good way. She sighed and turned back to Mary-Ann.

"I wish I was more like you. To be happy living in your own sphere, without the need to question anything. It would make life so much easier."

Chapter 17

MARY STOOD ON THE PAVEMENT as William and Harriet climbed into the carriage that would take them back to Handsworth. Even now he was a married man, tears still filled her eyes as the carriage turned into Summer Lane and disappeared from view. With a final wave she let out a deep sigh before she reached for a handkerchief to wipe her eyes. Mary-Ann and Alice waited for her to turn around before Mary-Ann put her arm around her mother's shoulders and walked her to the front door.

"Do you want us to come in with you?" Mary-Ann said.

"No, I'll be fine. I haven't got much tidying up left and I need to talk to Mr Wetherby. I'll see you later."

She waited for Alice and Mary-Ann to disappear down the entry before she went indoors and continued to clear the table.

"You're quiet," Mr Wetherby said from his seat by the fire.

"I'm fine, but I never did like waving William off."

"I remember. I'll never forget the day I brought William down to Birmingham. I didn't think you'd ever forgive me." Mr Wetherby smiled at the memory.

"I didn't think I would either. It seems such a long time ago."

Mary gave the table a final wipe before she sat in the chair opposite Mr Wetherby. "Do you remember when we used to walk out every Sunday afternoon?"

Mr Wetherby smiled and put the newspaper on his lap. "I do, it was always my favourite time of the week."

"Why did we stop? I wonder. I don't remember now."

"I suppose once we were married there was no need to."

"And once we moved back to Birmingham, walking the streets in the middle of winter wasn't as appealing as strolling to the wood in Handsworth during the summer."

Mr Wetherby stood up and went to the window. "Considering it'll be November next week, it is a lovely day out there. Why don't we go for a walk now? There might be a band playing in the park."

"We'll be lucky to see a band this late in the year, but yes, I'd like that." Mary smiled. "Do you think Charlotte will be all right in the court? I can't imagine she'll want to come with us."

Mr Wetherby walked back to the chair and helped Mary up. "Why don't you go and find someone to keep an eye on her? Be quick though. I don't want it clouding over before we go."

Ten minutes later the two of them left Frankfort Street, Mary's arm linked through his.

Halfway down Summer Lane, Mr Wetherby turned to Mary. "You're still quiet. You're not thinking of William, are you?"

"No, not at all, but I've got something to tell you and I'm not sure how to put it."

A frown rested on Mr Wetherby's brow. "What is it?"

"Part of the problem is that I'm not sure I should be telling you and if I do, I worry how you'll react."

"Well, you've no choice now, so out with it."

Mary took a deep breath. "You know I took Harriet to visit Sarah-Ann when she was with us? Well, Sarah-Ann was in quite a state." Mary could tell by the tension in his arm that she had his undivided attention.

"What sort of state?"

"Well, firstly she got cross with Charlotte, which isn't like her."

"She shouted at Charlotte?" Mr Wetherby turned and glared at Mary.

"No, not directly; at me for letting Charlotte wake Elizabeth up. I had to intervene to stop her arguing with Harriet as well."

Mr Wetherby gritted his teeth. "What's that damn husband of hers been up to?"

"How did you know it had anything to do with Mr Flemming?"

Mr Wetherby didn't miss a beat. "It doesn't take a genius. You've seen how he's been with her lately. He's the only one who would upset her like that."

"He's taken to spending every evening in the beerhouse, often not returning home until after closing time."

"Sarah-Ann should be pleased. It means she doesn't have to see so much of him."

"It's not that simple." Mary paused until Mr Wetherby turned to face her. "If anything upsets him when he gets home, especially Elizabeth, he takes it out on Sarah-Ann. She showed me some bruises."

The blood drained from Mr Wetherby's face as he stopped and pulled his arm free. "He beats her?" His voice turned low and cold. "I'll kill him."

"No, please calm down." Mary took hold of his hands. "This is why I wasn't going to tell you. Sarah-Ann asked me not to."

A steadiness returned to his voice. "What does she want then?"

"I don't think she wants anything. She wouldn't have told me if I hadn't seen her in such a state. I got the impression it's been going on since Elizabeth was born, which is over a year now."

"Elizabeth? What's it got to do with her?"

Mary shrugged. "She wouldn't say, but it wouldn't surprise me if Mr Flemming thinks she's not his."

Mr Wetherby's eyes almost popped from their sockets. "What on earth makes you say that?"

"She went bright red when I asked what had happened to upset Mr Flemming."

"But she didn't say anything?"

Mary shook her head.

"So what makes you think there's another man involved? You can't go around saying things like that when you've no idea what happened."

"It was just a feeling I got. He was always jealous when you paid Sarah-Ann any attention."

"That's enough. I don't want to hear any more of it." Mr Wetherby started walking again, the fist of his right hand hitting the palm of his left.

"What will you do?" Mary said as she ran to catch him up.

"I need to teach him a lesson."

Mary pulled on his arm, forcing him to stop. "You can't make a scene. What will people think?"

"You should be more worried about Sarah-Ann."

Mary flinched under his glare. "I am, but I'm also worried about you. You can't get into a brawl with him."

"I've got to do something; we can't let him carry on like this."

Mr Wetherby stared at the pavement as they continued walking, deep in thought.

"Perhaps I can help," Mary said. "If we both go and see him …"

"Don't be ridiculous." The ferocity of his words took Mary by surprise.

"Why is it ridiculous? I could keep the peace while you talk to him."

Mr Wetherby's face was crimson. "I'll do more than talk to him."

"Calm down. I don't know why you're so agitated. Stand still and take some deep breaths."

Mr Wetherby glanced up and down the street before he did as he was told. After a moment he took out his handkerchief and wiped his brow.

"I'm sorry, I didn't mean to shout. I haven't liked the man since the day he first came to our house, and this is intolerable. If I hadn't introduced them …"

"You couldn't have known. Everyone else liked him when we first met him; we didn't know he'd change."

Mr Wetherby let out a sigh but when he said nothing, Mary continued.

"If you won't take me with you, why don't you take

someone else? It's a shame William isn't closer, he'd be ideal."

Mr Wetherby grunted. "Leave it with me, William might be visiting again next week."

A week later Mr Wetherby was ready to pay Mr Flemming a visit. To keep Mary happy, he waited until William was with him, but he had no intention of letting him listen to the conversation.

"You stand guard outside the door to make sure nobody comes in." Mr Wetherby checked his pocket watch before he pushed open the door.

The bell over the door brought Mr Flemming into the otherwise empty shop. As soon as he saw Mr Wetherby, he put his hands together and cracked his knuckles.

"What do you want?"

Mary had told Mr Wetherby what to say and so taking a deep breath he tried to remember how to start.

"Mrs Wetherby's concerned about Sarah-Ann and wanted me to come and speak to you."

"It's Mrs Flemming to you, and what are you on about?"

"I hear you've been beating her."

"What's that got to do with you?" Mr Flemming spat the words out.

"It's got everything to do with me. In case you've forgotten, I introduced you and frankly it was one of the worst things I ever did."

"If you'd wanted her for yourself you should have done something about it before she married me."

Mr Wetherby counted to five. "For some reason your

wife wants you to go home earlier in the evening. I was asked to tell you."

Mr Flemming's eyes looked black as he glared at Mr Wetherby. "It was my going home early that got us into this mess in the first place."

"Without reason." Mr Wetherby took a deep breath to control the tone of his voice. "Several parties, my wife included, have told you I escorted Sarah-Ann home from our house that evening because I didn't like her being out on her own while she was so obviously expecting a child."

"Maybe you did, but there was still something going on. You can deny it all you like. I won't believe you."

"Nothing was going on then and nothing has gone on since. If you remember, you moved to Highgate after she lost the baby. I didn't see Sarah-Ann for years. In fact, from the time you moved I didn't see either of you until after Elizabeth was born." Mr Wetherby wasn't sure if mentioning Elizabeth was a good idea, but it was too late now.

"You keep Elizabeth out of this. She's my daughter." Mr Flemming walked across the shop, his fists clenched in front of him.

"I've just said that. I didn't see Sarah-Ann for months before she found out she was expecting Elizabeth. That, I presume, is why she wants you to go home of an evening. She wants you to see your daughter grow up. She was sobbing when she told Mrs Wetherby how she never sees you."

"How do I know you're not lying?"

"Go home and ask Sarah-Ann. Believe her if you won't believe me, or do I need to ask Mrs Wetherby to talk some sense into you?"

"You bring your wife in here and I'll make sure she knows all about you."

Mr Flemming stood within a foot of Mr Wetherby, and Mr Wetherby grabbed the front of his jacket with both hands. "You're pushing my patience. I promised Mrs Wetherby I wouldn't lay a finger on you today, but if I don't hear that you've started behaving like a civilised human being, I'll be back, and next time there'll be no guarantees."

"You can't come in here threatening me."

Mr Wetherby pushed Mr Flemming away and he banged into the display cabinet behind him. "I can and I will. If you don't stop hitting Sarah-Ann, I'll be back to give you a taste of your own medicine. Have I made myself clear?"

Mr Wetherby glared at the silent Mr Flemming before he turned and left the shop. He was so distracted he forgot William was waiting for him and walked straight past him.

"Is everything all right?" William had to run to catch him up.

"I did what your mother asked if that's what you mean."

"I thought she only wanted you to give him a message. It looks as if you've done more than that."

Mr Wetherby rubbed his right fist with his other hand. "No, all I did was give him a message, but if I need to come back, I won't be quite so lenient next time."

Chapter 18

Handsworth, Staffordshire.

HARRIET SAT IN THE BACK room of her uncle's house, the latest edition of *Cornhill* on her knee, but try as she might she couldn't concentrate. The baby was particularly active this afternoon and her swollen limbs throbbed in the heat. Against all her expectations, she'd been pleased in the New Year to learn she was expecting her first child. William was happy, and at least it meant she was normal. At first, it had been easy, but she hadn't enjoyed the last few months and was now downright miserable. The doctor had told her the baby would be born in July, but today was the first day of August and there was still no sign of it. She put her magazine down and pushed herself up from the chair. As she did, there was a sharp pain in her side and she let out a loud shriek.

"Whatever's the matter?" her aunt said putting down her embroidery.

Harriet bent forward to ease the pain. "I don't know, but something hurts. Do you think the baby's coming?"

Her aunt appeared lost for words. "You sit back down and I'll fetch the midwife," she said after a minute. "William should be home soon; if we need the doctor he can go for him."

"You can't leave me on my own." The panic in Harriet's voice was clear. "What if the baby arrives while you're out?"

"I can't deliver a baby." The colour drained from her aunt's face. "Surely you can hold on for ten minutes while I get some help."

Harriet had no idea whether she could or not.

"I'm going anyway," her aunt said. "The sooner I'm gone, the sooner I'll be back."

Harriet sat back in her chair, her heart racing. *What's going to happen to me?* Nobody had told her how the baby was going to come out, but if the pain in her stomach was anything to go by, she wasn't going to enjoy it. Why hadn't she asked any of her old friends in Birmingham what happened at the birth? Enough of them had children, yet she'd been so uninterested she hadn't bothered to ask. She'd heard a couple of girls she'd known at Sunday school had died giving birth. At the time she'd just shrugged as if it was one of those things. But it wasn't when it was you. *How bad is having a baby if it could kill you?*

By the time the midwife arrived, Harriet was struggling to breathe.

"Calm down, Mrs Jackson," the midwife said. "Working yourself up into a state like this won't make it any easier. Now, give me a few deep breaths and we'll get you upstairs and check whether the baby's on its way."

"I can't walk up the stairs. What if the baby falls out?"

"That won't happen, not with your first; now stop talking and give me some deep breaths."

Harriet put her hands on her swollen belly and breathed

in, but between each deep breath the shallow breathing returned. After a minute the midwife helped her to the bedroom to lie down.

"Nothing to report yet," the midwife said once she'd examined her. "You've started but there's a long way to go."

"A long way to go?" Harriet said. "What's going to happen to me?"

"You'll be fine. When the time's right, you need to push the baby out."

Harriet propped herself up on her elbows. "How do I do that? How will I know when the time's right?"

"You'll know once it happens and I'll be back with you. Now I suggest you get some rest. If the baby decides to come tonight, you won't get much sleep."

Sleep was the last thing on Harriet's mind but she stayed in bed waiting for William to come home.

Harriet lay on the bed for over an hour before William got home.

"How are you?" he said as he walked into the bedroom and sat on the bed beside her.

"Not too bad. I keep getting pains across my stomach but then they disappear. I'm thirsty though; will you help me downstairs so I can have a cup of tea?"

"Are you sure that's wise? Let me sit you up and I'll bring something for you."

William leaned forward and pulled at the pillows but as she moved Harriet gave a loud cry.

"I think I'd better lie down again."

William's brow puckered. "Do you think the baby's coming?"

"I've no idea, but can you fetch the doctor? I'm scared."

❧

When William returned with the doctor fifteen minutes later, the midwife was already there. Harriet was propped up in bed, tears glistening in her eyes. As soon as William stepped into the room she held her hand out to him.

"It's on its way," the midwife said. "Mr Jackson, you need to leave."

Stopping William from reaching Harriet, she turned and pushed him out of the room. For a moment William stared at the door that had been closed behind him before he went back downstairs and poured himself a glass of whisky. He didn't normally drink spirits but tonight he needed to calm his nerves. Before long, Mr and Mrs Watkins joined him.

"I hope she's quick," her uncle said. "I won't be able to sleep with that noise going on."

"It's not her fault," William said. "I just hope she's all right."

Mr Watkins grunted. "She'll be fine; she's a good, strong woman. There's nothing to it."

William stared at him. "How can you say that?"

"Well, there wouldn't be so many of the little blighters if it was difficult."

"It's not easy; there are plenty of women who die in the process."

Mr Watkins was unrepentant and turned to his wife. "They love it, don't they, dear?"

"There isn't a woman alive who wouldn't want a child of her own if the Lord looked favourably on her." Mrs Watkins wiped a tear from her eye. "He denied me the privilege and it's a pain far worse than any experienced by a mother."

"That's enough," Mr Watkins said. "You brought Harriet up as if she were your own."

"I did, thanks to your brother, but it's not the same. Not on a day like today. How can I know what she's going through? She was asking me questions earlier and I couldn't answer her." Mrs Watkins blew into her handkerchief. When she continued to wipe her eyes, William went to the sideboard and poured her a glass of port.

"Here," he said. "It'll help settle you."

The three of them sat, mostly in silence, for the rest of the night. Mr Watkins dozed off several times but William and Mrs Watkins remained awake, listening to the noises above. Eventually at half-past five in the morning the doctor came down the stairs.

"Congratulations, Mr Jackson, Mr Watkins. Mrs Jackson's given birth to a baby boy. Both appear to be doing well. You can go up and see them, but please don't stay long."

A smile spread across William's face and he thanked the doctor before he raced up the stairs. When he went into the bedroom, Harriet looked exhausted but she smiled when she saw him.

"We have a son." She turned the baby to face him.

"So I believe. Let me see him." William looked at the baby before he sat on the edge of the bed and kissed her forehead. "You're so clever; I do love you."

"I think he'll have your hair." She pulled back the blanket to reveal a shock of black hair. "I hope he does."

Several minutes later Harriet's aunt and uncle joined them.

"What will you call him?" her uncle asked, without preamble.

Harriet turned to William; they hadn't discussed it.

"I know what I'd like to call him," William said. He looked to Harriet, not sure how she would react. "The most important man in my life, who's given me everything, is Mr Wetherby. I'd like to name my son after him. William-Wetherby Jackson."

"Don't you want to name him after your father?" Harriet said. "It's going to be confusing with so many Williams in the family."

"I did think that, but I didn't know my father and he left my mother in a terrible mess. I know it wasn't his fault, but if it hadn't been for Mr Wetherby we would have ended up in the workhouse. I wouldn't be sat here with you now. I'll never forget that I owe the man my life."

"William-Wetherby Jackson it is," Harriet said with a smile.

William had never been much of a letter writer, but once he left Harriet he went downstairs and penned a short note to his mother. The mail wouldn't go until Monday, but at least it was done and he would post it when he went out.

Minutes later he walked to church with a spring in his step, his tiredness forgotten. He thought about his stepfather and hoped he'd be pleased with his choice of name. If there was one man in the world he hoped his son would be like, it was Mr Wetherby.

Chapter 19

WILLIAM STEPPED OUT ONTO THE pavement and looked up and down Grosvenor Road before he took out his pocket watch and checked the time. Mr Wetherby had hired a private carriage to bring his mother and sisters from Birmingham and it was due soon. Within minutes he saw it approaching and a smile lit his face as he stood to attention, waiting for the coachman to open the door. Mary-Ann and Charlotte were the first out and Mary-Ann squeezed William's hand as they waited for Mary to join them. William beamed at his mother and bent forward to kiss her cheek.

"I'm so glad you could come," he said.

"Of course we were going to come. Do you think I'd delay seeing my first grandchild for any longer than necessary?"

"I want to see the baby," Charlotte said.

"Of course you do," Mary-Ann said, taking the child's hand.

"Congratulations, my boy," Mr Wetherby said as he joined them and shook William's hand. "You have your first son and I believe you've done me a great honour. William-Wetherby Jackson."

William smiled. "If my son can grow up to be half the man you are, I'll be very proud of him."

Mr Wetherby put his hand on William's shoulder, momentarily lost for words. "I'll have to make sure I'm a good influence on him."

They went into the house and straight into the back room where Harriet sat holding William-Wetherby. Most of the swelling from her pregnancy had gone but the extra weight she carried suited her, it gave her a round, cheerful face that was so different from the pale, drawn features of a year earlier.

Mary-Ann walked straight over to the baby and took him from her. "Come to Aunt Mary-Ann, young William."

"It's William-Wetherby, not William," William said. "We don't want to confuse him with either myself or William Junior."

Mary-Ann ignored him as she sat down and showed him to Charlotte. For several minutes Charlotte entertained everyone as she poked and prodded the baby. Eventually, when she made him cry, she lost interest and went to sit with her father.

After they had eaten, the ladies returned to the back room and Mrs Watkins invited everyone to make themselves comfortable.

"I'm so glad I'm no longer carrying a child," Harriet said as she sat down. "What an ordeal it was. I thought it would never be over. Did you feel like that, Mrs Wetherby?"

"I was fine with William and Mary-Ann, even with William Junior, thinking about it, but it was hard when I had Charlotte. I lost several babies before I had her so Mr Wetherby confined me to my room."

"Thank the Lord I didn't have to go through that; I think I'd have died."

"Well, at least you have a baby." Mary-Ann slumped in her chair. "Have a thought for those of us who'd love to have one."

Harriet reached for her hand. "I'm sorry, I'm being tactless again. I'm sure you'll have your own baby soon. Did William introduce you to anyone? I asked him to."

"He didn't mention it and I didn't want to ask."

"What's all this?" Mary interrupted. "You've not said anything to me."

"There isn't much to say," Mary-Ann replied. "It was Harriet's idea to involve William."

Mary turned to Harriet for an explanation.

"It was only a suggestion," Harriet said. "Mary-Ann doesn't meet many young men and I thought William could help."

"It's not that I don't meet any," Mary-Ann explained. "It's just that I never have the opportunity to get to know them, and Mr Wetherby is too busy to worry about finding me a husband."

Mary studied her daughter. How could she have let her down so badly? She should have spoken to Mr Wetherby long ago about introducing her to potential suitors, but she hadn't because it suited her to have Mary-Ann close by. She turned to Charlotte and imagined what a different life she would have. Mr Wetherby was certain to make sure she married well and would want for nothing. Mary-Ann wasn't one of his priorities.

"Let me talk to him," she said.

"Please, don't make a fuss …" Mary-Ann said, but she was interrupted when the door to the back room opened and Mr Wetherby walked in.

"I'm sorry to disturb you, but we must be going."

"Is that the time? I didn't realise. You must come and visit us next time," Mary said to Mrs Watkins. "I'm always accepting your hospitality without giving any in return. Next time you come to Birmingham you must call."

"I'd like that, but I expect you'll be coming here again soon." Mrs Watkins paused but continued when a puzzled expression crossed Mary's face. "For the baptism."

"Of course; how could I forget?" Mary turned to Harriet. "Do you have a date in mind?"

"No … not yet," Harriet said. "Probably not for a while."

"You can't leave it too long," her aunt said. "He should be baptised while he's still a baby."

Harriet stood up and took William-Wetherby off Mary-Ann. "He'll be a baby for long enough. I'll let you know when we decide."

The following week Harriet thought all her birthdays and Christmases had come at once. Not only was her pregnancy over and she had a healthy baby boy, but the previous evening her uncle had announced he was going to Birmingham for a couple of days. What he was doing, she didn't know and frankly she didn't care. As a bonus her relationship with her aunt had improved, although she wasn't sure how long that would last.

Unbeknown to anyone, she'd made up her mind not to have William-Wetherby baptised at the Parish Church, at least not while the rector was there. Try as she might she couldn't forgive him for the way he had treated her before her wedding. It didn't help that the comments and criticisms kept coming every Sunday morning. She hadn't discussed her decision with William, but as they went to bed that evening, she prayed he would support her.

"Did you tell me once your father was a Quaker?" she started.

"I don't specifically remember telling you, but yes, he was. Why?"

Harriet sat down to brush her hair, turning her back on him. "They don't have their children baptised, do they?"

"They don't believe it's necessary. They think a person's faith should be a lifelong journey, not a one-off event."

"So why were you baptised?"

"I've never thought about it, to be honest, but I would imagine it was down to my mother. You know what she's like; besides, my father was baptised despite being a Quaker."

Harriet put the brush down on the dresser and took a deep breath. "I've given it some thought and don't think we should have William-Wetherby baptised."

"Of course we have to have him baptised. My mother and your aunt would never forgive us if we didn't."

Harriet turned to face him. "I'm not having him baptised for them; we should only have him baptised if we believe it's the best thing for him."

"But having him baptised *is* the best thing for him." Incomprehension crossed William's face.

"Why is it? He should be able to make his own mind up when he's ready. The Congregational Church don't baptise people until they're adults."

"Who've you been talking to?"

"Nobody." Harriet turned back to the mirror. "I don't want him baptised at the Parish Church, not as long as the rector's there. If we have to go through with it, I want it to be at another church."

"As far as Mother's concerned that will be as bad as not having him baptised at all. Why do you bring these things upon yourself? Couldn't we simply do what everyone expects and move on?"

Harriet spun around to face him. "That's the worst suggestion of all. You have to make solemn vows at a baptism about bringing the child up within the church; if you don't believe what you're saying you're lying to God. You shouldn't go through with it just to make life easy."

"Has the rector been round to see you? Is that what this is about?"

"Not yet, but it's only a matter of time. They'll expect me to go to church on Sunday as well, but I'm not going. Every time I see the rector he has another verse from the Bible to quote at me. Did you hear him last week? *The Lord says let your women keep silent, for it is not permitted unto them to speak, but they are commanded to be under obedience.* He doesn't even know his verses; the Bible says we should be silent in church and yet he dares to tell me to be quiet at all times. I've a good mind to go to the Congregational Church from now on."

"You'll do no such thing," William said. "You're still my wife and the arrangement was that I'd be tolerant with you in private as long as you behaved yourself in public. You're not leaving the church and William-Wetherby will be baptised there."

Harriet sat where she was, her heart pounding. That hadn't gone well. If William couldn't understand her point of view, she needed to think of something else because it was going to be much harder to tell everyone else. Perhaps Mary-Ann would understand. After all, it was her family too that had been Quakers. She would ask her advice next time she saw her.

Chapter 20

Birmingham, Warwickshire.

MARY-ANN LET HERSELF INTO THE front house and laughed when she saw Mary covered in flour.

"What on earth are you doing? You've got flour everywhere. It's even on your nose."

Mary wiped the sleeve of her dress across her face. "Is that better? I put too much water in the dough so I needed to add more flour to get it off my hands. Put some water over the fire to boil; I'm nearly done."

Mary-Ann did as she was told before she sat down by the fire. "I've had a letter from Harriet." She waved the letter in the air. "She's asked me to go and stay in Handsworth for a few days."

"How lovely. I'm glad the two of you get along. It makes life so much easier."

"It was never me who had a problem with her if you remember, it was you."

Mary shrugged. "It didn't last long; I'm fond of her now. When did she suggest you go?"

"She didn't say, just sometime in the next few weeks. Hopefully William will be coming to Birmingham soon and I can travel back with him. You don't mind me going, do you?"

"Of course not, except for the fact that I wish I could go with you. I think Mr Wetherby might be wavering, but he's not ready to move yet."

"Well, let's hope it won't be too long." Mary-Ann stood up to make the tea. As she went to the door to throw the remains of the old tea into the gutter she saw a young man looking lost.

"Can I help you?" she asked.

"I hope so." He smiled and ran his eyes up and down her. "I'm looking for a Mr Wetherby. Do you know where I can find him?"

Mary-Ann returned his smile. "He lives here, but he's at work at the moment."

"Could you tell me where he works then? I have a delivery for him."

Mary-Ann hesitated. "I'll take you if you like. It's not far. Just let me put this teapot down."

The young man was about to respond but Mary-Ann disappeared back into the house without giving him a chance. A minute later she reappeared, wearing a bonnet and a decorative shawl.

"It's this way." She pointed up Frankfort Street. "It's quite a large workshop if you know what you're looking for. You're not from around here, are you?"

"No, I'm not. My horse and waggon are up the road, but when I couldn't find what I was looking for I jumped down to take a closer look. Are you Mr Wetherby's daughter?"

"No, not me. My father died shortly after I was born

and Mother married Mr Wetherby several years later. He's taken care of us ever since."

"I'm sorry … not about Mr Wetherby … about your father I mean."

"You don't need to apologise; it was a long time ago. Right, here we are."

"Is this it?" The young man looked up at the workshop.

"Yes, this is it. I told you it wasn't far, Mr …"

"Diver. Mr Diver … from Saltley. And your name is?"

"Miss Jackson." Mary-Ann smiled. "It was a pleasure to meet you, Mr Diver."

"Likewise, I'm sure. I suppose I'd better get these crates delivered. I hope Mr Wetherby likes them. If he does, he might want me to deliver some more."

Sensing her cheeks colouring, Mary-Ann stared at the pavement. "I'll let you get on then, Mr Diver. Good day."

"Good day to you … and thank you for showing me the way. It was lovely talking to you."

It didn't take long for Mary-Ann to walk back, but as she turned to go into the house she glanced back. Mr Diver was still watching her. She stopped and gave him a small wave before she disappeared indoors.

"What was that all about?" Mary asked as soon as she saw her. "One minute you're making a pot of tea and the next minute you've taken my best bonnet and shawl, and disappeared."

"Oh, nothing. Only a deliveryman looking for Mr Wetherby."

"Since when did you personally escort delivery drivers to the workshop? You usually just point them up the road. Who was he?"

Mary-Ann shrugged. "He said his name was Mr Diver and he's from Saltley. Other than that, I don't know. He wasn't dressed like a usual deliveryman though, his suit was too smart."

"We'll have to ask Mr Wetherby when he comes home."

Mary-Ann's cheeks went scarlet. "You can't do that."

Mary smiled at her daughter. "I think you rather liked him. There's nothing wrong with that. Let's ask Mr Wetherby what he thinks of him."

"Please don't ask him while I'm here, I couldn't bear it. If you have to ask, wait until I've gone home and tell me what he says tomorrow."

Mary laughed. "Well, can I ask him about William and when he expects to see him again?"

"Yes, of course. If he can think of a reason for William to come here next week, that would be wonderful. I want to visit Harriet as soon as I can."

৩৶

Handsworth, Staffordshire.

By the following Thursday, Harriet was in the back room of the house in Handsworth with Mary-Ann sitting opposite her.

"I'm so glad my aunt arranged to go out this afternoon. If ever she knows I'm having visitors she seems to make a point of staying in. It drives me mad. I wanted to talk to you and so I didn't tell her you were coming until Tuesday. By then it was too late to change her plans."

Mary-Ann laughed. "You are terrible."

Harriet put her hands on her hips. "I am not! It's self-preservation. Would you like it if your mother sat in on all your conversations?"

Mary-Ann's cheeks coloured. "I don't suppose so."

"You've gone red. What have you been up to? You must tell."

"Nothing much …"

"But …" Harriet prompted, her eyes shining.

"But … I met someone last week who I thought was rather dashing."

"A man!"

Mary-Ann laughed. "Yes, a man. His name's Mr Diver."

"Did William introduce you?"

"No, nobody did. He was looking for Mr Wetherby's workshop and I showed him where it was."

Harriet was on the edge of her seat. "So, what's he like?"

Mary-Ann took out her fan and, much to Harriet's amusement, waved it in front of her face.

"Is he *that* nice?"

"Better." Mary-Ann laughed. "He's about William's height. His hair and moustache are a lighter brown, but he has lovely blue eyes. Mother found out from Mr Wetherby that he works for his father making boxes. They had a deliveryman who didn't turn up for work last week so he had to do the round."

"Are you going to see him again?"

Mary-Ann's shoulders slumped. "I don't know. Mr Wetherby said the boxes were good quality and he may order some more, but I doubt Mr Diver will deliver them."

"He might. If he liked you, he may surprise you. You need to know when Mr Wetherby places the order and how long delivery will take. You'll have to be ready."

"I think I'd better take some lessons from you. How do you know all these things?"

"It's amazing what you can learn from the pages of a magazine." Harriet smirked. "Anyway, before we go into that, I need to ask you a question."

"That sounds ominous." Mary-Ann shifted in her seat.

"William told me your family were once Quakers, and a couple of your elderly aunts still are. What you do think of their beliefs?"

"A nice easy question then." Mary-Ann rolled her eyes. "Why do you want to know? You're not thinking of converting, are you?"

Harriet laughed. "No, not at the moment, but they have different views on things like Christmas, Easter … baptisms, that sort of thing. They don't celebrate them as we do. Do you agree with them?"

Mary-Ann shrugged. "I've never thought about it. I wouldn't like to not celebrate Christmas or Easter."

"And what about baptisms?"

"I think they're wrong. A new baby needs to receive the blessing of God. They shouldn't deny them that."

"But they believe God blesses all their children without the need to have them baptised. Don't you think that's a better idea?"

"Is this about William-Wetherby? You're not thinking of not having him baptised, are you?"

"Would it bother you if we didn't?"

"Of course it would. He needs God's blessing to keep him safe. God needs to know you'll bring him up within the church."

Harriet sank back into her chair. *Doesn't anyone understood my point of view?*

"What's the matter?" Mary-Ann asked. "Have I said something wrong?"

"No, it doesn't matter." Harriet smiled. Despite the fact Mary-Ann was a year older than her, she was innocent in so many ways. She needed to get out of the shadow of her mother and Mr Wetherby; maybe then she would understand her point of view. What better way to do that, than to find her a young man? "Let's change the subject. This Mr Diver, we have to make sure you're ready for him when he calls."

"We don't know he will."

"You need to make sure Mr Wetherby asks him to call. I can see I have a lot to teach you. Right this is what you should do …"

Chapter 21

Stroud, Gloucestershire, England.

M R WETHERBY HADN'T SEEN HIS hometown since the day he left, over twenty years earlier. There had been no reason for him to make the journey, but now, as the winter turned into spring, he had no choice. The wind was cold as he stood and stared across the grave at the woman opposite him. He hadn't seen her in all that time, but he still recognised her. He would never forget those piercing steel eyes. He had never wanted to see her again, but given the event he supposed it couldn't be avoided. She shouldn't be at the graveside though; it wasn't her place. She should have stayed in church with the rest of the women. She'd probably only come to annoy him.

As if she sensed his eyes were upon her she looked up and smiled, not a pleasant smile but one that was cold and calculating. He remembered that smile. It usually came before she beat him and even now, despite the fact he was standing with his eighteen-year-old son, he felt like a child again. How he wished Thomas was with him; he would have understood, but the last letter from his brother had been months ago from South Africa. No one knew his current whereabouts and they hadn't been able to tell him of his father's death.

Mr Wetherby checked his pocket watch and touched William Junior's elbow as they turned to lead the mourners back to the church. They hadn't gone far when he heard a dreadful high-pitched voice behind him.

"I must say you don't have the manners of your father. Won't you escort me back to the church?"

Every muscle of Mr Wetherby's body tensed as he turned to face her. "Pardon me, I assumed you had an escort, otherwise you'd have stayed at the church."

"He was my husband; it was right I was here."

Mr Wetherby took a deep breath and walked back around the grave. "Allow me." He extended his arm to her.

"You haven't changed," she said. "You have the fancy clothes now, but you still have the arrogance I used to hate. I suppose this is your son. He's got those dreadful green specks in his eyes, just like you. Is your wife here? I've always wondered what sort of a woman would have you."

Mr Wetherby refused to take the bait. He wasn't going to dishonour his father's funeral by arguing with her.

"My wife is with my sisters at the church, where all women should be. I expect you'll meet her soon enough. She's fortunate enough to know everyone here except you."

"Yes, I believe you're quite a host when it suits you, although why everyone wants to travel to Birmingham to visit is beyond me. I can't stand the place myself. I hear it's getting worse as well, nearly as many vermin as there are people. Heaven knows what it smells like in the summer. Your father was always telling me how well you were doing, but frankly I didn't believe him. If you were doing so well you wouldn't still be there. If you want my opinion it's no place for a self-respecting gentleman, but then …"

"Madam, I have a business to run that is based in Birmingham. I also own numerous properties there; I can't move on a whim."

"As you like, but you wouldn't find me living there. Your wife must either be very tolerant or else …"

"Don't say a word about my wife. Our neighbourhood is quite respectable although you'll never be invited to see it. Now if you don't mind I have some people I want to talk to."

With that, Mr Wetherby unhooked his arm from hers and without another word strode purposefully back to the church.

"I am not travelling to the wake in a carriage with that woman," he said to Amelia and Betsy when he joined his sisters in the entrance to the church. "I don't care what the protocol is."

"She's not changed, has she?" Betsy said, "Still as evil as ever."

"I've never hated anyone so much in my life, although I suppose I've a lot to thank her for. If she hadn't turned our lives upside down I may never have moved to Birmingham. Having said that, I can't help thinking she's out to cause trouble. I won't rest until I leave this place."

"Do you know that man over there?" Amelia nodded towards the corner of the church. "He's been watching us for the last few minutes."

Mr Wetherby turned in the direction Amelia was pointing. "I don't think so, although perhaps he is a little familiar."

"He's coming over; it looks like he knows you," Betsy said.

Mr Wetherby watched as the man walked towards him and extended his hand. "Mr Wetherby, isn't it? May I offer my sincere condolences? Your father was a good man."

"Yes, thank you, Mr …"

"You don't recognise me, do you? Mr Havers, George Havers; we went to Sunday school together."

"Good Lord, yes, I remember. That was a long time ago."

"You haven't changed a bit. I'd have recognised you even if it wasn't your father's funeral."

Mr Wetherby smiled. "Do you still live around here?"

"No, I'm in Balsall Heath now, but I worked with your father and wanted to pay my respects. I hoped I might bump into you as well. I have a proposition for you."

"Splendid. Why don't we lead everyone to the wake and you can tell me all about yourself over a pint of best."

Chapter 22

Birmingham, Warwickshire.

MARY-ANN STOOD IN FRONT OF the mirror at her mother's house adjusting her bonnet.

"What's the matter with you tonight?" Mary asked. "You've retied that bonnet half a dozen times and each time there was nothing wrong with it."

"I can't get my hair to sit right underneath it. I want it to have a bounce, but instead the bonnet's making it flat."

"Mr Diver's seen you before, so it's not as if he doesn't know what to expect."

"I want to look my best."

"You want to be careful." Mr Wetherby glanced up from his newspaper. "If you appear too keen you'll send out the wrong signals; he'll think there's something on offer."

"Mr Wetherby!" Mary-Ann said. "Mr Diver would never behave like that. He's a proper gentleman."

"Maybe he is, but you mark my words, at the end of the day he's still a man."

Mary-Ann's cheeks went scarlet and she was about to object when there was a knock on the door.

"That'll be him." She glanced at herself one last time,

patting her cheeks to reduce the redness, before she went to the door. "Mr Diver, how good to see you again."

"Good evening, Miss Jackson, I was thinking the same about you. You look lovely." He stepped into the room where Mr and Mrs Wetherby were sitting on either side of the fireplace. "Good evening, sir, ma'am." He removed his hat and gave a slight bow. "I trust you're well."

"Yes thank you, Mr Diver." Mr Wetherby stood up to shake his hand. "Where are you taking Mary-Ann this evening?"

"I thought we'd go over to the recreation ground on Berners Street. They have a band playing and it's such a lovely evening."

"Indeed it is. I was going to take a walk myself. Do you mind if I join you?"

"Not at all." Mr Diver couldn't look at Mary-Ann. "It would be a pleasure."

Mary-Ann was less than pleased and turned to her mother for help.

"Must you go, dear?" Mary said. "I hadn't planned on spending an evening alone."

"Ask your sister to come round; she hasn't been here for a few days. I need some air." With that, Mr Wetherby picked up his hat and ushered Mary-Ann and Mr Diver out of the house.

As they walked, Mr Wetherby talked about the weather. It was the hottest summer for many a year and they discussed what effect the heat and lack of rain would have on the farmers and the price of food. After a suitable period of time, Mr Wetherby turned to the subject of work.

"How's business going, Mr Diver? Are you selling many boxes?"

"Yes sir, we can't make enough of them at the moment. Father says we'll have to take on more workers."

"Are the premises big enough?"

"They are for one more expansion. We can probably take another twenty women before we need to move."

Mr Wetherby thought for a moment. "How's your father? Is he still in good health?"

"He can't complain. He still has the terrible cough he developed last year, but otherwise he's tough as old boots."

"I'm glad to hear it. You may know, I lost my father earlier this year and it brought home to me how vulnerable we all are." Sadness passed over Mr Wetherby's face.

"I did, sir. I'm sorry."

"It'll happen to us all one day. Remind me, do you have any brothers at home?"

"I have a younger brother and sister."

"As the eldest I presume you'll inherit the business if anything should happen to him? Are you ready to take over?"

"My father has taught me all I need to know. I do most of the day-to-day running and my brother isn't interested in the business."

"I like to see somebody prepared. Now, Miss Jackson here, she's an attractive young woman, I think you'll agree."

Mary-Ann stared at Mr Wetherby, her mouth gaping.

"Indeed I do, sir," Mr Diver said.

"And with that, Mr Diver, come some challenges. I trust I can leave her in your safe care without the need to be concerned for her well-being."

"Absolutely, sir, you can trust me."

"I don't want to be left with any damaged goods, if you know what I mean."

Mr Diver flushed. "I wouldn't dream of it."

"I wouldn't take kindly to any improper behaviour. Do you have any plans for the future yet?"

Mr Diver hesitated and glanced at Mary-Ann.

"No, you're right, this isn't the time," Mr Wetherby said. "We'll talk again. Now, I think I'll stop off at the beerhouse over there. Enjoy your evening." Mr Wetherby raised his hat and crossed over the road in front of them.

Once Mr Wetherby had gone, Mr Diver gave a sigh of relief. "I think he was checking me out," he said when he was sure Mr Wetherby was out of earshot.

"He was. He always does it; it's so embarrassing."

"You mean you've walked out with other men?" Mr Diver looked perturbed.

"No! Most men don't make it this far. He must like you or he wouldn't have left us alone together."

"How do you think I did?"

Mary-Ann smiled. "You sound like you have good prospects, which he'll like, but you left yourself open to a second interrogation."

He smiled back and tweaked her nose. "I didn't want to give away too much, not without telling you first."

Chapter 23

Handsworth, Staffordshire.

I T WAS THE MIDDLE OF the afternoon but Harriet lay on the top of her bed staring at the ceiling. She had no idea why she was surprised, these things happened, but she wasn't happy. At least this time the worst of it would be over the winter. William would be happy though; he loved William-Wetherby and often talked about him having a brother. Her aunt and uncle would be less so. Harriet had been two or three years old when she came to live with them, and she wondered if this was why they had so little patience with William-Wetherby. The only time her uncle was happy with him was when he was asleep and sadly for all of them that didn't happen often enough.

Then there was the baptism to worry about. With no one to support her view that William-Wetherby needn't be baptised, it had taken all her charm to persuade William it wasn't necessary. It was probably one of the reasons for her current predicament. Knowing she wasn't going to win any arguments, she tried to forget about it and hope everyone else did too, but so far it hadn't happened. Now William-Wetherby had turned one, her aunt repeatedly told her that if she left it much longer he would be too old. She prayed for the strength to hold out a little bit longer, but having another baby would raise the question all over again.

As she'd predicted, William was overjoyed when she told him.

"When will it be born?" he asked.

"Sometime around February or March. It seems a lifetime away."

William smiled. "It might seem a long time to wait but it'll come around soon enough."

"It's not that, it's just, well … naturally I'm excited about the baby, but … I hate carrying it."

There was a look of incomprehension on William's face. "Why? It's perfectly natural."

"Maybe it is, but you're not your usual self anymore and you grow fat and can't do the things you want to. Then you can't sleep and at the end of it all, you have to go through the birth. What if I can't do it again? What if I die? What will happen to you and William-Wetherby? I'm frightened, William."

"Don't be silly; you were fine last time."

He put his arms around her and held her, but he had no idea. He hadn't been there when William-Wetherby was born and she hadn't shared any details with him. As far as he was concerned it was all quite straightforward and she couldn't tell him any different. She buried her head in his shoulder and sobbed quietly, only faintly reassured by the strong arms holding her.

The following day she was late downstairs, by which time her aunt had given William-Wetherby a drink of milk.

"What time do you call this?" her aunt asked.

Harriet looked at the grandfather clock. "Half past eight."

"There's no need for your lip. You know perfectly well that's not what I meant."

Harriet picked up the teapot and felt its weight before she poured herself a cup of tea.

"That'll be cold," her aunt said. "It's been made half an hour."

"It'll be warm enough. I'm not feeling my best this morning."

"What's up with you? You don't have the excuse of William-Wetherby keeping you awake last night. William said he slept through."

Harriet flopped into a chair by the fire, her face averted from her aunt. "I'm having another baby."

"Oh … William didn't say. When did you find out?"

"Yesterday afternoon when you were out. It's due in the spring."

"You don't seem very pleased." Her aunt stood up and went to sit beside her.

Harriet shrugged. "These things happen. I'm sure I'll be fine once it's over."

Mrs Watkins shook her head. "I'll never understand you. Any normal woman would be pleased."

"Just because I don't want a house full of children doesn't mean there's something wrong with me."

"You might not think so, but plenty around here would think you're mad. You should thank your lucky stars."

Harriet closed her eyes. *Am I going to have another nine months of this?* She was relieved a moment later when the postman called and her aunt left the room to meet him.

"There's a letter for you," she said when she returned. "It's from Mary-Ann."

Mrs Watkins handed her the letter and Harriet tore it open. "She's getting married! She thought Mr Diver was about to propose last time she wrote and she was right. What marvellous news."

Mrs Watkins frowned. "Have they set a date? You may not be able to go."

Harriet stared at her aunt. "Of course I'll go."

"Not if the wedding is when the baby's due."

Harriet slumped in her seat. The thought hadn't crossed her mind. She picked up the letter and reread it. "It's in May. I'll be well over it."

Her aunt raised an eyebrow. "It sounds like a close thing to me."

"I don't care. As long as it isn't on the day I give birth, I'm going."

Chapter 24

M ARY SMILED AS SHE SAT by the fire listening to Mary-Ann talk about her plans for the wedding. She wasn't an extravagant girl, but she knew what she wanted. Her most difficult wish was that she wanted the service to be in Handsworth.

"Do you think Mr Wetherby will agree to move before next May?"

"I've no idea," Mary said. "I keep asking, and I've told you before, I think he's weakening, but you know what he's like."

"I do so want to be married in the same church as you and William." Mary-Ann paced the room, her hands clasped beneath her chin. "It's not much to ask, is it?"

To Mary it wasn't much to ask but then it wasn't her decision. "Have you thought about bridesmaids?"

"Of course." Mary-Ann sat down opposite her mother. "Naturally Harriet will be matron of honour and we have to have Charlotte, Catherine and Elizabeth. I'm sure Aunt Martha and Aunt Sarah-Ann will love seeing Catherine and Elizabeth in their dresses. I'll have to ask Mr Diver's sister too and I'd like to ask Mrs Harris. She's been a good friend over the last few years."

"Do you have to have Mrs Harris?"

"I can't leave her out."

Mary sighed. "We need to invite a lot to the wedding itself. I'm going to have to make sure Mr Wetherby's in a good mood when I mention it."

Mary knew that Mr Wetherby was often in his better moods straight after tea. She chose an evening when they were alone and he was settled by the fire.

"Mary-Ann's been thinking about her wedding," she started. When the only response she received was a grunt, she continued. "I'd like it to be special for her. I'm afraid we've neglected her over the years, especially since we had Charlotte."

"Hmm."

"She's going to ask her friend Mrs Harris to be a bridesmaid … as well as Harriet, Charlotte, Catherine, Elizabeth and Mr Diver's sister."

Mr Wetherby remained silent for a whole minute, before he banged the newspaper onto his lap.

"What on earth does she need six bridesmaids for?"

"It's her special day and God willing she'll only be married once. I don't imagine you'll moan about Charlotte's wedding, even if she has ten bridesmaids."

Mr Wetherby straightened out the paper again. "I'll think about it."

Mary smiled. That was as good as a yes. "I'd like to treat Mary-Ann to a dress as well. Something special. I've been wondering if we could take her to London for one. I'd like to go as well. You've never taken me before."

Mr Wetherby had only just picked the paper up before he dropped it again. "Are you trying to bankrupt me? I'm not made of money."

"Of course you are," Mary said. "And if you're not, you put on a good act. Besides, you don't want people to think you can't afford a grand wedding, do you?"

"They won't think that."

"Once folk's tongues start wagging you know what they're like. It'll only take one person to set them off." Mary pulled her chair closer to his and took hold of his hand. "What will they think if we only have one carriage with two little bridesmaids? You should want to be proud of your daughter on her wedding day."

"She's not really …"

"Yes she is. You've brought her up as your own since she was seven years old."

Mr Wetherby took a deep breath. "Is there anything else on your list?"

Mary stroked his hand in hers. "Well, we have the wedding breakfast to arrange. I'm not sure how many we'll have to invite from Mr Diver's family, but I would imagine we need to invite at least sixty people."

"Sixty? Where are we going to house that many people?"

"Well, that's my next dilemma. We can't have it here but where do I look? Mary-Ann has her heart set on getting married at St Mary's."

"St Mary's?" A puzzled expression rested on Mr Wetherby's face. "On Whittall Street? What on earth does she want to get married there for?"

"Not in Birmingham. In Handsworth." Mary let the words sink in. "She wants to be married in the same church as us."

Mary had always thought Mr Wetherby was intelligent, but this evening he was determined to be obtuse.

"She can't get married in Handsworth. Neither she nor Mr Diver live in the parish."

Mary took a deep breath. "Not at the moment, but if we move before the marriage, then I'd arrange everything up there."

Mr Wetherby closed his eyes and let his head rest on the back of the chair. "We are not moving to Handsworth. How many times do I have to tell you?"

"You've said yourself how much nicer it is compared to here. Isn't it about time you started acting like a gentleman rather than a foreman?"

Mr Wetherby stood up and reached for his hat. "I'm going to the tavern. You can have five bridesmaids ... and a trip to London, but we are not moving to Handsworth."

৵৶

Mary-Ann smiled at the postman as he handed her a letter. As soon as she closed the door, she turned to Mary.

"It's from Harriet," she said. "And about time too. It's over a week since I asked her to be my matron of honour."

"That's not like her," Mary said. "Is she all right?"

Mary-Ann read the letter and passed it to Mary. "She's having another baby. It's due right before the wedding, so she can't do it."

"Another grandchild. What marvellous news." Mary's eyes glistened as she smiled.

Mary-Ann stamped her foot. "What am I going to do for a matron of honour? Why didn't she tell me before I set the date."

"We'll have none of that, madam. Now sit down. You should be pleased for her."

"I am, but I was so looking forward to her helping me get ready. She's such fun."

"Well, you'll have to make do with Mrs Harris. At least Mr Wetherby will be pleased. Only five dresses to buy now."

Mary-Ann sat down and folded her arms across her chest.

"Don't be upset; it's not the end of the world," Mary said. "I'll tell you what, how would you like a trip to London?"

Mary-Ann's eyes widened. "London? Me?"

"Only if you promise to stop sulking."

"When … and why?"

"Mr Wetherby has said we can travel to London to buy you a dress for the wedding. We can go whenever we like and stay overnight. Would you like to?"

Mary-Ann jumped from her chair and threw her arms around her mother. "Thank you so much. That's the best present anyone could give me. I'd love to go."

Chapter 25

London, England.

IT WAS EARLY FEBRUARY BEFORE the snow cleared sufficiently for Mr Wetherby to escort Mary and Mary-Ann to London. It was a bright but cold day and Mary was thankful to be travelling on the train. She was even more thankful they had a compartment to themselves.

"Will you come to the shop with us?" Mary asked Mr Wetherby as the train approached London.

"I'll deliver you and pick you up again, but I have no intention of staying. I'm a member of a club nearby. I haven't been recently so I thought I'd call in and drum up some business."

Mary rolled her eyes at him. "Trust you to still be thinking about work."

"Someone has to. How else am I going to pay the bill for all this?"

"I do appreciate it, Mr Wetherby. Thank you so much for everything," Mary-Ann said. "I hope I'll make you proud."

Mr Wetherby smiled back. "I'm sure you will. Just remember, only the wedding dress from here. You can take a drawing and have the bridesmaids' dresses made in Birmingham."

Once the train drew into Euston station, Mr Wetherby climbed down from the carriage and held out his hand to help Mary and Mary-Ann onto the platform.

"I'm glad we're not wearing wider skirts," Mary-Ann said as they walked down the platform. "I don't think we'd have got through the door."

Mary laughed. "They wouldn't have been easy to manage in this wind either."

"I'd like one of the new designs with layers of material arranged around the back of the skirt for my wedding. Not white though. I want to be able to wear it again and again."

"I'm sure Mr Diver will be pleased about that," Mr Wetherby said, as the coachman helped the ladies climb into the back of a Hansom cab. As soon as they were seated, he joined them.

"It'll take about an hour to get to where we're going. We'll take a few detours to see some sights and avoid the most unsavoury places."

"We live in Birmingham; it can't be much worse down here."

Mr Wetherby shuddered as the carriage moved off. "You've no idea. I tell you they make the houses on Summer Lane look comfortable. Why people keep coming down here, I don't know. It's as well so many of them die. It would be even worse otherwise."

"How awful." Mary pulled her cloak more tightly around her shoulders. "Isn't anyone doing anything about it?"

"The only way to improve things is if all those lazy

good-for-nothings got themselves a job. If they earned themselves some money, they could move on and wouldn't be in this position."

"What about those who can't work? Those who are ill or mothers with no husbands."

"Most of the time they've brought it on themselves. Women have children out of wedlock and many men and women do nothing but drink themselves into a stupor. They need to take a look at themselves. If they got their lives in order, the guardians could concentrate on those who need it."

Mary knew from experience it wasn't so easy, but it wasn't worth arguing. She'd heard Mr Wetherby's views on overcrowding often enough and didn't want to upset him on a day like today. Instead, she turned and looked out of the window.

They travelled in silence except for the commentary of Mr Wetherby as they passed a range of impressive buildings. The city certainly made Birmingham look small, but nothing they had seen so far prepared her for the sight that was now before her. Towering above everything else on the horizon was a large dome standing on a circle of columns.

"What on earth is that?" Mary asked, unable to take her eyes from it.

"Magnificent, isn't it?" Mr Wetherby said. "Saint Paul's Cathedral. It's the tallest building in London."

"It's beautiful," Mary-Ann said. "It was worth coming to London just for this."

"You wait until we're closer and pass alongside it. It's such a size you won't be able to see the top out of the windows."

As the cathedral drew closer, the dome disappeared behind a large façade of roman columns, flanked on either side by two large towers. The dome reappeared as they drove past and watched the cathedral fade into the distance.

Mary sighed as the cathedral disappeared from view and she and Mary-Ann turned back to face the front of the carriage. "What a wonderful sight that was. Can you imagine going inside?"

"I'm afraid that will have to wait for another day. We're almost at the dress shop."

Once he left them, Mary and Mary-Ann spent the afternoon with the dressmaker, choosing the material and design. By the time they were finished, they were exhausted.

"I hope you're both hungry," Mr Wetherby said when he came to collect them. "There's a little restaurant not far from here. I've booked a table for five o'clock."

"How lovely," Mary said as she fastened her cloak and pulled the accompanying cape over her shoulders. "I always thought something must have come out of all your trips to London a few years ago."

"They did have their advantages. The workshop wasn't far from here, so I got to know the area. It's close enough to walk and we can take in the Bank of England and Royal Exchange on the way. They're not quite as impressive as Saint Paul's, but they are splendid buildings nonetheless."

By the time they reached the restaurant, it was dark and their excitement had been dented by the cold. They soon recovered when the waitress offered them a seat near the fire.

"Isn't this marvellous?" Mary said, looking around. "It's busier than I expected.

"Office workers often come here after work. I think we got here just in time."

Once they had given their order Mary sat back and ran her hands over the starched white tablecloth. "Did you notice the outfits the waitresses are wearing? Black dresses with a white apron. If we ever have any servants, I think I'll get them to dress like that. They look very smart. I could get used to someone cooking for me and doing all the tidying up."

"Well, don't get too used to it," Mr Wetherby said. "We'll be back in Birmingham tomorrow."

Mary sighed and shook her head. "I know, but might this be an appropriate time to tell you about our plans for the wedding?"

"It's as good as any, I suppose. What are you thinking?"

Mary-Ann told Mr Wetherby what they had discussed, but when she talked about being married in Handsworth a frown settled on his face.

"My dear," he said. "We're now only a few months away from the wedding and there is no possibility we'll be living in Handsworth by then. What's wrong with St George's?"

Mary-Ann's shoulders dropped. "It won't be the same. I wanted to be married in the same church as you and Mother, and William and Harriet. Why could William move to Handsworth before he was married but I can't?"

Mary took hold of Mary-Ann's hand. "There's an idea. Perhaps you don't need us to move to Handsworth, you only need to move yourself. Why don't I ask Mrs Watkins if you can move in with them for a couple of months? Unless

I'm mistaken, William's old room is still empty. They may let you stay there."

Mr Wetherby smiled at his wife. "What a splendid idea. I'm sure Mr Watkins will oblige, especially for a little extra rent."

Mary-Ann wasn't so sure. "Harriet said she was going to move William-Wetherby to that room once the new baby arrives."

"Can't you share with a two-year-old for the sake of getting married in Handsworth?" Mary raised her eyebrow at her daughter. Mary-Ann smiled back.

"Yes, of course I can. Oh, I do hope they let me stay. Harriet wants me to tell her everything about London when I get back too, which could take weeks knowing what she's like. You will write and ask them as soon as we're home, won't you?"

Chapter 26

Handsworth, Staffordshire.

MARY LEFT MARY-ANN'S BEDROOM WITH a smile on her face. The trip to London had been worth every penny. Mary-Ann's dress, with its fitted bodice trimmed with beads and lace, and full skirt pulled into layers around the back, looked every bit as expensive as it was. The young bridesmaids, who left the bedroom with Mary, wore a similar style in pale blue. What a show they would give.

Downstairs in the front room Mr Wetherby was in his element. Although it was Mr and Mrs Watkins' house, they had told him to treat it as his own, and he was taking full advantage of the situation.

"Look at you," he said to Charlotte when she walked into the room with Mary. "Pretty as a picture."

"Thank you, Papa. Mary-Ann looks pretty too."

"She does," Mary said. "The dress is fabulous."

Mr Wetherby smiled. "I should hope it is."

"They all look lovely," Martha said, seeing Catherine and Elizabeth. "You've done the family proud, Mr Wetherby."

"It's a shame Mr Flemming couldn't join you today,"

Mary whispered to Sarah-Ann. "Didn't he want to see Elizabeth in her new dress?"

Sarah-Ann shrugged. "Whether he did or he didn't, he couldn't leave the shop. To tell you the truth, I'm happier on my own."

"I thought everything was fine between you." Mary said.

"It is really. He doesn't drink so much anymore and he's good with Elizabeth, but somehow things are a lot easier without him."

Mary put her hand on Sarah-Ann's shoulder, but as she turned back to face the room she noticed the sadness on Alice's face. She supposed it must be hard for her twin sister to be the only woman in the room without a daughter. Not for the first time, her heart went out to her, although she couldn't help wondering how much she had brought it on herself. A moment later, William, and Martha's husband, Mr Chalmers, came into the room.

"Is there no sign of Mary-Ann yet?" William asked.

Mary glanced at the clock. "She's got time yet. Have the carriages arrived?"

"Not yet, but they shouldn't be long now."

In the bedroom upstairs, Mrs Harris, assisted by Mr Diver's sister, Isobel, was putting the final pins in the hair knot arranged on the back of Mary-Ann's head. Harriet sat on the bed nursing her new daughter, Eleanor.

"It's as well I'm not a bridesmaid," she said with a laugh. "I wouldn't fit into one of those dresses."

Mary-Ann rolled her eyes at her. "We'd have made it fit.

Besides, given that Eleanor isn't two months old yet, you're looking in pretty good shape."

"You're most kind, but even if the dress did fit, I don't think pale blue would have worked well with feeding a baby every couple of hours. At least I won't miss anything. One of the benefits of living in the same house as the bride." She smiled. "My aunt and uncle still don't think I'm ready to go to the wedding breakfast, but they can think what they like, I'm going."

"So you haven't grown any more responsible now you have another baby?" Mary-Ann laughed at her friend.

"Don't be silly. Why should I be serious when I have those two watching everything I do? I've got to give them something to moan about."

"I'm glad you're here to take my mind off my nerves," Mary-Ann said. "I'm worried Mr Diver won't turn up."

"He won't change his mind; he adores you," Isobel said. "He'd have me to answer to if he did."

"I do hope today goes well. Mother's put so much into it, and Mr Wetherby as well, to be honest. It must have cost him a fortune. She's invited so many people; I don't think I'll recognise everybody. All my father's side of the family are coming."

"That'll be interesting; I still haven't met some of them," Harriet said.

"Carrying such a sweet baby around with you I don't think there'll be a woman in the room who won't want to talk to you. I can't wait for that to be me," Mary-Ann said.

"Well, come on then," Harriet said. "Mrs Harris, have you finished Mary-Ann's hair? She's in a hurry."

Mrs Harris and Isobel led the way down the stairs and announced Mary-Ann's arrival.

"You look beautiful," Mary said as she walked to the bottom of the stairs and took hold of her daughter's hands. "I knew the dress would be perfect for you. I think cream was a good choice."

"Is my hair all right? It doesn't want to stay in place this morning."

"It's perfect."

"I have a confession to make," William said as he stepped forward. "I've somehow missed the fact I have such a beautiful sister. Where've you been hiding yourself?"

Mary-Ann smiled. "It's the dress that makes the difference. I've never worn anything so beautiful in my life."

"It suits you," Mr Wetherby said as he walked into the hall. "I'm glad. I hope you enjoy your day. Now, the carriages are here so we'd better start moving. William Junior, Mary and Harriet you come with me in the first carriage; Alice, Sarah-Ann, Martha and Mr Chalmers, you'll be in the second carriage. Mrs Harris, you'll be in the third carriage with the rest of the bridesmaids, leaving William to accompany Mary-Ann in the final carriage."

News of the wedding had spread and as Mary and Mr Wetherby stepped onto the street a number of onlookers broke into a round of applause. Mr Wetherby smiled and raised his hat, while Mary gave a wave before Mr Wetherby took her arm and helped her into the carriage.

Once the first two carriages had left, Mrs Harris checked the younger bridesmaids to make sure they were still presentable. Catherine Chalmers was the eldest of the three and she helped to look after her cousins, Charlotte and Elizabeth. Isobel gave them their flowers and showed them how to hold them without damaging them, something that was proving a challenge. As the only two in the room with nothing to do, William turned to his sister and took her hands.

"We've been through a lot together over the years, haven't we? I can't believe I'm giving you away; Mr Diver's a lucky man. You will travel to Handsworth to see us from time to time, won't you?"

"Of course I will, but you and Harriet must visit us as well. Mr Diver's found a marvellous house and we'll have two servants. I'll need something to keep me busy."

William sighed. "Harriet will be so envious. She'd love us to have a house of our own."

"Well, why not? You must earn enough money by now."

"It's not that easy." William studied the engagement ring Mary-Ann wore on her third finger. "I can't go into details, but we need to stay with Mr and Mrs Watkins."

"Is Harriet aware of the problem?"

William shook his head.

"Perhaps you should talk to her. If she understood your reasons …"

"I can't tell her; she'll think I'm a fool."

"She won't think much of you if you insist on staying with her uncle. Seriously. Don't underestimate her. She may be able to help."

William gave Mary-Ann a weak smile. "I'll think about it. Now, we'd better be going while these flowers are still in one piece. Charlotte, don't do that; you'll break them."

Chapter 27

WILLIAM STOOD AT THE TOP of the aisle studying the congregation before him. The church was full and he wasn't surprised he could sense tension in Mary-Ann's arm as she stood by his side. As expected, all his father's sisters were sitting near the front with their families, as were Mr Wetherby's. Even his mother's brother and sisters were present, yet there was one notable exception. His father's brother, Uncle Richard. *Where is he?* He hadn't seen him for years but he'd expected him to be here today.

As the organ sounded, William put his left foot forward and led Mary-Ann down the aisle. Mr Diver smiled as they approached and when the time came, William happily passed him the hand of his sister. The service was elaborate with four hymns, two readings and a sermon, and so it was over an hour later before William went with the newlyweds, Mrs Harris, Isobel and William Junior to sign the register.

With the formalities out of the way, they made their way to a local inn for the wedding breakfast. Mary-Ann and Mr Diver waited by the door to receive their guests, and it was half an hour later before everyone was seated. As the bride and groom prepared to make their way to the top table, Uncle Richard walked in, followed by his wife, Mrs Richard, and their four grown children.

"My dear, we're sorry to be late." He walked across the room to Mary-Ann. "I had to finish my round before I could get away and it's been a busy day."

Mary was about to take her seat when Richard's voice caused her to freeze.

"What the hell's he doing here?" Mr Wetherby said, making no attempt to keep his voice down. He slammed his napkin onto his chair before he marched to the end of the table. Mary regained her composure and followed close behind. Thanks to Mr Wetherby, she hadn't seen Richard for almost eight years, and she'd purposely invited him without telling her husband. They had once been close and she had longed to see him again, but now he was here, her heart was racing. *How does he do this to me after all these years?*

"How good of you to come," Mary said rather too loudly before Mr Wetherby had a chance to say anything. "And Mrs Richard too. I thought you were avoiding us."

Richard's smile sent a tingle down her back. "Not at all. We got your invitation and wanted to see everyone again. It's been a long time ... thanks to Mr Wetherby. I'm surprised he let you invite us."

Mr Wetherby glared at Richard. "I didn't let her invite you; I didn't know she had."

"I thought it was about time we were all together again." Mary fidgeted with her wedding ring.

Mrs Richard smiled and linked her arm through Richard's. "Yes, it's been too long," she said.

"Where's Emma?" Richard ignored Mr Wetherby as he surveyed the tables looking for his sister.

"She couldn't make it today," Mary said, also ignoring Mr Wetherby. "But the children are here."

"She's the only one not here? It's not like her to miss a family gathering."

"I'm afraid she's not well."

Richard sighed. "Perhaps we should take it as a sign that life's too short to hold grudges. What do you say, Mr Wetherby?"

❧

William had followed Mary down the room and when he saw the expression on Mr Wetherby's face he stepped between the two men.

"Uncle Richard, it's good to see you again. I hoped you'd be here." As he spoke, Harriet walked towards them. "May I introduce my wife? I don't believe you've had the pleasure of meeting each other."

"Mr Jackson, how nice to meet you," Harriet said. "There's no question you're related to William with those eyes." The vein in Mr Wetherby's neck pulsed. "Why didn't I meet you at our wedding?"

"I don't believe we were invited … were we, Mary?"

"You were, but … there was a mix up with the invitations." Mary noticeably struggled to find the right words. "I didn't realise until too late that yours hadn't been sent."

"That was convenient; I can't imagine how it happened."

"That's enough." Mr Wetherby took a step towards Richard, causing Mrs Richard to let out a yelp.

"Stop." Mary put her arm in front of Mr Wetherby and turned to Richard and his family. "There are seats for you at the end of the table on the left. If you'd like to sit down, the food's about to be served."

❦

Harriet was seated opposite William at the end of the top table, adjacent to the seats of Uncle Richard and his wife. Once she had exhausted the conversation with those closest to her, Harriet turned to Uncle Richard.

"That was quite an entrance," she said, once she had his attention. "Did you miss the church service on purpose?"

"No, nothing so grand," Richard replied. "Like I said, I was working. I had a full cart of coal to deliver."

"I didn't think he was ever going to get home," Mrs Richard said.

"I thought you belonged to the Society of Friends. I'd imagined you didn't want to attend the a Church of England church."

William kicked her under the table.

Richard appeared not to notice. "No, most of the family have converted now. Since Aunt Rachel died, only Aunts Lucy and Rebecca are still Friends. We prefer the structure of the Church of England."

"It's not for me," Harriet said. "I'd like to move to the Congregational Church."

"You should be ashamed of yourself," Sarah-Ann said as she overheard her.

"Why?" Harriet replied. "You used to be a non-conformist."

"Only until I knew better." Sarah-Ann pulled her shawl around her shoulders.

"She didn't mean it." William apologised to his aunt.

"Yes I did, and I'm not prepared to have our children baptised in the Anglican Church."

"You have children?" Richard turned his head to William. "Why didn't anybody tell me? Are they here?"

"I'm sorry," William said. "I'm not a great letter writer and I assumed somebody would have told you. We have a son who's nearly two but we left him with a neighbour. We have a daughter as well, born a couple of months ago. She's here. Harriet, what have you done with her?"

"She's with Mrs Storey over there." Harriet pointed towards Mr Wetherby's sister, Betsy.

"Did you name the boy after your father?" Richard said as Mrs Richard turned in her seat to look at Eleanor.

"No, I ... well, we named him William, after ... myself." William couldn't bring himself to say he'd named his son after Mr Wetherby.

"William-Wetherby," Aunt Sarah-Ann said. "I thought you named your son after Mr Wetherby."

"Is she joking?" Richard stared at him, his eyes wide. "You named your son William-Wetherby, after your stepfather?"

William wanted the ground to swallow him up. "He's been good to us over the years."

"The man's a bully. Can't you see it? Did you know he had me run out of Birmingham?"

William's eyes bulged. "No!"

"Don't be so dramatic, Richard," Sarah-Ann said. "He did no such thing."

"Yes, he did, but you wouldn't know; you were still in Aldridge at the time." Richard turned his back on his sister and wife and lowered his voice. "The way he dominates your mother too, he won't let me talk to her and we used to be ... friends."

"He's always been fair with me, and generous," William said. "Without him we'd have been in the workhouse."

"Did he tell you that?" Richard couldn't contain himself. "My mother and father would never have let that happen. In fact, I wouldn't have let it happen. Your mother had family with her all the time she was in Birmingham, people looking out for her, even if she didn't realise it. I don't mean to sound hard, but Mr Wetherby is one of the nastiest people I've ever come across. Please be careful, and if you ever need anything, I may not have his money, but I'll be there for you."

Chapter 28

Birmingham, Warwickshire.

SINCE THE WEDDING MARY HAD been restless. It was nothing to do with the wedding itself; in fact she was pleased with the way things had gone once she had separated Richard and Mr Wetherby. No, the restlessness was to do with the house. Why were they living with only one downstairs room, amongst squalor and filth when they didn't have to? Mr Wetherby had told her often enough that they had money, and so why wouldn't he move?

She studied the cup in her hands, long empty of its contents, and placed it back on the saucer. As she stood up to take it to the sink, the postman knocked. She didn't recognise the handwriting on the letter he handed her, but when she opened it she found it was from her niece, Jane Dainty. Her mother, Emma, had passed away. Having spoken to Jane at the wedding, it wasn't a surprise, but it was sad; she had always liked Emma. She'd lived in Birmingham for the last few years and so the funeral would be local. The only problem was, Richard would be there, which meant another encounter between him and Mr Wetherby.

It was turned seven that evening when Mr Wetherby

arrived home and as usual he sat straight down to eat. Mary picked at some bread while she waited for him to finish, her pulse racing. As he moved to his seat by the fire, she coughed the tension from her throat.

"I had a letter this morning to say Emma's died. The funeral's on Monday; I'd like to go."

"Out of the question. I can't go on Monday and you're not going on your own." Mr Wetherby picked up the newspaper.

"Is there a problem?"

"I have a meeting with a builder and you're not going without me."

Mary was about to argue until the significance of his words struck her. "A builder, whatever for?"

"I need to expand the workshop again and the best thing to do is expand into this house and the house at the back."

"So we're moving?" Mary clapped her hands together under her chin.

"I expect so; I don't suppose you want to live in the workshop."

"Where will we go?"

"I've been giving it some thought. I don't want to move too far, for obvious reasons, and I don't want anything that will cost me too much. I've been looking around Summer Lane but I haven't seen anything yet."

Mary's heart sank, not Summer Lane. None of the houses were up to much, but there were parts of it, particularly the courts, that were positively overcrowded. It made Frankfort Street look smart.

"What about Alice? Where will she go?"

"I've a room in a house further down Frankfort Street she can have. She doesn't need her own house now Mary-Ann's moved out and she doesn't need to move with us."

Mary thought about leaving her sister on her own. "I'll have to speak to her. I suppose she does have a few friends around here now. Do we have to stay around Summer Lane? Isn't it time we moved to Handsworth?"

"How can I oversee the work here when I'm living in Handsworth? No, we'll be staying here; there's no question about it."

"Will we ever move to Handsworth, do you think?"

Mr Wetherby stopped what he was doing. "What is your fascination with the place?"

"It's so much nicer than it is here, the air especially. Susannah's happy there and look where William lives. We could have a house like that. You could have your own carriage too. It would make the travelling easy enough. It would be lovely to entertain without fearing the house is too small or we'll be overrun with rats."

"I don't want to spend money on a house like that. If we did move, it wouldn't be to a grand house."

"But why do you have to buy it? You already own property; you could buy some more houses here if you wanted to and rent a bigger house in Handsworth."

Mr Wetherby stared at her. "You may have an idea there. I've been thinking I'd buy the house we lived in but I needn't. In fact, if I don't worry about living in them, I can buy so many more. I think you've hit on a marvellous idea there."

"So does that mean we can move to Handsworth?" Mary's eyes sparkled with delight.

"Don't let it go to your head, just because you've had a good idea. I still need to be here to keep an eye on the building work, and we'll have to stay in Birmingham while that goes on, but let me think about it."

Mary tidied the table with a smile on her face. The possibility of a move to Handsworth was growing.

Ever since they'd been children, one of Alice's favourite meals had been slices of beef, stewed with vegetables and savoury suet balls. Not that they'd had it very often. The price of meat meant their mother had only served it on special occasions, but maybe that was the attraction. This evening, Mary had invited Alice around for tea to tell her they were moving house. She hoped the stew would put her in a good mood. She smiled as she chopped the vegetables and thought back to the last time she'd eaten it with her family in Shenstone. Her mother had prepared it for her and Alice's nineteenth birthday. She could almost smell the flavours as she remembered them all sitting around the kitchen table. They were happy times, but less than two months later everything had changed. How had it gone so wrong?

She knew of course *why* it had gone wrong, but what had caused it? The day her beloved Charles had arrived at her father's farm had been the start of it. It hadn't taken long before she'd fallen in love with that crop of dark hair and his deep brown eyes, not to mention his muscular physique. Even now, the thought of seeing him with his shirt off sent a tingle racing through her body. In those early days, they had been careful not to be seen alone together, especially when they went into the barn, and yet her father had walked in and found them at the worst possible moment. It was as if he was looking for them. She shivered as she remembered her father attacking Charles and then afterwards, once Charles had gone, the shame of being accused of losing her virtue to him. She hadn't, but they wouldn't believe her and her life had fallen apart.

Why her father had gone to the barn at that time of day she had never been able to fathom. She'd wondered for a time whether it had anything to do with Alice, but her sister had denied it so often, she supposed she must be telling the truth. Anyway, she couldn't dwell on it now. It was nearly thirty years ago. So much had happened since and she needed to be thankful for her second chance. She pushed all thoughts of Charles to the back of her mind, put the vegetables into the cooking pot and lifted it over the fire.

When Alice arrived, over four hours later, the smell of the casserole filled the room.

"Have you made a beef stew?" A smile stretched across Alice's face.

"I have. Like Mother used to make. We haven't had one for such a long time I thought it would be a treat."

"What's the occasion?"

Mary stood up to pour them both a gin. "Does there have to be an occasion?"

"I don't suppose so but this brings back such happy memories. Do you remember our birthday?"

Mary smiled. "I do. I was thinking about it earlier."

"I'm sorry I spoiled everything."

Mary stopped where she was. "What do you mean?"

Alice's face turned scarlet and she struggled to find the right words. "I'm sorry … I was thinking of Mother … of not contacting you. I shouldn't have mentioned it."

"Are you sure that's all it was?"

Alice was about to answer when the door opened and Mr Wetherby and William Junior walked in.

"My, that smells good," Mr Wetherby said. "Is this to celebrate the move?"

Mary glared at Mr Wetherby before she turned back to Alice. "No … no of course not. I just wanted to make something different."

Alice took the cup of gin that was still in Mary's hand. "It looks like it's you with some explaining to do, not me."

Chapter 29

WITHIN WEEKS, MARY WAS PACKING the last of their personal property into crates, unable to believe things had happened so fast. The evening with Alice hadn't gone quite as she had planned but strangely Alice had been relieved they were moving away. She was happy to move into a room further along Frankfort Street and said it was probably for the best. Mary suspected she was hiding something from her, but Alice had been keen to move as soon as possible and Mary hadn't had a chance to talk to her since.

In many ways, Mary envied Alice staying in Frankfort Street. Mr Wetherby had found what he considered suitable accommodation on Great Charles Street, but his idea of suitable accommodation was not the same as hers. For one thing, it meant William Junior would have to share a room with Charlotte, something he was not happy about. It also meant they were back in the town centre. Not only was it more congested than Frankfort Street; the railway station was practically on the doorstep.

"Why are we going all the way down there again?" she asked.

"Because the house is better than many I've seen, and

it's cheap. I told you I don't want to spend too much." With that the debate was closed.

Once Mary had her own belongings in the house it was slightly better than she had imagined, but she still wasn't happy. It was small, and even the smell of the steam engines couldn't mask the stench from the privies.

"It's because it's the end of a hot summer's day and the ashpits haven't been emptied," Mr Wetherby said when he came home on the first evening. "They'll do it tonight and everything'll be fine in the morning."

When Mary went into the court the next morning, she had to put her hands over her nose and mouth to stop herself retching. The stench was overwhelming and she knew the water on the ground wasn't due to overnight rain.

"This place is disgusting," she said to Mr Wetherby when she returned to the house. "You go out into the court and see how you like it. I'll have to go to the park. I can't stay here."

"I'm sure they'll sort it out today." Mr Wetherby stood up from the table and beckoned to William Junior to do the same.

"They'd better, or I'm not staying."

Mr Wetherby didn't have to go into the court until Sunday, by which time Mary was ready to walk out.

"I've never known anything like it," he said. "Those pits should have been emptied weeks ago. I'll call the night soil office first thing in the morning and demand they come and clean them."

"At least you and William Junior can go to Frankfort Street each day," Mary said. "Me and Charlotte have to endure the place all week. I can't let Charlotte out to play and I can't stand it much longer."

"All right. I'll make it a priority."

৵৶

A week later the ashpits were more than overflowing. Raw sewage ran in channels down the middle of the court, collecting in the potholes and against the walls, attracting flies and rats alike. As the days passed, Mr Wetherby was determined to clean the place up. More than anything, he wanted Mary to settle into the house, but at the moment there was no chance of that. His visits to the night soil office continued to have no effect and before long many of the children and some of the adults became sick.

The following Monday when he returned from work he was horrified to find Charlotte lying on her bed, showing no signs of movement except for a pitiful writhing as her stomach cramped. Mary sat wiping her down with cool water, but watching her suffer was more than Mr Wetherby could bear.

The following morning, without going into the workshop he went straight to the Inspector of Nuisances to report the night soil office for neglect.

"What did they say?" Mary asked when he got home that evening.

"Nothing. The fool said it was nothing to do with him and all he could do was send my report to them. I told them that half the people of the court are ill, but he still denied any involvement. I'll give them one more day to respond and then I'll go to the Magistrates' office to see if wc can force them to come and empty it."

"We can't last that long." Mary inhaled the fumes from her gin before taking a large mouthful. "I've felt sick since the day we arrived and Charlotte's getting weaker. We've got to get out of here."

"Can you go and stay somewhere; with Sarah-Ann perhaps?"

"She says it's much the same where she is. If we want Charlotte to recover, the best place to go is Handsworth, if Mr Watkins will have us, of course."

Mr Wetherby paused to think. Was it now becoming inevitable that they should move to Handsworth? It was apparent that most of Birmingham was in some distress and the night soil office couldn't cope with the situation. If anything happened to his daughter he would never forgive himself and so reluctantly he agreed they should go.

"Why don't you write and ask Mrs Watkins. I don't want you to go but I can't bear Charlotte suffering like this."

The following evening Mary came from sitting with Charlotte with a rare smile on her face.

"Mr Watkins has said we can stay with them for a few weeks. I've packed our things so we're ready to go first thing in the morning. Will you arrange a carriage for us?"

Mr Wetherby put his arms around her. "I wish you didn't have to go. I went back to the night soil office earlier and demanded to speak to the inspector. He said the man who does the work was off sick and they've no one else to do it. It could be weeks before it's sorted out."

"Well, thank the Lord we can go to Handsworth. Can I take Mr Watkins a bottle of port as a thank you?"

The following morning Mr Wetherby delayed going to the workshop to help Mary.

"What on earth are you taking all this for?" He surveyed all the personal property she had by the front door.

"I don't know how long I'll be. You said yourself, it might be months."

"It had better not be months. I'm not giving up on the night soil office."

"Whatever you do, this place has got to be spotless before I come back. I'm not leaving Handsworth and coming back to live in squalor."

When the carriage arrived, Mr Wetherby gave up arguing and carried Charlotte to the carriage. He laid her on the seat and as he did he finally understood the pain Mary had gone through all those years ago when he had taken William from her. He would miss his daughter dearly; in fact if he were honest, he would miss her more than Mary, something years ago he wouldn't have believed possible. As the carriage door closed he conjured up his best smile and stood back to wave.

Chapter 30

Handsworth, Staffordshire.

MARY STOOD AT THE GATE looking at the house in front of her. An imposing detached property on a wide tree-lined thoroughfare. There was a small garden to the front and a larger one to the rear with a grassed area, a coach house and stabling for up to four horses. The building stood three storeys high and had impressive bay windows to either side of the front door both on the ground and first floors. Above the front door was another window and there were three small windows protruding from the roof.

When she'd arrived in Handsworth, six months earlier, she'd planned to find the grandest house she could, to persuade Mr Wetherby to move from Birmingham. In her wildest dreams, she hadn't expected to find a house like this, and when she had, she hadn't imagined he would buy it, but he had and here she was.

The house on Wellington Road, now named Wetherby House, was more than she dared dream of. On the ground floor the hallway ran between two large reception rooms to the front and led to a smaller sitting room, a morning room and kitchen at the back. The kitchen was larger than any Mary had seen and housed an impressive range for cooking and a sink with running water. On the first floor there were four bedrooms and a bathroom, while on the second floor were six smaller bedrooms. The house was too much for Mary to take care of herself, and Mr Wetherby had employed two domestic servants. It was as if she were living in a dream and she worried that one day she would wake up to find herself back in Great Charles Street.

One of the first things Mr Wetherby did after the move was buy a distinctive pair of chestnut horses and a carriage. If he was to travel to Birmingham regularly, he needed his own transport. He also found a reputable school in Birmingham for Charlotte. Although she was only seven, he'd decided she would travel down to Birmingham with him on a Monday morning and return on a Saturday. As a result, other than visitors, the only company Mary had during the week were the two Scotch Collie dogs, Prince and Pippin, bought specifically for the purpose. They were similar to the dogs her father used to keep on the farm and she loved them.

Mary walked through the front door and reflected on the afternoon she had just spent with Mrs Watkins and Harriet. On the surface, it had been pleasant enough, but the tension between Harriet and her aunt was evident. Even by her standards, Harriet was becoming increasingly difficult, mainly because of the children's baptisms. In an act of sheer defiance the previous Sunday, she had taken both children to the Congregational Church, swearing that neither would be baptised into the Church of England.

Although Harriet claimed a moral victory, the strain was showing. Her cheerful, confident nature had disappeared and had been replaced by a withdrawn, anxious shadow of herself. Mary wondered why William hadn't ordered the children to be baptised, but she knew how she would have reacted in those circumstances. As Mary put a pan of water on the range, she realised it was time they talked.

The following day, Mary was in the kitchen kneading some dough when there was a knock on the door. Knowing the maid would answer it, she continued her work but stopped abruptly when Emily came back into the kitchen waving an envelope.

"Mrs Wetherby, you have a telegram."

"A telegram; oh my, I hope it's not bad news. Who's it from?" Mary tore it open to read:

Baby boy born last night
Mr Diver

"Praise the Lord; it's good news after all." Mary placed her hand on her chest. "Mary-Ann's had her baby, a boy. I'll write to her as soon as this bread's resting. A letter I think rather than a telegram; they're no good for my nerves."

Believing news of his new nephew would be a perfect excuse to speak to William, Mary put on her cloak, hoping to catch him on his way home from work. The light was fading as she left, but she didn't have to go far before she saw him with Mr Watkins. He didn't notice her until they were practically upon her, but when he did, his face dropped.

"Mother. What are you doing out on your own at this time of day?"

"It's nothing to worry about. I just have some news for you. Have I disturbed you?"

William glanced at Mr Watkins before he spoke. "It'll keep."

"It will," Mr Watkins said. "There's a lot more talking to be done yet."

William took his mother's arm as they continued walking. "What news do you have?"

"Why don't you join me for some tea and I can tell you?"

"I have to get home," William said, looking at Mr Watkins. "Harriet will expect me at the same time as her uncle."

"Can't you be a little late, just this once? Mr Watkins can tell her where you are."

Mary sensed William tense.

"Why don't you tell me your news while we walk?" he suggested.

Mary let out a sigh. "Mary-Ann had her baby last night. You have a nephew."

"That's marvellous. Is she all right?"

"I assume so; I haven't heard anything to say she isn't."

"Is that it?"

"What do you mean, is that it? I thought you'd be more excited. I hope to go and visit her soon. Mr Wetherby said I can go whenever I want. I'll probably stay with her for a few days."

"I'm sure she'll like that."

"She will. I don't see nearly as much of her as I would like, but then I don't get the chance to talk to you much either. I had hoped you'd be able to join me for half an hour."

"I'll tell you what, why don't I go and get Harriet and we can both come and visit you?"

"Do you have to?" Mary spoke rather too quickly.

"What's wrong with bringing Harriet?"

"Nothing … only, by the time you go there and back, Mr Wetherby will be home and we won't be able to talk properly."

"We won't be long. Harriet enjoys going out for a walk as soon as I'm home."

"Doesn't she let you eat before you go out again?"

"I didn't mean that, of course we eat first."

"We're here now." Mary stopped outside Wetherby House. "Would you see me in?"

William hesitated. "Will you give me a minute, Mr Watkins?"

"You see to your mother," Mr Watkins said, "I need to call on Mr Johnson about his order. We can talk again later."

Mary waited for Mr Watkins to cross over the road before she turned to William. "What was all that about? Mr Watkins doesn't seem very happy."

"It's nothing for you to worry about; he's just angry about these new bank holidays. He doesn't think he should have to pay the workers when they don't turn up for work. He's thinking of retiring."

"Retiring?" Concern crossed Mary's face.

"He's been struggling over the last year or so and I think the bank holidays are the final straw. He has a point, but I don't think he can do much about it. I don't suppose Mr Wetherby's happy about it either." William opened the front door for his mother and placed his hat on the hall table before he followed her into the back room. She gestured for him to take a seat by the fire.

"But what will you do if he retires?"

William shrugged. "That's what we were talking about. He wants to pass the business to me, but in truth, I'm not ready for it. I'm going to have to tell him I can't take it."

"Why ever not? It would be a good opportunity for you."

"I don't know …"

"If you stay a little longer Mr Wetherby should be home. Why don't you talk to him?"

William glanced at the clock. "Not tonight. I can't."

Mary sat down opposite him and leaned forward. "What's the matter? You haven't settled since the moment I met you."

"Harriet's expecting me."

"Can't she spare you for five or ten minutes? I'm worried about her myself; that's why I wanted to talk to you. The last couple of times I've seen her she's been withdrawn again; is she expecting another baby?"

William let out a sarcastic laugh.

"No, she's not expecting another baby; apparently two are enough for her."

"What do you mean, two are enough? You can't choose how many children you have; it's down to the Lord."

"Then the Lord has clearly underestimated Harriet." William stood up to leave but Mary continued.

"It's a year now since Eleanor was born; that must be what she needs."

William said nothing.

"I'll call and see her, tell her that having more than two children is a blessing."

William went white. "Please don't say anything of the

sort. She's still bitter about the way everyone expects the children to be baptised and feels her life isn't her own. Please don't let her know I've told you."

"But why won't she have the children baptised?"

"Mother, please, don't start; we've been through it a thousand times. I didn't come here for an argument, but when you say something like that I can understand why Harriet is so reluctant to have any more children. I'm sorry, I must be going; Mr Watkins will be home soon and I can't be late."

"How is Harriet's relationship with her uncle nowadays?"

"It's … fine, as long as I'm there."

"That doesn't sound fine."

"No, it is, honestly; now I really must be going."

Chapter 31

T WO WEEKS LATER, MARY WAS sitting in the back room of Wetherby House with Harriet opposite her. Having failed to find out anything from William, she hoped her new tactics would be more successful. She put her cup and saucer down on the small table at her side.

"I had a lovely couple of days with Mary-Ann last week," she said. "The baby's so placid. We hardly knew he was there."

Harriet smiled. "That's hard to believe given the way William-Wetherby was."

"I'm pleased she named him after her father. Although she never knew him, she said she wanted to remember him."

"I know she wasn't happy with us when we named William-Wetherby. She thought we should call him Charles. Anyway, I'm glad she's used the name; I'll write and tell her I'll visit them both soon."

"He's being baptised two weeks on Saturday. You will be there for that, won't you?"

Harriet shifted uncomfortably. "I'll speak to William about it. I'm sure my aunt will mind the children."

"How are things with your aunt and uncle now?"

Harriet screwed her face up. "All right, I suppose.

Sometimes I think things are improving, but at other times I can't say or do anything right. I had thought everything would change once I was married, but they haven't. To be honest, I don't know what to do about it. I try to stay quiet and say nothing, but even that's wrong. I've no idea what to do for the best. The only time I relax is when William is with me."

"What will you do if your uncle retires? William won't be able to stay at home with you all day."

"Don't think I haven't thought of it. It wouldn't be a problem if we moved to a house of our own, but William won't hear of it. I don't know why he's so reluctant because he won't discuss it. Has he spoken to you?"

"No, I don't often see him on his own and when I do he doesn't share anything. If you were to have another baby he may be more inclined to move, to give you more room."

Harriet coughed back a laugh. "Well that's not going to happen."

"How can you be so sure? You can't affect these things."

"You can if you want to. I'm not prepared to go through another childbirth and that's the end of it."

Realisation spread across Mary's face. "You don't mean … surely not; William has his rights. You can't deprive him, not after all he does for you."

Harriet sighed. "I thought you'd understand. Why does everyone always feel sorry for William but never for me; why are my feelings always ignored?"

"Men have rights, you know. You promised to love, honour and obey him. Is he angry with you?"

Harriet shrugged. "I don't think he's happy but he understands. He's good to me and I do love him."

Mary's mind drifted back to the time before Charlotte was born. "Well, don't take him for granted; the last thing you want is for him to fall out with you."

Chapter 32

MARY-ANN GAZED AT HER BABY and smiled; he was all she'd ever wanted. He was almost three months old now and was always smiling. Many a time she had found him lying in his cot without demanding anything. She knew it was time for her to go back to bed but when she finished feeding him she put him in his cot and sat staring at him, thanking the Lord for her blessings.

She wasn't surprised the following morning when he didn't cry. It was usual for her to find him awake and smiling, but this morning something was different. His eyes were closed, and when she touched him, he was cold. Freezing cold. The blood drained from her face and her stomach somersaulted. *Dear God, this can't be happening. Not my baby. Not Albert and Edwin all over again.* The image of her baby brothers jumped to the front of her mind. No, this wasn't happening to her. She needed to warm Charles-Jackson up; then he'd open his eyes and give her that adoring smile. She bent to lift him from his cot but as she straightened up, her vision blurred. Moments later she hit the floor.

Mr Diver was downstairs and heard a thud from the room

above. He took the stairs two at a time and found Mary-Ann in a heap on the floor, Charles-Jackson lying beside her. He looked from one to the other, unsure who to help first, but as he knelt between them, Mary-Ann moved her head.

"What happened?" he asked when she opened her eyes.

Mary-Ann didn't speak but when she saw Charles-Jackson next to her she reached for his hand. A moment later she pulled herself towards him, covering his tiny body with hers. Mr Diver saw tears streaming down her cheeks.

"Mary-Ann, let me see him. Shall I fetch the doctor?"

Mary-Ann shook her head as Mr Diver took hold of his son's icy hand.

"I can't live without him," Mary-Ann wailed. "He was my life … and now it's over."

Mr Diver watched helplessly before he spoke. "Let me put Charles-Jackson back in his cot and I'll help you back to bed."

"Noooo." Mary-Ann let out a sob and held the baby closer to her. "Don't take him from me. Leave me here to die with him."

Mr Diver stroked the back of Mary-Ann's head. There were no words to make it better. After a moment he lay down beside her, enveloping her in his arms and wiping his tears on her nightdress. He was aware of nothing but her sobs as they consumed her energy, leaving her breathless.

He had no idea how long he stayed there, but eventually he sat up and reached into his pocket for a handkerchief. He wiped his eyes before he offered it to Mary-Ann. "You can't leave me; please don't talk like that. We'll get through this, I promise."

Mary-Ann cried harder. "I can't go on. It's so unfair. Why did this happen to us? To Charles-Jackson. Oh God, we were so happy. What have You done?"

৵৶

As soon as she saw the telegram asking her to go to Birmingham, Mary knew there was a problem. There was no explanation as to why she was wanted, but even for such a short note, the tone was urgent. She put a change of clothes into a bag and prepared to travel to Birmingham with Mr Wetherby first thing the next morning.

When she arrived, minutes after seven o'clock, Mr Diver looked as if he hadn't slept.

"Thank goodness you're here," he said as he met her at the door. "Charles-Jackson's been taken from us. Mary-Ann's in a terrible state."

"Oh my dear Mr Diver. What happened?"

"He passed away in his sleep. Mary-Ann found him yesterday morning."

"Thank the Lord for the telegram so I could get here so quickly. Let me go and see her."

"She's had some laudanum to help her sleep, but I don't know what to say when she wakes up. She wants answers and I can't give her any."

A shiver ran through Mary's body as the faces of Albert and Edwin appeared unbidden. She would never forget the anguish their deaths had caused. Her daughter shouldn't have to go through such pain.

Mary-Ann didn't move when Mary went into the bedroom, and she could do nothing but sit and admire the paleness of Mary-Ann's skin alongside the dark brown curls surrounding it. Mary-Ann remained asleep when the doctor called and only woke late in the afternoon.

"I was just dreaming about you," she said when she opened her eyes. "You'd come to see me and you were sat exactly where you are. What are you doing here?"

"Mr Diver told me you were in bed and needed some company."

"Why am I in bed? It's not dark." A puzzled look formed on Mary-Ann's face as she tried to climb out of bed. "I need to see Charles-Jackson; he'll need feeding."

Mary put her hand on Mary-Ann's arm.

"You stay where you are; your legs may be weak."

"But I need to see him, I had a terrible dream and …"

Mary couldn't hide the sadness in her eyes. "It wasn't a dream, my dear. I'm so sorry …"

"No, it was …"

Mary-Ann battled with Mary over the bedcovers.

"Mary-Ann, be still." Mary stood up and held Mary-Ann's arms. "The Lord's taken him for reasons we don't understand. I know how you feel, but believe me, the pain will ease."

Mary sat down on the edge of the bed and for the first time in her adult life Mary-Ann felt the arms of her mother wrap around her, comforting her, loving her. As reality hit her, she collapsed into the embrace and let her tears fall. *Why has this happened*? Had she been too happy? Was the Lord jealous of how much she loved Charles-Jackson? Why did her brother have two healthy children when he hadn't even had them baptised? In that moment she hated God more than anything else in the world.

"I thanked You for blessing us with a beautiful son,"

she sobbed. "We had him baptised; he would have grown up loving You … and this is how You repay me." Her head dropped back onto Mary's shoulder as her body shook. When her tears finally subsided, Mary gave her another dose of laudanum and prayed that sleep would take her.

Despite his sympathies for his sister, Mary-Ann's problems were inconvenient for William. He had wanted to talk to Mr Wetherby for weeks, but with his mother in Birmingham he had been staying in one of his houses on Summer Lane. It was over three weeks later, while he and Harriet were out walking one evening, that they met Mr Wetherby arriving at Wetherby House.

"Mr Wetherby, what are you doing here?" William said. "I thought you'd be in Birmingham."

"I'm expecting some mail and I wanted to check on the dogs. I don't trust Emily to feed them properly. Your mother's not with me, of course. Why don't you come in? I've been meaning to have a word with you."

William and Harriet followed him into the house and waited while he took off his hat and coat and instructed the maid to provide some tea.

"How's Mary-Ann?" Harriet asked.

"In a bad way to be honest with you. The doctor keeps dosing her up with laudanum to help her sleep, but when she comes around it's as if she's hearing about Charles-Jackson for the first time. I want her to come back here so your mother can come home, but Mr Diver won't have any of it."

"I'd come and sit with her if she was here," Harriet said. "I'd like to help."

Mr Wetherby nodded. "I'll pass the message on, although I'm not sure it will make any difference. Do you want to go into the morning room with Emily while I talk to William?"

Harriet nodded but stayed where she was while William went into the back room with Mr Wetherby.

"Your mother told me Mr Watkins is thinking of retiring."

"He's made his decision. He's been struggling for a while and this business with the bank holidays has been the final straw."

Mr Wetherby nodded. "Well, quite, it's outrageous. What will you do? Your mother tells me you're not keen to take over from him."

"It's not that I don't want to, but it's such a responsibility. Getting enough work in to pay the men. I've never dealt with that side of the business before; I'm only used to running the workshop. I worry I won't be able to do it."

"What about if you take over the business from Mr Watkins and we work together?"

A puzzled expression settled on William's face. "What do you mean?"

"Once you're in charge, we'd merge the companies and work together as partners. Then I could teach you everything about running the business yourself."

William's eyes lit up. "Could we do that?"

"I don't see why not. Although I'd suggest you don't mention it to Mr Watkins ahead of him handing it over to you. He may not view things quite the same way as I do."

Chapter 33

AFTER SPENDING A MONTH IN Birmingham, Mary wanted to go home. Mary-Ann was showing little sign of recovery, despite being on laudanum for the whole time, and Mr Diver reluctantly agreed she should go to Handsworth with her mother.

By the time they got to Wetherby House it was approaching midday and Mary insisted Mary-Ann stay downstairs and have something to eat. She'd barely eaten since Charles-Jackson had died and she was painfully thin. The maid brought in some bread covered with butter and Mary broke off a small piece and pushed it into Mary-Ann's mouth. Immediately she spat it out.

"Mother, can't you see I don't want it? My mouth is dry and I can't swallow. Why won't everyone leave me alone? Please give me some laudanum and let me go back to sleep."

"You've been asleep for the last month; you have to get back to normal."

"How can anything ever be normal again?" Tears fell from Mary-Ann's already swollen eyes. "My baby is dead and my heart is broken. The only thing that gives me any relief is the laudanum. Why won't you give me any?"

Mary sighed. "You can have some tonight, but you have

to try and get over this. I know it's hard, but you have to deal with it."

"I'll never be back to how I was." Mary-Ann paused and fanned her face with her hand. "It's hot in here. I'm going outside for some air."

Mary jumped from her seat to restrain her daughter. "You're not well enough to go outside. You can't stand up."

"Stop fussing me; I can manage."

"No you can't. Besides, the dogs are outside and they'll knock you over if they jump up at you."

Mary-Ann struggled to stand up, but when her legs wouldn't hold her she slumped back down. "Why won't you help me? Is it too much to ask?"

"Why are you angry with me? I'm only trying to help."

"Nobody can help. Can't you see that? Nobody."

Mary released her arms and sat back down as Mary-Ann fidgeted with her skirts. A moment later she tried to stand up again.

"What have you done with my handkerchief; I can't find it and my nose is running."

Mary said nothing but disappeared to find a handkerchief. When she came back Mary-Ann was on the floor shaking violently.

"What are you doing?" Mary asked. "Why are you being so difficult?"

"Why won't you let me go to bed? All I want to do is curl up and die."

Mary tried to stop Mary-Ann from shaking but when she saw the perspiration covering her face she went for the maid.

"Emily and I are going to help you up the stairs," she

said when they returned. "If you're no better by tomorrow I'm calling the doctor."

The following morning Mary-Ann was calmer but as the day wore on she deteriorated. By mid-afternoon, Mary had no choice but to send for the doctor.

"How long has she been taking the laudanum?" he asked once he'd examined her.

"About four weeks. I stopped giving it to her two days ago so she could travel here. She had some last night to help her sleep but she's had none since."

"I wonder …" he said, scratching his head. "I've read reports of this condition but I've never seen it before. Some people become so used to taking it that when it's stopped their bodies have difficulty adjusting. What dose are you giving her?"

"She's had thirty drops four times a day for a month. Last night I gave her another thirty drops."

"Quite a high dose. I suggest you start dropping the evening dose first to twenty drops and then to ten. Once she's comfortable with that, try and stop it completely. She may be uncomfortable for a few days once it's stopped but give her plenty to drink. That should help."

Concern settled on Mary's face. "Will she be all right?"

The doctor shrugged. "It may have some lasting effects but let's hope it doesn't come to that."

It had been over a week since Mary-Ann arrived in Handsworth and Harriet decided it was high time she paid her a visit. After all, she had offered to sit with her. She was in high spirits when she got to Wetherby House and she helped William-Wetherby and Eleanor off with their coats before the maid showed them into the back room.

"Is Mary-Ann not here?" Harriet was surprised to find Mary sitting alone.

"She's in bed. She's been very poorly."

"I thought she'd be all right by now? Can I go and see her?"

Mary dropped her knitting onto the table and stood up. "No, I'm afraid you can't go upstairs."

"Why ever not?" Harriet's frown was enough to show she wasn't happy.

"You know how much she wanted a baby and when he died she was devastated. The only thing that kept her calm was laudanum. Unfortunately, she's had too much and we're having trouble stopping it. For the last week I've sat and watched her writhe around the bed in agony, at times drenched in perspiration and half an hour later shivering with the cold. I did wonder if she would ever recover, but I'm pleased to say she seems to be making progress. This is the first afternoon I've been able to leave her alone since she got here and that's only because she's asleep."

Harriet's frustration turned to concern. "When can I see her?"

"I don't know." Mary walked to the window before she continued. "I worry that seeing you with the children, will remind her of what she's lost."

"But that's nonsense."

Mary took a deep breath. "Maybe it is, but things have changed. Mary-Ann has lost a son she adored and she's asking why. She's blaming herself and she's blaming God, wanting to know why a child who was baptised has been taken from her ... and I worry how she'll react when she sees two healthy children who are not baptised. I don't want to talk about the rights or wrongs of your choices, but that's how she sees things at the moment. She's angry and she's lost all sense of fairness."

Harriet's mood changed in a moment. "Why does it always come back to me? It's not my fault she lost her son. It happens to many women whether the children have been baptised or not. I'm sick and tired of being criticised. I won't hide William-Wetherby and Eleanor away, but I won't be made to feel guilty any longer either. If you can't stop criticising me, our relationship is over ... and if you don't like the fact the children haven't been baptised then I won't inflict them on you."

"Harriet, please, it wasn't meant as a criticism. I'm simply telling you how she feels."

"Well, when she feels she can accept me on my terms, she knows where I am. I won't trouble her again unless I'm invited."

Chapter 34

EVEN THOUGH IT WAS SEVERAL hours later before Mr Wetherby came home, he could tell Mary had been crying, and demanded to know why.

"I will not have her talking to you like that." His face was scarlet as he paced the room. "William needs to be told of this and he needs to do something about it. I'll call and see him after we've eaten."

"Please don't do anything to make things worse."

"How can it be any worse? She's threatened to stop you seeing your grandchildren; she's no right to do that. She needs to be disciplined and by God I'll make sure she is."

Once he had eaten, Mr Wetherby marched around to Grosvenor Street and demanded to see William. He was shown into the front room and a minute later William joined him.

"Mr Wetherby, what brings you here? Is everything all right?"

"No, everything is not all right. I left your mother at home in tears, worried that she might never see her grandchildren again."

The colour drained from William's face. "What? Why would she think such a thing?"

"Because that is precisely what your wife told her when she visited this afternoon."

William stumbled into the nearest chair. "What happened?"

"Your mother's been like an angel these last few weeks. Mary-Ann's been desperately ill but never once has your mother complained. When she told Harriet she couldn't see Mary-Ann, she was subjected to the cruellest verbal attack. It was completely unprovoked and I fear your wife is losing her mind. I want you to see to it that she's disciplined in the most severe way. Your mother doesn't deserve to be treated like that and I won't stand by and watch it happen."

"I noticed Harriet was upset about something when I came home, but I haven't had a chance to speak to her. I'll talk to her tonight and see what caused it."

"I'm sure your mother wouldn't provoke such an attack. Your wife needs more than a talking to; if I had anything to do with it she'd get a thrashing. If I hear you haven't dealt with her severely enough, I'll not hesitate in talking to Mr Watkins. He'll know how to deal with her. I want your assurance that you'll sort her out."

The bile rose in William's throat. "Please don't make me beat her."

Mr Wetherby stood over William. "You need to start asserting yourself. You take far too much notice of her. Mr Watkins has the right idea."

William subconsciously wiped the palms of his hands on his trouser legs. "Mr Watkins treats her worse than you treat your dogs."

"I treat my dogs very well."

"That's beside the point. She doesn't deserve it.

Whatever she said, she won't have meant it. She's just impulsive."

"That doesn't excuse her behaviour. I want to hear that you've dealt out sufficient punishment and I don't want her coming near Wetherby House unless we specifically invite her. Have I made myself clear?"

William sank further into the chair as he nodded his agreement. Was he ever going to be able to stand up to Mr Wetherby?

༄༅

Later that evening, when William walked into the bedroom, Harriet was sitting in front of the mirror brushing her hair. She'd been quiet all evening, despite the fact she knew Mr Wetherby had called specifically to see William. Normally this would have aroused her curiosity; tonight it hadn't.

"Mr Wetherby called earlier," William said.

"Yes, you said."

William raised an eyebrow. "Don't you want to know why?"

Harriet shrugged. "Some business, I expect; nothing to do with me."

"As I think you probably know, his visit was very much to do with you."

Harriet said nothing but continued to brush her hair.

"I believe you visited Mother this afternoon."

"I went to visit Mary-Ann. I wanted to cheer her up but your mother wouldn't let me see her."

"Was that why you were nasty to her?"

Harriet spun around to face William. "I wasn't nasty. Is that what he told you?"

"If you don't think you were nasty, then you'd better tell me what happened."

"Well … your mother said Mary-Ann was too ill for visitors, especially as I had William-Wetherby and Eleanor with me. She said Mary-Ann didn't want to see me again because she thought it should be our children who were dead."

William raised his eyebrows. "Did my mother really say that?"

"Yes, she did. Not quite in those words, but that's what she meant. She said it was because they hadn't been baptised."

"And so you told her she couldn't see them again?"

"If she wished they were dead, she wouldn't miss them, would she?"

William's cheeks were turning scarlet. "I don't believe my mother said anything of the sort. She loves William-Wetherby and Eleanor. Of course she wouldn't wish they were dead, whether they've been baptised or not."

Harriet stood up. "Well, why does she keep bringing it up at every opportunity? I'm fed up of being criticised every time I see her. I was trying to be friendly."

William sighed. "I'm afraid they don't see it like that. Mother's upset and Mr Wetherby is so furious he's told me I have to discipline you."

Harriet turned to William, her eyes wide with horror. "Discipline me, how?"

"I don't know. He suggested you should be thrashed."

"Thrashed! I don't deserve that. William, please, the man's a brute."

William put his arms around her. "I'm not going to beat

you, but you can't talk to Mother like that. He said you're not to go to Wetherby House again without an invitation and that I have to deal out some punishment. If I don't he'll go to your uncle."

Harriet buried her face in William's chest to hide her tears.

"Please, William, forgive me. I didn't mean what I said, I was just angry. Of course I wouldn't stop her seeing the children. I won't ever upset her again, I promise."

"So what are we going to do to make it appear as if I've punished you sufficiently?"

Harriet didn't answer.

"I hope you know I'm trying to do what's best for you. I don't want to punish you but I have to do something. I think the best thing to do would be to keep you locked in here for the next two weeks. You'll see no one but me, you won't have your magazines and you'll be permitted no visitors. I'll bring you something to eat each evening."

"Can't I just have a few magazines? Nobody need know."

William sighed and tightened his hold of her. "Only if you promise to keep them well hidden. I'll have to keep the key to the door so nobody can come in unannounced."

Harriet nodded. "What about the children. Who'll take care of them?"

"I'll speak to Mother. She misses Charlotte when she's at school so I imagine she'd like the company."

"What about Mary-Ann?" Harriet's voice broke into a sob. "That's what all this is about. If your mother's to be believed, Mary-Ann won't want the children in the house."

"That's enough. I'll speak to Mother and we'll sort it out between us."

৵৶

Harriet cried herself to sleep that night. *Why am I always the one in the wrong?* She'd gone to see Mary-Ann with the best of intentions and it had all gone wrong.

By the end of the first week, she had read the three magazines William had allowed her and was bored. By the beginning of the second week, she didn't bother getting out of bed. She missed the children and couldn't bring herself to talk to William when he joined her in the evening. The only benefit of being upstairs was that she didn't have to deal with her aunt and uncle every day.

Two weeks later, when she was allowed back downstairs, she wished she hadn't bothered.

"I hope you've learned your lesson from this, young lady," her uncle said. "If it were up to me you'd have been up there a lot longer than two weeks."

Harriet glared at him. *Why can't he treat me like a normal human being?*

"Mother will be bringing the children back soon," William said. "Are you looking forward to seeing them?"

"Of course I am. I've never been away from them so long before."

"I'd better hear you begging Mrs Wetherby for forgiveness," her uncle added. "You'll get the back of my hand if you upset her again."

Oh to be back upstairs again, away from all this, Harriet thought. She stared at the pile of magazines in the corner. Dare she walk over, pick some up and go back to her room? A glance at William confirmed it wasn't an option and so, remembering her training from 'school', she sat down and put a smile on her face.

The children arrived within minutes and much to everyone's surprise Mary-Ann was with them.

"Mary-Ann, how lovely to see you," William said. "Are you feeling better?"

"I am, and it's in no small way down to you and Harriet." Mary-Ann sat on the couch next to Harriet. "Having William-Wetherby and Eleanor in the house lifted me out of my melancholy. There are still times when I'm sad and I'm not over the laudanum, but I'm on the mend and hope to go home in the next few days. One day I'll have more children and they'll be as precious as Charles-Jackson. Thank you for letting the children come and stay, Harriet. Mother told me how she talked you into it. You must have missed them dreadfully."

Harriet was lost for words and turned to Mary for an explanation. "Well … yes, I suppose … but if it helped you …"

"Haven't you got something else to say?" Mr Watkins snapped.

"Yes, of course." Harriet took a deep breath. "Mrs Wetherby, I owe you an apology."

Mary turned to Mr Watkins. "That won't be necessary. Harriet did us all a tremendous favour by letting the children come and stay."

"Mr Wetherby said …"

"I'm afraid Mr Wetherby misunderstood," Mary interrupted. "We have a lot to thank Harriet for."

Harriet was perplexed but smiled at Mary. Why had she been so angry with her? Despite everything that had happened, Mary had protected her. It also appeared that Mary-Ann knew nothing of what had been said. She would have to apologise and thank her properly when they were alone.

"It was the least I could do. I'm glad they helped." Harriet picked Eleanor up and placed her on her knee before she turned to her uncle. "Perhaps it's about time you apologised to me."

Chapter 35

HARRIET WAS OUT OF PATIENCE. Since her recent imprisonment she had tried on numerous occasions to talk to William about moving to a house of their own, but every time he closed down the conversation before it started. Tonight, as they were preparing for bed, she'd made up her mind she would be ignored no longer.

"Why won't you talk to me about moving house?"

"Because there's nothing to talk about. We have plenty of room here, your aunt helps with the children and it means I can keep in touch with your uncle. Why do you persist with this mad idea?"

"Don't throw it back at me; you know why I want to move. I'm sick and tired of being told what to do by everyone. I have no say in the running of the house, my aunt makes more decisions about the children than I do, and as for my uncle … do I have to go into that? We've been married for four years, you're thirty years old, we have two children and you're going to be a partner in a business. Don't you think it's high time we were living on our own? Everyone else of our age has their own house, so why won't you discuss it?"

"We're comfortable here. Why do we need to move?"

"I'm not comfortable, William. Remember me? I'm your wife. You promised to love and cherish me but you're letting a part of me die by keeping me here."

"Don't be so melodramatic."

"I'm not being melodramatic. I mean it and in case you doubt how important this is to me, I've decided that as long as we stay in this house I'm not sharing this bedroom with you. I'll sleep in the spare bed in the children's room until you start taking me seriously."

"Well, there won't be any difference there. I've been patient with you ever since Eleanor was born, but for all the affection you've shown me over recent months you might as well have your own room. Don't think I'm going to take this lightly though and don't think your uncle won't notice. In fact, I think it's high time I asked his advice on how I should deal with you."

"Why do you always have to ask what to do? It's got nothing to do with him … or is that why you don't want to move, because you're not *man* enough to make your own decisions? Even with the business you go running to Mr Wetherby for help. You're like a puppet doing whatever they tell you and you never stand up to them. You make me sick."

William had never hit her before but a blackness came over his eyes and before she could move, he brought his hand sharply down across her face, making her momentarily lose balance. A moment later he grabbed her arms, threw her onto the bed and climbed on top of her, pinning her to the mattress.

"On second thoughts, maybe I don't need any help," he said as Harriet struggled beneath him. "I'll show you how much of a man I am." He pushed her hands together and clasped them with one of his while his free hand grabbed at her nightdress. "You, Mrs Jackson, will do as you are told, whether you like it or not."

Harriet writhed around beneath him but when William hit her again she became still and allowed him to do his will. Once it was over, numbness enveloped her. She'd never been treated like that before and it frightened her that William would do such a thing. As he lay on the bed next to her, she heard his breathing but she couldn't look at him. She didn't know if she would ever be able to look at him again. Turning her head away, she let her tears fall onto the pillow. *How has it come to this? I loved him so much.*

She had to escape from this life. She was no longer prepared to live as a third-class citizen, constantly being told what to eat, what she could read, whom she should meet, how she should raise her children. She would also not live with a husband who treated her like that. Until half an hour ago, she had thought she would leave this house with William and the children; that they would move somewhere together and she would gain her freedom, but not now. It was never going to happen, not as she'd planned, but what were her options? She was a woman with no money and nowhere to go; after tonight she might be expecting another child. The thought made her stomach turn and she tried to dismiss it. Hadn't she told herself that if you wanted something badly enough, you could make it happen? Well, she wanted to leave this house, and come what may, she would do it.

By the time Harriet went downstairs the next morning, William had left the house. He only went out early on the rare occasions he went to Birmingham with Mr Wetherby, but he hadn't mentioned anything about it last night. As she walked into the back room she saw a note on the fireplace addressed to her. She opened it casually, sensing her aunt had followed her into the room.

> *Won't be home tonight.*
> *Mr Wetherby wants me to stay in Birmingham.*
> *I don't know when I'll be back.*
> *William*

A shiver ran through her as she took in what it said. *He's left me alone with my aunt and uncle. How could he?* She folded the note and put it into the pocket of her apron before she turned to smile at her aunt.

"Only William reminding me he has to stay in Birmingham overnight." Tears formed in her eyes but she held her smile until she walked past her aunt. "I'll go and see the children."

In a way she was relieved that she wouldn't have to face William tonight, but the tone of the note worried her. Why didn't he know when he'd be back? He had always been gentle and affectionate with her and stood up for her against her uncle, but not now. She'd obviously pushed him too far. They hadn't been intimate for many months and it must have got too much for him. She wondered where he would stay. Mr Wetherby still had a house in Birmingham and so she supposed he would go there.

She stayed out of her uncle's way all day, but as they sat for their evening meal she had no choice but to sit with him.

"What's up with you tonight? You've hardly said two words. Has William been giving you the hiding you deserve?" He nodded at the bruise on her face.

"I walked into the door last night when it was dark."

"It didn't sound like that to me." Mr Watkins smiled at his wife. "He sounded like he was giving you a right going over and about time too. I should've done it years ago, shouldn't have messed about with that school and wasted all my money. A regular beating every day, that would have brought you to your senses better than any school."

Harriet slammed down her knife and fork and stood up. "I'm sorry but I've had enough. What have I done to deserve all this? You never stop criticising me."

"Talking to me like that, for one thing. You don't know your place, you never have. Ever since you went to school you've thought you were better than everyone else, but you're not. You're a woman. Your function is to have children for your husband and keep the house tidy. You don't have the same brains as men, and we don't want to hear your opinions. Why can't you get that into your silly little head?"

"There are plenty of women who can think as well as men; in fact there are many women more capable than men. The way you constantly put us down makes me think you're frightened of something. Are you frightened that by letting me do more reading I'll show myself to be better than you? I don't suppose it would be difficult."

She knew what was coming before she felt his blow, but she didn't care. Maybe if he beat her enough, he'd put her out of her misery. "That's your answer to everything, isn't it? If you can't win the argument, beat us up. That's really clever. It takes a lot of brains to do that. Go on then, carry on. Show me how clever you are."

She could see the veins pulsing in her uncle's neck as he tightened his fists, struggling to decide what to do next.

"You'll live to regret that little outburst," he said after some deliberation. "Now get out of my sight. I'll deal with you tomorrow."

Harriet deliberately walked to the other side of the room and picked up a handful of magazines. A moment later she turned and looked him straight in the eyes. "It will be my pleasure."

Without a second glance she headed for the door, slamming it behind her.

Chapter 36

HARRIET HAD NO IDEA WHAT time it was, but it was dark outside. She guessed it must be between three and four o'clock. Lying in bed with her eyes open she doubted that sleep would visit her again before daybreak. Her mind refused to switch off as the events of the previous twenty-four hours filled her thoughts. Even by her standards she suspected she'd gone too far with both William and her uncle. Should she apologise? She didn't want to, it would be admitting she was wrong when all she was trying to do was stand up for herself, but it would make for an easier life if she did. After all, she did have to live with them both.

She must have dozed off at some point because she was woken with a start when a door slammed downstairs. It was light outside, suggesting she should be up, but she was in no hurry. She picked up a magazine and was onto her third article before she heard her uncle go out. She finished what she was reading before she got out of bed, pulled on her dress and sat in front of the mirror to brush her hair. She was putting some clips in her hair when she heard the front door open followed by footsteps coming up the stairs. *He must have forgotten something.* She thought no more of it until she realised there was more than one set of footsteps and they'd stopped right outside her room. She stood up to go to the door, but before she reached the handle the door burst open and her uncle stepped in, closely followed by the doctor and rector. Her aunt stood behind them on the landing. Harriet looked from one to the other, settling on her uncle as he started to talk.

"Here she is, doctor," he said. "She's been shut in her room all morning and spoken to no one. She's not even seen her own children. We've had to lock them in their bedroom for their own safety." Harriet tried to speak but her uncle continued. "Last night she was quite hysterical to the point where I'd say she needs treatment."

"I would suggest she's needed treatment for some time," the rector added.

"There's nothing wrong with me ..." Harriet's raised voice caused each of them to look at her.

"Listen to her, doctor; she's out of touch with reality."

"I am not out of touch with anything ..."

"This is what I have to deal with. Do you have anything to calm her down?"

"I'm not taking any medicine." Harriet's eyes widened as the doctor reached into his bag.

"You, young lady, will do as the doctor tells you."

"You can't treat me like this ..."

"That's enough! Doctor, even if you can calm her down now, I think the best thing would be a spell in the asylum. What do you think?"

"You can't send me there because I stand up for myself." Harriet shouted to make herself heard.

"The patient is quite hysterical," the rector said. "I could pray for her, but I fear it won't be enough ..."

"I'm not hysterical. You're not listening to me."

"I see what you mean, Mr Watkins," the doctor said. "I think it would be quite appropriate to send her to the asylum. It's fortunate we have the rector with us. Do you have the relevant paperwork?"

The rector held a prefilled sheet of paper out in front of him.

"You can't do that." Harriet glared at the rector as she moved to the far side of the room. "You have to speak to William. He won't let you."

"A carriage goes to Winson Green on the hour." The doctor spoke as if she wasn't in the room.

"I'm not going to Winson Green." Harriet's knuckles were white as she tried to grip the wall.

"I have my own carriage," Mr Watkins said. "I'll take her in that."

The doctor nodded. "It's probably for the best. I'll write out the certificate for you to present when you arrive there. They'll take her off your hands."

Harriet eyed the doorway, but there was no way through. "What about the children? You can't expect me to leave them with you."

"Thank you, Doctor. I'll get the horse ready straight away. The sooner she's there the better."

"I won't go; you can't make me. You have to talk to William."

Her uncle stared at her as if he had forgotten she was present. "Doctor, can you do something with her? I can't take her in this state."

The doctor lifted a bottle of laudanum from his bag.

"No … I won't take anything."

"Do you want to hold her down and I'll drip the tincture into her mouth," the doctor said.

Harriet's uncle grabbed her from the wall and threw her on the bed, sitting astride her before she had time to move. Harriet twisted her head from side to side as her legs kicked, but the rector hurried to hold her legs together while her uncle squashed her face between his hands allowing the doctor to pour the liquid into her mouth. As it hit the back of her throat she coughed and spluttered, but the doctor put his hand over her mouth to make sure she swallowed it.

The last thing Harriet remembered before falling asleep was the hand of her uncle across her face and a warning that if she didn't behave she might never be allowed back.

Chapter 37

Winson Green, Birmingham, Warwickshire.

ALTHOUGH WINSON GREEN ASYLUM STOOD less than two miles south of Handsworth, it might have been in another world. It had once been a desirable area with large houses for those who wanted to escape Birmingham, but now it was a place for those that Birmingham didn't want. The asylum stood in its own grounds, but the neighbours included a prison, a workhouse and a fever hospital.

Harriet was still dazed from the laudanum when the carriage turned into the main gate. She gazed at the symmetrical red-brick building, unable to comprehend what she was seeing. The central section stood three storeys high and was flanked on either side by additional blocks that were joined to the main building by two-storey walkways. The windows and doors were edged with stone and the taller parts of the building were topped with arched gables. As they drove towards it, Harriet sat up and became aware of a number of labourers. They were supposed to be working but were instead leaning on the wall watching her arrive.

"Here's another nutter," one shouted.

"Look at her, enough money for a carriage, but no brains to go with it."

"Make sure she's locked up; we don't want the likes of her escaping." The men laughed and Harriet tried to close her ears. Was this how everyone would see her from now on? A lunatic unable to take care of herself, let alone her children. Even her husband had left her. *Where is he?*

Once they reached the steps leading up to the front door, Harriet's uncle grabbed her left arm and pulled her from the carriage.

"Get in there and don't say a word." He pushed her through the door into a reception hall. A stern woman in a starched white uniform greeted him. Mr Watkins handed her the doctor's note and she nodded knowingly as she read it.

"Leave her with me, Mr Watkins; we'll deal with her for you."

Mr Watkins smiled coldly at his niece. "I'll see you when you learn how to behave yourself and not a day before."

The reality of what was happening hit her. "No, please, you can't leave me here … please, Uncle. Take me home." Harriet started to follow him out of the door.

"Come along now, dear," the woman said as she held her back. "Nurse Cooper, will you come and take Mrs Jackson for me?"

"No … leave me alone; you have no right."

"You come with me." Nurse Cooper pulled Harriet towards the stairs.

"You can't keep me here," Harriet screamed. "I need to see my husband. He hasn't agreed to this."

"Up the stairs, now, and that's an order," the nurse said. "Nurse Baker, can you come and help me? We need to get her to the shower-bath. Fifteen minutes under the cold water'll calm her down."

Nurse Baker was a stout woman who took Harriet by the arm and forced her up two flights of stairs. Harriet kicked at her legs as they entered a large bathroom, but Nurse Baker held her while the other nurse stripped her and strapped her under a shower. The icy water was powerful and as the first jets hit Harriet's warm body her shrieks filled the room. She pleaded for mercy and begged for William, but the walls were thick and nobody paid any attention to the screams of one more patient.

Ten minutes later Harriet was exhausted. She was frozen to the core but the straps were so tight around her wrists that she couldn't move her arms to shield herself. Finally, as she was ready to collapse, the nurse who had stood and watched, turned off the water, untied her right hand, and passed her a small towel. Harriet didn't have the energy to lift her arms, let alone dry herself, and after a minute the nurse gave her a quick rub-down before she released the other strap and put her in a cotton gown.

"Follow me," she said, as she opened the door and stepped out into a seemingly unending corridor. Harriet's legs were so numb that with every step she feared she would stumble and fall. Before long they stopped outside a room on the right-hand side that overlooked the front of the property. The nurse told her to wait at the door while she entered the room to talk to the doctor. Harriet didn't hear much of the conversation but one word jumped out at her. *Pauper.* Was that why the rector had been there, so he could admit her as a pauper? Harriet broke into a cold sweat. She couldn't be treated as a pauper. *It's bad enough just being here.* Several minutes later, the nurse ushered her into the room and told her to lie on a bed situated along the left-hand wall. The doctor thanked the nurse as she left but continued to work at a desk with his back to her. It was several minutes before he stood up, walked over to the door and locked it.

"We don't want anyone disturbing us, do we, Mrs Jackson?"

Harriet's eyes followed him across the barren room until he stood by her side. The doctor was a tall thickset man with greying hair and a pair of pince-nez perched on the end of his nose. He read her notes and after removing his glasses he stared down at her coldly. Without a word he walked behind her, pushed her into a sitting position and pulled the back of her gown open. The cold metal of the stethoscope made her jump as it touched her skin, but he grasped her shoulder to stop her moving. After a few seconds he moved his hands up to her neck and pulled the gown off. Harriet was so startled she let out a shriek.

"We'll have no more of that, Mrs Jackson." His voice was calm but Harriet noted the menace in his eyes. "I need you to lie down for me."

Harriet couldn't move and stayed where she was, holding her arms in front of her. Not even her husband had seen her like this.

"Do I have to force you down, Mrs Jackson? You can make this as easy or as difficult as you like, but I will examine you, all of you, whether you like it or not." His tongue flicked across his thin lips. "I have all the time in the world."

Harriet saw the anticipation on his face and her eyes

widened; he wasn't going to examine her at all. He rubbed his hands together and pushed her back onto the bed before he wiped the wet hair from her face.

"You must learn to do as you're told," he said. "We have ways of dealing with disobedient women like you and the more you struggle, the more often you'll come back to see me. Do you understand?"

Harriet opened her mouth to speak, but the words stuck in her throat.

"I'll take that as a yes." His eyes worked their way down her body before returning to meet her gaze. "It's always a pleasure to see someone for the first time."

Harriet froze as he reached for a cane resting against the bottom of the bed.

"Don't worry," he said, as he rapped it against his left palm. "I won't use it unless you scream."

Harriet had no idea how long she lay there while he worked to degrade every inch of her. Once he finished she lay motionless, unable to move.

"You can get dressed now." He threw her gown at her. "We're finished for today."

With all the energy she could muster Harriet sat up and reached for the gown but her arms were shaking and she couldn't pull it up high enough to fasten. The doctor appeared not to notice and called for the nurse before he left the room without a backward glance.

"Now, Mrs Jackson, let's get you dressed." The nurse pulled the back of her gown together as if there was nothing unusual about it draping on her knees. "The doctor will see you again tomorrow if you have trouble settling in." She helped Harriet off the bed and led her out into the corridor and into another room, this time much larger. It contained at least thirty beds, crammed in so tightly there was barely room for a chair between them. They were all occupied except for one on the left-hand side towards the end of the room. That was where she was heading. Harriet glanced around at the other women and her heart sank. She had always imagined the asylum would be full of lunatics but she didn't see any. What she saw were mostly young women, about her age, looking forlorn and desperate. How could it be right to treat them like this?

Harriet sat down on the bed and put her head in her hands. *How dare they treat me like that?* It wasn't just the doctor; it was her uncle, aunt, husband, and the nurses. *How dare they?* She wanted to scream, but it would only confirm she was hysterical, and she wouldn't give them the satisfaction. Eventually she got into bed and stared at the ceiling, her mind racing. She remained there for the rest of the day and was so still that when the nurses came around with the sleeping draught that evening, they thought she was asleep. It wasn't until hours after dark that sheer exhaustion carried her off into an uneasy sleep.

The day was breaking when she woke and it looked like it would be warm. Under normal circumstances it would lift her spirits but there was nothing that would take away the horrors of the previous twenty-four hours.

"There's breakfast on the trolley." A nurse pointed to the end of the ward. "Porridge with bread and cocoa. It won't be there all morning and so if you want anything you'd better go now."

Harriet glanced down the ward, but didn't move. She didn't remember the last time she'd eaten, but she wasn't hungry; besides, she wasn't sure her legs would make it to the end of the ward and back.

Shortly afterwards, the same nurse came to take her to the needle room. "You've been put to do the mending. The doctor must have liked you."

Harriet glared at her.

"There's a lot worse jobs he could've given you; I'd take this one if I were you."

Harriet gave the nurse such a vicious glare that she backed away. "Suit yourself, but I'll warn you now. The best way to get out of here is to keep yourself busy."

Harriet said nothing and lay back down on the bed. She needed time to think but the images of the doctor, and the memory of how he'd touched her, were too fresh. It was vital to focus and blank it out. She spent the rest of the day staring into space, lying perfectly still except for the movement of her fingers, which continually twisted the bed sheets into tight knots. Women from the ward would occasionally stop by her bed to make conversation, but when she refused to speak, they left her alone.

As evening approached a nurse came to tell her she had a visitor. Her interest was aroused for a second before she decided there was nobody she wanted to see. A minute later, William walked towards her. As soon as he reached the bed he sat down and took hold of her hands.

"Harriet, what happened? I came as soon as I heard. I'm so sorry, I shouldn't have left you as I did."

No, and you shouldn't have treated me like you did either.

"Harriet, look at me."

Silence.

He reached for her chin and turned her face to his, but she looked away.

"I'm sorry, Harriet. Please forgive me. I shouldn't have treated you as I did, it was just that … well, it doesn't matter. We need you out of here. I only found out about your hysteria when I got home tonight. Your uncle told me how concerned he was and that he called the doctor because he didn't know what to do."

Harriet couldn't help herself and turned to William, incredulity obvious on her face. She wanted to tell him the truth but there was no point; he wouldn't believe her. In frustration she turned away again and blinked back her tears.

"I missed you when I was away and the children miss you. We want you to come home."

Well, I don't want to come home; in fact I don't want to see you or speak to you ever again.

"I can see you're upset right now, but I'm sure you'll feel better in a day or two."

It's going to take a lot longer than that.

"I'll come back on Saturday. I'll be finished work earlier so I can stay for longer. Perhaps we can go for a walk in the grounds. You'd like that, wouldn't you?"

Chapter 38

Handsworth, Staffordshire.

WILLIAM LEFT THE HOSPITAL WITHOUT hearing a word from Harriet. It wasn't like her; she really must be ill. As it was still a pleasant evening he walked back to Handsworth. He wasn't in any hurry to talk to Mr and Mrs Watkins about his visit. In fact he was embarrassed Harriet hadn't wanted to talk to him and he didn't want to admit it. She hadn't looked at him, except for a moment when he thought she was going to say something but seemed to change her mind. He also didn't want to talk to the children about her. They hadn't been told much about her absence, but it didn't stop them asking questions.

After walking the long way home, he approached the front door and took a deep breath. Mr Watkins was waiting for him as soon as he entered the hall.

"Here you are. How is she? Has she got over her little outburst?"

William took off his hat and walked into the back room before he answered. "She's comfortable enough, although the ward's overcrowded."

"But did she behave herself while you were there?"

"Yes, quite impeccably. I expect she'll be home in a couple of days."

Mr Watkins's eyes widened. "The doctor assured me she'd be there for longer."

"What do you mean he assured you? Do you want her to be locked up for longer?"

"No … of course not, but I thought she might need a longer stay … to make sure she fully recovers."

William sighed. "Yes, of course. Maybe it's my wishful thinking that she'll be back sooner."

"Don't be too hasty with her. She needs to learn her lesson … I mean she needs to learn that we want the best for her."

At that moment Mrs Watkins joined them. "Well, that's the children in bed for the night, thank goodness. They're so full of questions. I've told them Harriet's gone to visit your sister in Birmingham. They seem satisfied for now, but want to know when she'll be back."

"Tell them Mary-Ann still misses baby Charles-Jackson. That should work for a few weeks."

"I don't like lying to them," Mrs Watkins said.

"Well, you can't tell them the truth, can you?" her husband said. "Do you want them to know their mother's a lunatic?"

"With all due respect," William said, "she's not a lunatic."

"She's in an asylum for lunatics. Do you want to tell them that?"

William clenched his fists behind his back and took a deep breath. "Of course not. Now, if you'll excuse me, I think I'll call it a night."

The following evening, after they had eaten, William couldn't wait to leave the house. The conversation constantly revolved around Harriet's state of mind and he couldn't take another moment of it, not when Mr Watkins took such delight in the situation. As he left the house he had no plans as to where he might walk, but before long he found himself on Wellington Road. His mother always welcomed a visit.

"Do you mind if I come in?" William said when the maid showed him into the back room.

"William, how lovely to see you." Mary jumped from her chair and plumped the cushions up on the couch beside her. "Mr Wetherby's in Birmingham for a Conservative Association meeting. Come and sit down."

William let her fuss with a pot of tea before he spoke. "Did you know about Harriet?"

"Did I know what about her?" A puzzled expression rested on Mary's face.

"Did you know she's been sent to Winson Green Asylum?"

Mary almost dropped the cup she was handing to William. "She's not. What on earth happened?"

"I was hoping you might be able to tell me."

Mary sat herself next to William. "I know nothing of it. When did it happen?"

"Tuesday, the day I was in Birmingham for Mr Wetherby. I should never have stayed; I knew the situation with Mr Watkins was volatile, but I went anyway."

"Mr Wetherby told me you offered to stay so that he could come home. I didn't think he forced it on you."

William put down his cup of tea before he pushed himself up from the chair.

"What was I thinking?" he said. "It was all her fault. She'd made me angry the night before and I thought it would do her good to be without me for a couple of days … to make her realise how much she needed me. Why did she have to have an attack of hysteria when I wasn't there?"

"Maybe it was precisely because you weren't there. She must have done something terrible to make you so angry."

"She did." William turned away. "I don't want to talk about it. Perhaps she's in the best place after all, although I wish she wasn't."

"When do you think she'll be home?"

"That's another good question. I had hoped it would be in a day or two, but Mr Watkins was horrified when I suggested it. He said the doctor had assured him she'd be in for longer. He's so pleased she's in there; I'm beginning to wonder if he deliberately caused the hysteria."

Mary raised her eyebrow. "He wouldn't do that, surely?"

William returned to his chair. "Wouldn't he? I'm not so sure. I know she upsets him but she doesn't deserve the treatment he gives her. If it wasn't for the fact I live under his roof I'd go round there and confront him right now."

"Why do you still live with him?" Mary recalled the last conversation she'd had with Harriet. "I believe you're the one who refuses to move. You might have to consider it in the future if relations between the two of them don't improve."

"They'll have to improve; we can't move out and that's the end of it. We're comfortable enough where we are."

"You might be comfortable, but Harriet isn't happy.

She thought things would change when you got married, but they haven't, have they?"

William put his head in his hands. "I want to make her happy, really I do, but ..."

"But what? Why can't you tell me?"

William stood up again and went to the window. "You know when you were married to my father, did you ever live together in a house, just the two of you, or did you always live with Grandfather?"

"We lived together in Birmingham for a couple of years before he became ill. That was where you were born."

"And was he happy running the house?"

Mary smiled. "He was always happy, at least he was with me. Always up to something. We'd have stayed in Birmingham if we could."

"So I've no one but myself to blame." William's shoulders slumped as he went to the door. "I need to go. I'll see you soon."

Chapter 39

Winson Green, Birmingham, Warwickshire.

HARRIET DIDN'T REALISE IT WAS Saturday until she sensed William standing at the foot of her bed. Since she'd arrived she'd done nothing and spoken to nobody, and was irritated at the disturbance. She glanced up, saw him smile and turned away. He walked to the side of the bed and took a seat.

"Hello, Harriet, are you any better?"

Silence.

"Come now, you're not still playing these silly games, are you? You're never usually lost for words. Once you start acting yourself again, you'll be able to come home. You want that, don't you?"

When Harriet refused to answer, William glanced over his shoulder to check nobody was watching. He'd failed to see an older woman walk to the bottom of the bed and he jumped when he saw her.

"No point wasting your breath on her," she said. "She ain't spoken to nobody since she came in, not one word."

"She's upset; she'll speak to me soon."

"Have it your way." The woman shrugged as she walked away. William's eyes narrowed as he turned back to Harriet.

"Speak to me, damn you. Can't you see you're making a fool of yourself?"

Harriet couldn't stop her hands from twitching and she pulled on the sheet. Why was she the one making a fool of herself? She hadn't asked to be here.

"I've had enough of this." William pulled the sheet from her hand. "It's about time you had some home truths. Don't you realise you've brought all this on yourself? You can't carry on blaming everyone else. You know how easily your uncle gets upset and yet you carry on taunting him … after all they've done for you as well. It's your fault the children haven't been baptised and yet your aunt is looking after them as we speak. When did you last give her a word of thanks? If you don't want to come home for yourself you should want to come home for them; they miss you. You're nothing but selfish and ungrateful. Take poor Mary-Ann; she's still devastated after losing Charles-Jackson and yet you don't care for your children."

"Stop right there." Harriet made no attempt to keep her voice down. "I've had enough of this. You've no idea what happened the other day because you weren't there. It was nothing to do with me having an attack of hysteria or the doctor's recommendation; it was all down to him. He made the decision to send me here. He planned it down to the last detail. He knew you weren't at home on Tuesday morning and he walked right into our bedroom, with the doctor and rector, before I had gone downstairs. An hour later I'd been forcibly drugged, strapped under freezing cold water and stripped of everything, including my dignity."

"That's not what your uncle told me …"

"I don't care what my uncle said. I know precisely what

happened because I haven't stopped reliving the nightmare of it. It's so much easier to blame me, isn't it, but let me tell you I've been systematically humiliated from the moment I arrived here. I can't sit here minding my own business without doctors coming and prodding and poking me without the courtesy of a greeting. And do you know why that might be?" Harriet gestured around the ward with her arm. "Take a look around and tell me what you see. No privacy, no personal belongings, just a group of sad women squeezed into a room far too small for them. Have you any idea why that is?"

William shook his head as he glanced around the ward.

"I'll tell you why. It's because this isn't a ward for private patients. No. My guess is that he couldn't find another doctor to certify me insane and so he paid the rector to falsify the documents and sign me in as a pauper. It was much more convenient. Can you believe that or do you want to check I haven't made that up as well?"

William studied the ward with its stark white walls, threadbare curtains and grey bedcovers, while Harriet continued.

"After everything he's put me through, do you think I'm in any hurry to go back and live in the same house as him? Do you think he'll forget all that's happened and start treating me like a human being again? Of course he won't; in fact, he's likely to make life more miserable than before."

"I'll speak to him …"

"You needn't bother. I've had plenty of time to think while I've been here and I've decided that as long as you're living under the same roof as him, I'm staying here. They can't do anything more to humiliate me."

"You can't stay here forever …"

"That's where you're wrong. Mary-Ann may have lost her baby, but at least she has a husband who cares enough to provide a house for the two of them. They don't live with your mother and Mr Wetherby so why do we have to live with my aunt and uncle? If you care about me, you'll find us a house of our own."

"I do care for you; you should know that. Let me speak to Mother. Maybe we can move in with them."

"No!" Harriet's voice drew the attention of everyone on the ward. "Didn't you hear me? I want a house of our own. Do you think Mr Wetherby will treat me any better than my uncle? He's already said he doesn't want to see me at Wetherby House without an invitation."

"Please, let me try." There was desperation in his voice. "Getting a house of our own is the one thing I can't do."

Harriet glared at him. "Maybe if you give me an honest explanation as to why that ludicrous statement is true I might have a chance to understand, but until you do, I won't believe you."

"You'll have to take my word for it."

"I don't have to do anything of the sort. If you want me to come out of here, you'll find a house for us and it'll be ready for me to move into straight away. I won't spend another night under the same roof as that man."

William grabbed her hands. "You'll do as you're told …"

"No actually, on this occasion I won't." Harriet pulled her hands from his. "Can I remind you that people around here think I'm a lunatic and while nothing is further from the truth, the fact is if I want to stay in here I can have an attack of hysteria anytime I like. That means the chances of me coming out of here when I'm not ready are non-existent. Now, I suggest you go home and think about it, but let me tell you this; I don't want to see you here again until you have a house for us."

Chapter 40

Handsworth, Staffordshire.

WILLIAM HADN'T SEEN HIS WIFE for weeks, but he thought about her constantly. He knew now she'd been telling the truth about her uncle, which made the situation at home worse. Although he desperately wanted to confront Mr Watkins, to tell him to leave her alone, the process of transferring the business to him was underway and he didn't want to cause any trouble.

Now when he thought of Harriet, it was with affection. He remembered the days before they were married, when she was exciting and energising. In those days she had told him her secrets with a glint in her eye that made him feel special. Occasionally he thought of the mischief she caused, and his fear when he thought she would cause him trouble, but now he smiled. How he missed her. He wanted nothing more than to bring her out of the asylum, for them to live as man and wife again, but he couldn't do it without moving house.

A month after she was admitted, Mr Watkins came to the workshop to tell him the transfer of the business was complete. Guilt pricked at William's conscience as he thought about the arrangement he had made with Mr Wetherby. He also worried about how long he could stay on good terms with Harriet's uncle once she came out of hospital. That was up to Mr Watkins though. If he could resolve these differences with Harriet, there needn't be a problem. As a gesture of goodwill William bought a bottle of port on the way home, hoping it would also make amends for the recent animosity.

When he got home Mr and Mrs Watkins were in the back room. Unusually the children were with them. He was about to walk into the room when he overheard William-Wetherby talking.

"So is Mother a madwoman?" he asked.

Mr Watkins answered, "I'm afraid she is."

"So will I ever see her again?"

William burst into the room. "Yes, you will see her again, and soon." He glared at Mr Watkins. "What have you been saying to them?"

"Just telling them the truth," Mr Watkins said. "They need to know."

"They don't need to be told lies. Your mother is not a madwoman, William-Wetherby, and she never was. She was tricked into going to the hospital but I'm going to make sure she comes home soon."

"I don't think so," Mr Watkins said. "Mrs Watkins went to visit her this afternoon, and says she sits there like a deaf mute doing nothing but twitching and playing with the bedcovers. She doesn't so much as look at you. No doctor is going to discharge her when she behaves like that."

"And is it any surprise she doesn't want to speak to one of the people responsible for sending her there in the first place? I'm going to see her tomorrow and she'll be coming home soon."

"Well, let me remind you that when she comes back here she lives by my rules. I am not having her …"

"You don't have to worry about her doing anything because she won't be coming back here."

Mr Watkins stopped in his tracks. "What do you mean?"

"I'm going to find us a house of our own. I'm sick and tired of you treating her worse than you would a dog, and you won't fill my son's head with lies about her. Now if you'll excuse me, I'll take the children to bed myself."

The following day William walked onto the ward with a fresh pair of eyes. Sitting on her own looking vulnerable and frightened was the woman he loved. The last thing he wanted to do was run his own house, but he had to. There was no going back.

"Hello, Harriet."

Nothing.

"Please don't be angry with me, not anymore." William sat down and took hold of her hand. "I'm sorry. I've let you down; I can see that now."

Harriet did not respond immediately and William wondered if she had returned to being silent. Eventually she turned to him.

"Have you found us a house?"

William squirmed in his seat. "I'm going to look on Monday. I promise."

The flash of hope on Harriet's face disappeared and she shrank back into the bed.

"I've not stopped thinking about you over these last few weeks. I want to make you happy, but it'll be hard for me. Will you help me?"

Harriet turned to him with a puzzled look on her face. William took a deep breath before he continued.

"Ever since I went to school, I've known that I don't understand numbers the way other people do. They get mixed up in my head. I used to struggle with sums, even the easy ones, and I'd forget how to do things. Learning my times tables was about the only thing I could do, because I could remember them." William stopped and stared into the distance, his eyes filling with tears. "The teachers used to cane me if I got things wrong. Fortunately, I had a friend who helped me and I managed to make it to the end of school." William glanced up at Harriet, but she said nothing. His voice was a whisper when he continued. "I mentioned it to Mother once, but it was in the early days and I made her promise not to tell Mr Wetherby. When it didn't improve, I was so ashamed I couldn't tell anyone."

William stopped and buried his face into his handkerchief. "You don't know what it's like … always feeling like a fool … pretending everything's all right when inside you're praying that nobody will ask you any questions." He blew his nose and took a deep breath. "Even now I struggle with money. I've worried for years about how I'd manage the bills if we had our own house, never mind running a business. It's easy living with your uncle; I give him half my wages and he does the rest. That's why I didn't want to move."

"Why didn't you tell me?" Harriet's face remained stern.

"The same reason I didn't tell anybody else." William struggled to control his voice. "I was ashamed."

"But you've changed your mind now?"

"I have … if you'll help me. I want you to come home."

It took her a few seconds, but for the first time in over a month, Harriet smiled.

"Of course I'll help you. I love doing sums. I'll keep everything written down so we can go through things together."

William let out a long breath as he wiped his eyes. "I'm sorry I've let you down. I feel like such a fool."

"It would have been a lot easier if you'd told me sooner. I'd have helped you years ago and none of this would have happened."

"I'm sorry, really I am. Will you forgive me?" William clung to Harriet's hands.

"Only if you get me out of here. You've no idea what they've put me through. I won't ever forget it."

"Of course I will. I'll speak to the matron tonight before I leave."

Harriet smiled. "I'll start talking to a few of the women here then. Let them know there's nothing wrong with me. In a day or two, I'll go to the airing courts and by this time next week, assuming you've found us a house, I'll even agree to do some needlework."

William smiled. There wasn't much wrong with her. She wasn't even worried about his confession; in fact it had cheered her up to think she would be useful.

"I won't wait until Monday," he said. "I'll walk home now and start looking for a house tonight."

The evening was drawing in as William left the asylum but

he still decided to walk. As he approached Handsworth, it was too early to go home and so he called on his mother.

"So how is she?" Mary asked once he sat down.

"She's fine. Hopefully she'll be out in a few weeks and we can put this nightmare behind us. The only thing that might slow her down is me finding a house."

"So you've agreed to it?"

"I have. She refuses to live with her uncle any longer."

"Do you want me to speak to Mr Wetherby about you coming here? I'm sure he's calmed down enough over what happened."

"I thought of that, but she's adamant. If we don't have our own house, she won't come out."

"Can she do that?"

William shrugged. "Apparently. You know what she's like."

"Where will you go? You'll stay in Handsworth, won't you?"

"I will if I can find the right house."

Mary thought for a moment. "I walked past a house on Church Hill Road earlier and it looked like the tenants were leaving. It might be worth seeing if it's available."

"They're a little small but I don't think it'd matter. Harriet would live in one room if it meant not being with her uncle."

"What about you? Would you be happy there?"

William gazed into the fire before his eyes met Mary's. "It's been horrible this last month. I want it to be over. If it makes Harriet happy, I'll be happy."

"I always worried that Harriet would bring you trouble, but I didn't expect this."

"It wasn't her fault. I've got to take some of the blame, but her uncle's got a lot to answer for. It's as if he thinks she's too clever and he can't tolerate being inferior."

Mary paused before she spoke. "Does she make you feel inferior?"

William stared back into the fire. "No, she doesn't. She's the best thing that ever happened to me. We're going to put this behind us."

Chapter 41

HARRIET HOVERED AROUND THE WINDOW at the end of the ward peering at the driveway below. The doctor had discharged her and she stood in her hat and cloak waiting for William. *What's keeping him?*

The last few weeks had been a whirlwind of activity. William had found a house and every evening he came and reported on the progress of the day. The sparkle and smile had returned to Harriet's face and she was no longer the silent patient nobody bothered with. She talked to anyone who would listen and acted as spokeswoman if there were any problems. There were other women on the ward who had been admitted for much the same reasons as her and she would talk to them for hours about using the situation to their advantage. Such was her change that everyone on the ward was sorry she was leaving.

She quizzed William about every aspect of the new house and had a clear image of every room in her head. She would be the lady of the house, looking after the day-to-day running as well as doing the bookkeeping and managing the finances. That wasn't the best of it though. For the first time in her adult life she would be free of her uncle telling her what to do. If she wanted to go out, she would. If she wanted to read a book, she would. If she wanted to have friends around to the house, she would, and how she was going to enjoy it.

Since his outburst at Mr and Mrs Watkins, life had been difficult for William. Fortunately, he hadn't needed to stay with them for long. He'd picked up the keys for the house on Church Hill Road within days and left Grosvenor Road, taking William-Wetherby and Eleanor with him. It was hard without Harriet, but Mary took care of the children and had a hot meal waiting for him every evening before he went to the asylum. Tonight was different though. He was going to bring her home. Unable to keep the smile from his face, he wondered how she'd persuaded them to release her so soon.

He had taken some clothes in last night and as he turned onto the ward she was next to the window wearing her cloak and bonnet. The place was empty except for Harriet and he coughed to catch her attention. As soon as she saw him she ran down the ward and threw her arms around his neck. Steadying himself he put his arms around her and returned her broad grin.

"I take it you're coming home with me?"

"I'm so excited; I can't wait to see the house. Will the children be there?"

"They're with Mother." He smiled at her with a twinkle in his eye. "I was hoping you could do without them for one more night. We have a lot of catching up to do."

Harriet kissed him on the cheek. "Only if we leave now. I have to inspect the house first."

William laughed as he took her hand and led her out of the asylum. The carriage was waiting for them and Harriet delighted in getting out before they reached Grosvenor Road.

"Which one is it?" She peered down the street before hurrying ahead of William. "Why does it have to be so dark? I hope you have plenty of candles."

Within five minutes they stood outside their new house. It was a small two-storey cottage in the middle of a row of five. A bay window protruded from the room downstairs while a second window jutted from the roofline above it. There was a fence to the front with a short path leading to the front door.

"What are the neighbours like?" Harriet asked as they went in. "Do they know where I've been?"

"They seem friendly enough. I haven't told them anything and I don't think anyone outside the family knows. I asked your uncle not to tell anyone, but whether he did or not, I don't know."

"That'll be the worst thing, meeting people again who think I'm a lunatic."

William put his arm around her. "Anyone who knows you, knows you're not a lunatic."

Although it was mild for November, the house was cold and William knelt in front of the fire to light it. While he was busy, Harriet lit her own candle and walked from room to room, adjusting the furniture as she went.

Once the fire was burning, William found her in the bedroom. "I hope you like it."

"I love it, even though I can't see it very well in this light. Thank you."

William wrapped his arms around her. "I'm sorry for the way I treated you when we were last together."

"I'm sorry too. I spoke out of turn but I didn't mean it. I was just desperate for us to have our own house. I thought talking to you like that would make you see sense. I was wrong and you were right to be angry with me."

"I should never have hurt you though … or left you, I've regretted both ever since." William took her face in both hands, gazing into eyes that sparkled back at him in the candlelight. "I've missed you so much … come here." He took the candle from her hand and placed it on the dresser before he turned and guided her to the bed. "We can't waste our only night alone."

As soon as the following day dawned, Harriet was out of bed. William had done his best with the furniture, but it wasn't right and she needed to sort things out. The place needed cleaning too. When she was happy with the house she collected the children and when they went for their afternoon nap, she started work on the bookkeeping. William had listed everything he'd bought and how much it had cost; he'd also bought her a notebook to keep her accounts. Despite the recent outlay, it didn't take her long and she brooded about what he had done with the business. Why had he effectively handed it over to Mr Wetherby? *Why didn't he say anything to me? I could have helped him.* That was something for her to deal with another day. At the moment she was happy and didn't want to spoil it.

With Christmas approaching, Harriet decided to make

a real celebration of it. Christmas Day was on a Monday and with Boxing Day being a bank holiday it meant the men would have three days off work. She invited the whole family, and Mary-Ann came to stay with them for a few days at the beginning of December to help plan the whole event.

"Will you invite your aunt and uncle on Christmas Day?" she asked as they were making mince pies.

Harriet stopped in her tracks and shook her head at the notion. "I most certainly won't. They're not spoiling my Christmas."

"I thought it would be a good time to make amends," Mary-Ann said, not seeing the disgust on Harriet's face. "You can show them how well you're doing in your own house."

"I don't want to ever see them again, not after what they did."

"I understand you're still angry, but perhaps if you hadn't gone to the asylum William wouldn't have made the decision to move house. Maybe you should thank them."

Harriet bit her tongue. Even to Mary-Ann she couldn't share the conversation she'd had with William.

"I will not thank them. As far as I'm concerned they may as well be dead."

Chapter 42

Nine months later

Harriet sat by an open window fanning herself with a magazine. It was almost ten o'clock, but it was still warm and having such a heavily swollen body didn't help. *When will this baby be born?*

"Will you help me upstairs?" she said to William when she finished her glass of gin. "I haven't got the energy to do anything tonight."

William helped her onto the bed, but before he left she felt a tightening around her abdomen. For a moment, her spirits soared, but they were quickly dampened when a pain shot through her body. As a fresh wave of perspiration covered her face she knew her third child was about to be born.

"It's coming," she said. "You'd better get the midwife. I don't want to do this on my own."

The labour was longer than expected and it was late the following morning before William joined Harriet as she sat cradling their new son.

"Another boy; what marvellous news." William's smile was broad. "Let me see him."

Harriet turned the baby towards him as William took the seat beside the bed.

"Do you mind if we call him Charles after my father and in memory of baby Charles-Jackson," he asked after a few moments.

Harriet frowned. "You don't think it'll upset Mary-Ann, do you?"

"No, she'll be pleased. She always wanted us to use the name. I'm going to Birmingham tomorrow; I'll call in and tell her."

"I'd like to see her," Harriet said. "Will you ask her to come here for a couple of days when I'm allowed visitors?"

Two weeks later Mary-Ann travelled to Handsworth. She was staying at Wetherby House but went straight to see Harriet.

"You're looking pleased with yourself," Harriet said as soon as Mary-Ann walked into the living room.

"I am, and seeing you here with a new baby has made me more excited." Mary-Ann clapped her hands together when she saw Charles in his cot. "I saw the doctor earlier this week and I'm having another baby. Probably around February next year."

Harriet jumped from the chair and threw her arms around Mary-Ann. "That's wonderful."

"I haven't had a chance to tell anyone yet, not even Mother. I'll tell her later when I go round. At least I'll be able to hold my head up high again. I do hope I get another baby like Charles-Jackson."

Harriet hesitated. "William told you we're going to call this baby Charles?"

"He did and I'm delighted. I won't be using it again. Have you heard from your aunt and uncle since he was born?"

"I thought you were here to cheer me up, not make me miserable!" Harriet put a scowl on her face.

"I am, but I presumed your aunt would have called to see you."

"She did ... yesterday, but I didn't open the door."

"Did she know you were in? I bet she was upset."

Harriet shrugged. "She should have thought of that, shouldn't she? I've asked William to call and tell her not to bother me again."

❧

Once they had eaten tea, William walked Mary-Ann around to Wetherby House. When they arrived Mary was delighted to see them. Mr Wetherby was once again in Birmingham and so for the first time in many years the three of them spent the evening alone together.

"It's as if all of my prayers have been answered over the last few days," Mary said when she heard Mary-Ann's news. "You know what. Mr Wetherby had a case of sherry delivered the other day. We have two reasons to open a bottle; I'm sure he won't mind."

"Why is Mr Wetherby in Birmingham again?" William asked. "He's never here."

Mary stood up to fetch some glasses. "He's at another council meeting. Since he's been involved with the Conservative Association, he's interested in everything the council does. He's on the housing committee now. He's worried about the deterioration of the houses around Summer Lane and is determined to clean up the area. Most of his workers live there and he's having a lot of trouble with sickness. It was bad enough when we lived there, but he says it's worse now."

"I still don't think he should leave you on your own."

"Stop worrying about me. I've got Emily and Cook with me and the dogs don't let anyone walk up the drive without me knowing. I'm going down to Birmingham in a couple of weeks as well. I'm staying with Aunt Alice and spending time with Aunt Sarah-Ann as well. It's been too long since I saw them."

Chapter 43

Birmingham, Warwickshire.

MARY SAT IN THE LIVING room of her sister's house cradling a cup of gin. She studied the peeling wallpaper and wondered what on earth she was doing there. It was her second night and she'd planned to stay for one more, but she wasn't sure she could bear it. For one thing there was the smell. With the exception of Great Charles Street, she didn't remember Birmingham being as bad as this. Even the tallow candles, once common in her own house, made her stomach turn. On top of that, as much as she hated to admit it, she now found it hard work being with Alice. Conversation didn't come as easily as it had when they lived next door to each other. Did Alice resent the life she now had in Handsworth, she wondered, or was there more to it than that?

Mary raised the cup to her lips and purposefully breathed in the fumes of the gin as she took another mouthful. "Are you still happy in Birmingham?" she asked Alice.

"I'm not unhappy. I have a job and Mr Wetherby doesn't charge me much for the house. It could be worse."

"It's much nicer in Handsworth. Won't you come and live with us again? I'd like the company."

"It wouldn't suit me. You're a proper lady now, up there in your big house. I'd be more like the servant. I know you mean well, but I'm better off here."

Mary couldn't argue and thought of her elder sister who lived a few doors down from her in Handsworth. "What about moving in with Susannah then? She's not far from me."

"I wouldn't want people talking."

"What is there to talk about if you move in with your sister? At least let me ask Susannah if she has room. I don't like you being here."

"I do have a few friends in Birmingham, people I'm comfortable with, and that'll do me. Anyway, less of me; how was your visit to Sarah-Ann?"

Mary sighed and put her cup on the table. "I think there are problems again with Mr Flemming. She wouldn't go into details but she wasn't happy. Fortunately she has Elizabeth and they have one of their nieces staying with them. A pretty young thing she is; Mr Flemming has her working in the shop."

"Did Sarah-Ann have any gossip?"

"She had some news about old Aunt Lucy. You won't remember her but I lived with her when I first came to Birmingham. It was when William and Mary-Ann were still babies. She was very generous to me, gave us a roof over our heads and kept us fed. After a few years she made me manageress of a sewing business she set up with her sister. It was all going well until I told her I was marrying Mr Wetherby. She knew I wouldn't run the business once I was married and said I had to choose between her and Mr Wetherby. When I chose Mr Wetherby I had to move out. That was when I first went to Handsworth."

"I don't think you'd have done as well staying with her as you have with Mr Wetherby. Anyway, what about her?"

"Apparently she's ill and Sarah-Ann thinks she's starting to say goodbye to everyone. She's sending invitations to the family asking everyone to visit her. Sarah-Ann's going next week."

"Have you had an invitation?"

Mary laughed. "I doubt she'll want to see me again, even if she is on her death bed. I don't suppose I'd go either; I certainly wouldn't go with Mr Wetherby's blessing. He doesn't dislike many people as much as her."

"She must have upset him then, because I've seen him angry with a lot of people over the years."

Richard for one, Mary thought. "Well, quite …"

As they spoke, there was a knock on the door and Mr Wetherby walked in.

"Good afternoon, ladies," he said. "I hope I haven't disturbed you."

"What are you doing here?" Mary said. "I thought you'd be at one of your meetings."

"I'm on my way to the Town Hall now, but there was a letter for you at the workshop. I thought I'd drop it in."

Mary glanced at her sister before taking the letter from Mr Wetherby.

"What's the matter?" Mr Wetherby asked. "Do you know who it's from?"

"I have an idea." Mary tore open the envelope and checked the signature.

"Aren't you going to tell us?" Mr Wetherby asked.

"It's from Aunt Lucy."

Mr Wetherby opened his mouth twice before any words came out. "What does she want?"

"Sarah-Ann was telling me about her earlier. She's ill and she wants to see everybody in case she dies. She's asked me to go next week."

"You'll do no such thing." Mr Wetherby's pale complexion turned a deep shade of pink. "You're not having anything to do with that woman, whether she's dying or not."

Mary studied the letter before answering. "It must have taken a lot for her to write to me. I wonder what she wants. Maybe she's going to apologise for the way she was with us."

"Don't fool yourself," Mr Wetherby said. "She wouldn't do that. She probably only wants to upset you again."

Mary tried to hide her disappointment. "I suppose you're right. Besides, I'm only in Birmingham for one more day. I couldn't possibly go at such short notice."

Chapter 44

WHY MARY HAD DECIDED TO visit Aunt Lucy, she wasn't sure. Maybe it was because the alternative was spending another morning sitting in her sister's living room or perhaps it was nothing more than idle curiosity. Either way, she wasn't turning back now. What she was sure of was that if Mr Wetherby found out she was here, she'd be in deep trouble. She had deliberately put on a new bonnet before she left the house and once settled in the carriage, she turned her face away from the window in case she happened to drive past him. As soon as she passed St Philip's church, she relaxed.

Since she'd received the letter from Aunt Lucy, she hadn't stopped thinking about it. Despite everything that had gone between them, Mary wanted to tell Aunt Lucy that she would always be grateful for the help she had given her when she arrived in Birmingham with William and Mary-Ann. Deep down she supposed she also wanted to be forgiven for walking away, although she knew she had made the right decision.

The carriage dropped Mary outside the house and she stood on the pavement looking up at the imposing three-storey building. It was a similar style to the houses around

Summer Lane, but it was bigger and there wasn't another house backing onto it. Mary had been told Aunt Lucy rented out at least four rooms in the house, but nobody knew quite how many people lived there. She walked to the door but hesitated as her hand reached for the door knocker. She hadn't sent word she was coming. The worst thing she can do is turn me away, she thought as she took a deep breath and banged firmly on the door. It was opened within seconds.

"Well, well. Look who we have here." Aunt Rebecca stood with her arms crossed in front of her, glaring at Mary. "Are you sure you've come to the right address?"

Mary swallowed the lump that had formed in her throat. "I got Aunt Lucy's letter … she asked me to call. I'm not in Birmingham next week, but I'm staying with my sister at the moment …"

"And so you thought you'd come unannounced so you didn't have to say anything to Mr Wetherby."

Mary's face turned red. "I leave later today … I didn't have time to write."

"You'd better come in," Aunt Rebecca said. "Never let it be said we turned you away."

Mary followed Aunt Rebecca into the back room and found Aunt Lucy sitting by the fire. She had one shawl pulled around her shoulders and a second over her legs. Her face was pale, but her eyes were as bright as ever.

"You came then." Her voice was hoarse and weak, and Mary took the seat next to her.

"I got your letter. Sarah-Ann said you were ill."

"I didn't think you'd come. Just here to see me off, are you?"

"No, not at all …"

"Well, you're out of luck anyway. The doctor thinks my chest is clearing. I'll be as right as rain in no …" A hacking cough cut off Aunt Lucy's sentence.

"I'm glad," Mary said. "I came because I wanted to thank you for everything you did for me."

"You've taken your time," Aunt Rebecca said as she added more coal to the fire. "Over twenty years it's been since you left us."

"I know, I'm sorry."

"Is that all you've got to say?" Aunt Rebecca continued.

"Enough." Aunt Lucy gestured for her sister to sit down. Once she got her breath back she turned to Mary. "I'm glad you came. I wanted to see you again. Are you still with Mr Wetherby?"

"I am. We live in Handsworth now."

"Martha may have mentioned it," Aunt Lucy said. "Are you happy?"

"Yes. We have a lovely house and William isn't far away with his wife. They have three children now; the third was only born last month. Mary-Ann's expecting as well."

"So why are you in Birmingham?"

A puzzled expression settled on Mary's face. "I'm visiting my sister, Alice."

"If everything in Handsworth is so splendid, why doesn't she visit you? I can't believe she lives a life of luxury if she's still around Summer Lane."

Mary shifted in her seat. "She's comfortable enough. I asked her only the other day to move to Handsworth, but she won't."

"So what's wrong with Mr Wetherby? There was no mention of him in your perfect life?" Aunt Lucy said.

"There's nothing wrong. Why?"

Aunt Lucy took a sip of gin. "He's no concern of mine, as I'm sure you'll appreciate, but I hear he spends a lot of time in Birmingham. Some say he never goes to Handsworth."

Mary's cheeks reddened. "He's always working, and he's busy with the Conservative Association as well."

"Well, I'd be careful if I were you. If people don't know what's going on, they tend to make things up. I heard rumours a couple of weeks ago that he'd left you."

"You didn't!" Mary moved to the edge of her chair.

"I thought you'd come to your senses and kicked him out, but obviously not." Aunt Lucy frowned.

"Is that why you asked me to call, so you could gloat and tell me 'I told you so'?"

"I'm not one for gloating but I did wonder if you were in trouble. I never did understand why you married him. You had no need to."

Mary stood up. "I had every need. I had two small children and no money. He's given them everything they could ask for. They both went to school and he's taken William into the business. In fact, he's a partner now. If you'd been in my situation you'd have done the same thing."

Aunt Lucy shrugged. "I would never have been in your situation."

"I don't care what you say, most women would have done the same as me. You must know how peculiar you are. It's not normal to want to live without a husband."

"Is that what he's drilled into you over the years?" Aunt Lucy let out a short laugh before she started coughing.

"Of course it is," Aunt Rebecca said. "Men like him need to control everyone around them."

"And what's wrong with that?" Mary snapped.

As she regained her breath, Aunt Lucy pulled her shawl more tightly around her shoulders. "It's so disappointing to hear you speak like that, but at least I don't need to concern myself with you. Rebecca, will you let her out? I need to rest now."

Chapter 45

M R WETHERBY STOOD TO ADDRESS the group of men in front of him. They were in the upstairs room of the Villa Cross Tavern in Birmingham and they were restless.

"Gentlemen, please, if I can have your attention." He knocked his fist on the table. "As you know, earlier today I asked for the public accountant to be appointed as receiver in the liquidation of Mr Hemming's plumbing business. We need to make sure we all receive the money he owes us and I'm pleased to report that although the judge didn't think the estate was in danger, our joint application persuaded him to carry out the order."

The room erupted into applause, which was followed by the clinking of glasses. Mr Wetherby waited for them to quieten down.

"The business will now be wound up and we should all receive our money by the middle of next year." More cheers but this time Mr Wetherby continued. "I believe the way we dealt with this case has been an excellent display of what can happen to unscrupulous traders who think they can carry on without paying their debts. I suggest we continue working to rid the town of these atrocious practices and I'd like to put myself forward as a point of contact. If any of you have any further problems with debtors, report them to me and I'll make sure they pay for it."

This time a toast to Mr Wetherby accompanied the cheering.

"Please spread the word to other reputable businessmen. We all need to know that the goods we provide will be paid for."

As the men began to leave, Mr Wetherby stayed at the front of the room, accepting the handshakes of those who came to congratulate him. William Junior was with him, but it was over twenty minutes later before he had the chance to ask him about the consequences for Mr Hemming.

"I understand he owes everyone money," William Junior said. "But what happens if he can't pay?"

"Basically they'll take his assets from him: his personal property, his plumbing equipment, his house. They'll sell them to pay the creditors. It's standard practice, nothing to be alarmed about."

William Junior's eyes were wide. "He could lose his house?"

"Only if he owns one. If he rents somewhere, he'll be able to stay until the landlord kicks him out. Frankly it's nothing more than he deserves. He could have put any one of the men here out of business by not paying them. He deserves no sympathy. They should never have changed the law to make it so lenient. In my opinion, anyone declared bankrupt should still be sent to prison."

"What happens if the sale doesn't raise enough money to pay everyone?"

"They work out how much he owes and how many

shillings and pence they can raise for every pound of debt they're owed. It means the creditors won't receive as much as they should, but that's one of the reasons we had to make this application when we did. If we'd waited until there was a real danger he couldn't pay us, the amount available for payment would be much less. Mark my words, when people owe you money you need to sort it out early to make sure you get back as much as you can. If you give way to sympathy you're storing up trouble for yourself."

Handsworth, Staffordshire.

The weather over Christmas and into January had been mild but over the last couple of weeks it had turned noticeably colder. William shivered as he got out of bed. It seemed particularly cold this morning and he scraped the ice from one of the panes of glass to reveal a thick covering of snow outside. He dressed quickly and went downstairs to light the fire. As he put a pan of water over the flames there was a knock at the door. He banged his hands together to remove the coal dust before he answered.

"Mr Wetherby, I wasn't expecting you. Is everything all right?"

"No, it's not." Mr Wetherby brushed the snow from his coat as he stepped into the hall. "Haven't you seen the snow? It's still falling too. I can't take the horses out in this and I doubt the omnibus will be running. I'll have to walk to Birmingham and stay there until the snow melts. I'll take William Junior with me but I need you to keep an eye on your mother while I'm away."

"It will be weeks before this amount of snow thaws."

"I have a business to run and I need to be in Birmingham. I want you to stay here and keep things going in Handsworth."

"Yes, of course." As soon as Mr Wetherby left, William put on his hat and coat and shouted up to Harriet that he was going to visit his mother.

William was greeted by the maid and shown into the back room to wait. Mary joined him a minute later.

"I imagine you've spoken to Mr Wetherby this morning," he said as he accepted a cup of tea. "I don't like you being here on your own at the best of times and certainly not in this weather."

"I'm not on my own this week, I have Charlotte with me; it was out of the question for her to walk to Birmingham."

William let out an exasperated sigh. "Having a nine-year-old girl for company doesn't count … and before you say anything, neither do the dogs. Harriet and I want you to come and stay with us, at least until Mr Wetherby gets home."

"You haven't got the room for us in your house. Besides, I might not be on my own for long. Mary-Ann's baby is due soon and when it arrives I'm going to stay with her."

William pointed to the window. "If the weather stays like this, you won't be going anywhere; besides, what will you do with Charlotte?"

"I'll take her with me," Mary said.

"I really don't think that's a good idea. We'll wait and see what happens to Mary-Ann, but if you go to Birmingham, Charlotte must come and stay with us. Is that clear?"

৵৶

A week later a telegram arrived from Mr Diver telling Mary that the baby was on its way. It was late afternoon but she wrapped herself and Charlotte in their thickest coats and walked around to Church Hill Road. Harriet was cleaning around the fire when they walked in.

"Why don't you go and find Eleanor," Mary said to Charlotte.

"She's upstairs," Harriet said over her shoulder.

Mary waited for her daughter to disappear before she spoke. "Mary-Ann's baby's coming."

Harriet jumped to her feet. "I hope you're not thinking of travelling to Birmingham. The roads are still frozen."

"I have to. What if she needs me?"

"Mr Diver will be with her. William will never forgive me if I let you go, and as for Mr Wetherby …"

"I can't worry about them today. I have to think of Mary-Ann."

Harriet put her arm around Mary. "Did you notice any carriages while you were out?"

"No … but it is thawing."

"Maybe it is, but let's wait and see what William says when he gets home. He should be here soon."

Mary went to the window to see if she could see him.

"Why don't you sit down and I'll pour us both a gin," Harriet said. "That usually relaxes you."

A look of resignation settled on Mary's face and she perched on the edge of a chair. "I can't bear to think of her going through so much pain. I just pray it's healthy and that it arrives without any trouble."

"She'll be fine, I'm sure. Mr Diver will have the doctor to her. You'd only be sat downstairs waiting there."

"You're right, of course, but at least I wouldn't have far to go if she needed me."

As she spoke, the front door slammed.

"Here's William," Harriet said, rushing from the living room.

William was in the hallway taking off his hat and coat when she appeared.

"How's the weather this evening?" she asked.

"It's still freezing but I think the roads are clearing. There was a carriage out earlier."

Mary followed Harriet into the hall, her eyes bright. "Do you think I'd be able to go to Birmingham? Mary-Ann's baby has started."

William hesitated before he spoke. "You may be able to, but you're not going on your own."

"But Mr Diver needs me. We're both concerned after what happened last time."

William thought for a moment. "You're not going anywhere tonight; it's too dark and cold but I'll tell you what, I'll go with you tomorrow. I need to talk to Mr Wetherby."

৵৶

Birmingham, Warwickshire.

When William and Mary ventured out the next day, the carriages that were out were moving slowly. Fortunately they didn't wait long before they found one going to Birmingham and they were at the Divers' before ten o'clock.

"The baby hasn't arrived yet," Mr Diver said. "I sent the telegram at the first sign of something happening. I wanted to give you plenty of time to get here. The midwife says it won't be long now."

Minutes later the midwife shouted for Mr Diver.

"Oh my, what does she want?" His face lost its colour as he dashed upstairs leaving Mary and William alone.

"I can't bear this waiting," Mary said. "I'd no idea when it was me having the babies what it was like for everyone else."

"The trials of being a man," William said.

Mary was about to respond when they heard the front door close. William walked into the hall to see who it was.

"There's nobody there. Perhaps it was the doctor leaving and he didn't realise we were here."

Mary couldn't contain herself any longer. "I'll go upstairs and find out what's happening. You wait down here ... just in case."

When she reached the top of the stairs, the bedroom door was ajar. Should she go in? She couldn't hear any harrowing cries. She crept towards the door and saw Mr Diver sitting on the edge of the bed looking at a bundle in Mary-Ann's arms. As she stepped on the floorboard nearest the door, it gave a loud creak causing Mary-Ann to look up.

"Mother, come in, I didn't know you were here."

"I'm sorry, Mrs Wetherby." Mr Diver jumped up. "I should have come and told you; we have a daughter. Isn't she beautiful?"

Mary shouted for William before she walked to the side of the bed. "She is indeed beautiful. Congratulations. Do you have a name for her?"

"Rose," Mary-Ann said. "We think it's such a pretty name."

❧❦

Once he learned of the birth of his niece, William wasted no time in calling on Mr Wetherby. He planned to spend some time with him and stay overnight in the house on Summer Lane, but he didn't get the reception he expected.

Mr Wetherby was sitting with a man William didn't recognise, while William Junior stood to his right.

"What are you doing here?" Mr Wetherby snapped.

"There's a problem with the order from Stathams. I didn't know when you'd be back in Handsworth so I thought it would be best to come and see you about it."

"There was no need; you could have dealt with it … in fact you should have dealt with it. It's not a complicated order."

"No, I'm sorry, but I thought …"

"I'm not sure you did think. I left express instructions for you to stay in Handsworth."

William shifted from one foot to the other. "I had to come to Birmingham with Mother. Mary-Ann's had the baby."

"Your mother's in Birmingham?"

"Yes … well in Saltley. She's staying with Mary-Ann until one of us can take her back to Handsworth."

Mr Wetherby stood up and walked William to the door. "There's no need for you to stay in Birmingham. I want you to take your mother back to Handsworth first thing tomorrow morning."

"I think she expected to stay for longer than that."

"Where's Charlotte. Is she with her?"

"No, she's with Harriet."

Mr Wetherby tightened his grip of William's shoulder.

"Well, tell her to go back to Handsworth and take care of her. I'm sure Mary-Ann can take care of herself."

"Can I tell her when you might be back in Handsworth?"

"Not at the moment. Can't you see I'm busy with Mr Havers?"

"What are …?"

"Ask no questions and you'll get no lies. This is my business."

William looked back at Mr Havers who was studying the books Mr Wetherby had been showing him. William hadn't seen him before and he got the distinct impression he was being excluded from something. Surely Mr Wetherby would tell him if there was a problem with the business?

William walked back to Saltley, replaying the scene in his head. What was Mr Wetherby up to and why did he want to hide it from him? With every possible scenario running through his head, and his heart thumping, he hoped Mary-Ann had a room he'd be able to stay in for the night.

Chapter 46

Handsworth, Staffordshire.

MARY PLACED THE STAMP IN the corner of the letter and stood up to go for her coat. She hadn't reached the hall when the front door opened and Mr Wetherby walked in, acting as if he'd only left that morning.

"I wasn't expecting you home. Why didn't you write and tell me you were coming? I've been worried."

"You should have known I'd be here. It's Saturday afternoon and I don't open the workshop on a Sunday." Mr Wetherby put his hat and coat on the stand.

"That's as maybe, but you didn't come home last Saturday. I was just on my way to post a letter to you."

"Yes, last week couldn't be avoided. I'm extremely busy at the moment."

Mary hesitated. Should she ask the question that was troubling her? She took a deep breath.

"Who's been looking after you? Did you have enough shirt collars with you?"

"I got someone from the court to do a bit of laundry earlier in the week."

"What about eating? Did you have someone to cook for you as well?"

"What is this all of a sudden?"

Mary's face flushed and she looked down to unbutton her coat. "I'm sorry, but you've been away for so long ... and then you didn't want William to stay in Birmingham ..."

"William had work to do here. Now, let's hear no more of it. A man should be able to come home to peace and quiet, not an interrogation."

Mary waited until he settled by the fire before she lifted out some cake and offered to make a pot of tea. "Has the snow all cleared now?"

"It has, thank goodness. That should be it for this year."

"So, will you start travelling home more regularly again?"

Mr Wetherby's mouth was full of cake, but he shook his head.

"No. Why not?"

"I've just told you, I'm too busy. I waste nearly two hours a day travelling so I'm going to stay down there more often."

Mary frowned. "What will you do with the horses? You can't keep them in Frankfort Street."

"It's all arranged. Mr Grimshaw has some stabling behind his workshop. I can leave them there."

So that's it. Mary put the teapot down on the table. *He's moving back to Birmingham. Aunt Lucy was right.* She looked around the living room, her eyes resting on her husband. His thinning hair and lined face betrayed his age, but where was the attentive, caring man she had married? The man who had loved her in a way she could never return.

Had he grown weary of her because she couldn't return his affection? Perhaps this was his way of dealing with it. Nowadays, nothing was as important as the business and making money, not even her. At least she was comfortable, but what would people think? If word had spread around Birmingham, it wouldn't be long before news reached Handsworth.

"People are going to talk," she said.

"Will you be quiet?" Mr Wetherby slammed the newspaper onto his knee. "Can't you see I'm trying to read? I've had a busy week and I'd appreciate some time to myself."

Mary sat down at the table and rubbed her eyes. She didn't want him to see her tears. After a minute she took Sarah-Ann's letter from the pocket of her apron and read it again.

Dear Mary

Aunt Lucy died on Wednesday. I hadn't seen her since before Christmas, but I believe the bronchitis she thought she'd beaten came back. Aunt Rebecca was with her until she breathed her last. The funeral's on Tuesday at the Friends' Meeting House. She told me you'd been to see her, so hopefully I'll see you there. It might be worth your while. It seems she left a will and it's going to be read after the service. Unless I see you at the church, I'll write again to let you know the news.

Sarah-Ann

Normally she would have shown the letter to Mr Wetherby, but that was out of the question. She hadn't planned on going to the funeral, but now she wasn't so sure. If Mr Wetherby was going to be away all week, why shouldn't she plan a trip to Birmingham? He wasn't likely to go near the Friends' burial ground. He need never know.

She watched from the corner of her eye as he turned the pages of the newspaper. When he reached the last page, she spoke again.

"Alice has invited me to Birmingham again next week. I wasn't going to go, but if you're not going to be here, can I travel with you on Monday morning?"

"This Monday?"

"Would that be a problem? I could help take Charlotte back to school at the same time. She's not been for weeks."

"Where is Charlotte?" Mr Wetherby asked as if he hadn't noticed his daughter's absence. "Why wasn't she waiting for me when I came home?"

"You forget, we didn't know you were coming. She's gone to William's house; she likes being with Eleanor at the moment."

"Then she does need to get back to school. Yes, you can come with me on Monday. You'd better write to Alice before the last post goes and tell her."

৸৶

Birmingham, England.

The last time Mary attended the Friends Meeting Hall, it was for the funeral of her beloved Charles. Now she stood at the door and scanned the room. It hadn't changed much. Most of the family were here as well as a lot of additional mourners, presumably other members of the congregation.

They'd have to open the balconies. Sarah-Ann sat with her head bowed a couple of rows from the front and Mary went and sat beside her. Aunt Rebecca sat alone, on the front row, the last of her generation.

As the oldest male in the family, once the service was over, Richard led the mourners to the burial site. Mary stayed where she was but studied him as he left. His dark hair was now streaked with grey, but he was still handsome. Would Charles have aged the same? she wondered. She liked to think so.

It was over twenty minutes later before they came back and Richard winked at her as he returned to the pew behind Aunt Rebecca. The solicitor walked in behind the mourners with Aunt Lucy's will in his hand. He took a seat on the platform at the front.

"This is it," Sarah-Ann said. "Let's see what she left."

"This is the Last Will and Testament of Lucy Jackson, spinster of the Coventry Road, Birmingham," he began. "All Miss Jackson's clothing and wearing apparel has been bequeathed to Jane-Ann Dainty and Emma-Louise Warner, the daughters of Miss Jackson's niece, Emma Dainty."

"What on earth are they going to do with them?" Sarah-Ann said. "They're only fit for the workhouse."

Mary shrugged and continued listening as the solicitor outlined Aunt Lucy's wishes for her property portfolio. Judging by the whispers in the pews around her, she had more leasehold properties than anyone suspected.

"She's given them all to a couple of friends!" Sarah-Ann whispered. "And men at that. Why didn't she leave them to her female relatives and let them have the freedom she did?"

"Maybe she worried their husbands would seize them?"

"The remainder of the chattels and personal effects will go to her sister, Miss Rebecca Jackson," the solicitor said.

"Well, that was a disappointment," Sarah-Ann said. "Nothing for the rest of us."

"Wait a minute." Mary put her hand on Sarah-Ann's arm to stop her talking. "Once Aunt Rebecca dies, everything is to be sold."

Silence descended on the room as details of the bequests were read out.

"It sounds like everyone in the family will get an equal share of the money," Sarah-Ann said when the solicitor paused for breath.

"Not everyone," Mary said. Sarah-Ann gave her a puzzled expression. "There were a few who'll receive nothing. I'm surprised you didn't notice."

"He read my name out." Sarah-Ann put her hand to her mouth. "She didn't leave anything to you."

"He didn't mention your Elizabeth either, or William and Mary-Ann."

Sarah-Ann studied the others in the room. "Were they the only ones?"

"They're the ones I remember, but looking at the Daintys, they weren't left much either."

"You're right, they only got the clothes."

"Charlie Dainty didn't even get that."

The solicitor continued reading, but his audience had stopped listening. For most, their names had been registered; all they needed now was for Aunt Rebecca to die.

As the family started to disperse, Mary slipped away and took the chance to visit the burial ground. It was a long time since she last visited Charles's grave but she found his headstone as if she had been there yesterday. She read the words on the headstone.

Remembered with dear affection
Charles Jackson
1820–1843
Beloved husband of Mary Jackson

"I thought I might find you here." The voice behind Mary made her jump.

"Richard." She smiled as he reached out and took her hand.

"I didn't think you'd be here. Mr Wetherby thought as much of Aunt Lucy as he does of me. I'm not surprised he didn't join you."

Mary stared down at her feet. "He doesn't know I'm here."

The corners of Richard's mouth twitched into a smile. "I'm glad you're taking no nonsense from him. Where does he think you are?"

"He knows I'm in Birmingham, but thinks I'm visiting my sister. I haven't told him about Aunt Lucy. I'll mention it when I get back."

Richard laughed. "What happened to the timid little girl I met all those years ago?"

Mary smiled back. "She grew up."

Richard touched her cheek. "Well, I hope she comes to stay with her sister a little more often. I'd like to see more of her."

Chapter 47

Handsworth, Staffordshire.

M ARY PLACED THE LETTER BEHIND the clock on the mantelpiece and sat back down in her chair. *Why do letters like this always come on a Saturday afternoon?* She knew Sarah-Ann was prone to exaggeration, but the tone of the letter sounded serious. She glanced at the clock again, approaching four o'clock. Mr Wetherby should be home by now. *Where is he?*

Five minutes later the front door opened and Mr Wetherby walked in holding Charlotte's hand. Seeing her mother, Charlotte skipped down the hall and waited for her to take off her cloak.

"Where's William Junior?" Mary asked as Mr Wetherby took off his hat and coat.

"He's coming. I asked him to help with the horses."

"We need to talk before he comes in," Mary said. "Something's come up."

Mr Wetherby nodded and walked into the back room just as William Junior came through the front door.

"Damn coachman," William Junior said.

"Excuse me. We won't have language like that in this

house." Mary pulled Charlotte towards her. "I don't know what's got into you lately, but whatever it is, you can leave it outside."

"If the coachman did his job properly …"

"William Junior. Enough." Mr Wetherby called from the back room. "Go and make yourself scarce; your mother wants to talk to me."

"Isn't tea ready?" William Junior said.

"No, it's too early yet," Mary put her arm across the door and looked at Mr Wetherby. "We need to talk."

Mr Wetherby turned to face William Junior. "You'll have to wait. Why don't you go down to the tavern for an hour, give your mother time to set everything out?"

William Junior glared at his mother and back to Mr Wetherby before he picked up his hat and coat and walked outside, slamming the door behind him.

Mary breathed a sigh of relief before she turned to Charlotte. "I've buttered some bread and left it in the morning room for you. Will you go in there for a few minutes while I talk to Papa? I'll join you as soon as I can."

Charlotte nodded. "Is my dolly in there?"

"She is, ready and waiting for you."

Mary smiled as her daughter disappeared, her blonde ringlets bouncing on her back, but the frown soon returned to her face.

"What's the matter?" Mr Wetherby asked as she joined him in the back room.

"It's Sarah-Ann. It sounds like she's in trouble again." Mary handed Mr Wetherby the letter.

"That damn man Flemming again."

"Will you stop using language like that as well? Is it any wonder William Junior's picked it up?"

"In this instance, it's justified. I thought he'd got over his issues, but if Sarah-Ann's as upset as she sounds, we can't stand by and do nothing."

"What should we do?"

"I'll have to pay him a visit. I thought I'd talked some sense into him last time, but it would appear he hasn't got the brains he was born with."

"We need to speak to Sarah-Ann first. We don't actually know what the problem is."

Mr Wetherby checked his pocket watch. "Try and get a letter in the post to tell her we'll call on Monday morning. You can travel down to Birmingham with me."

"We're probably too late. By the time I've got it written, the last post will have gone."

"Well, get a move on. Otherwise, we'll have to turn up unannounced."

♋

Birmingham, Warwickshire.

First thing on Monday morning, Mary and Mr Wetherby dropped Charlotte off at school before taking William Junior to Frankfort Street to open up the workshop. As soon as they reached Latimer Street, Mr Wetherby helped Mary from the carriage before he turned to talk to the driver. Mary knocked on the door and went straight in. Sarah-Ann stood in the middle of the room, still in her nightwear and let out a small yelp when she saw Mary. When Mr Wetherby followed her in she froze.

"I'm so sorry," Mary said, but Sarah-Ann didn't appear to hear her. She stood like a statue, her eyes fixed on Mr Wetherby.

"I didn't mean to come unannounced but I take it my letter didn't arrive. I only posted it late on Saturday." Mary reached for Sarah-Ann's arm, causing her to jump.

"It's fine … really." Sarah-Ann glanced at Mary, pulling her fingers through her hair as she did. Mary guessed she hadn't put a brush through it that morning.

Mary turned to say goodbye to Mr Wetherby, but was surprised when he closed the front door. "Aren't you going to work?"

"I'll go later. I was hoping Sarah-Ann might make a cup of tea."

Sarah-Ann's eyes widened as she looked between the two of them.

"Only if it's no trouble." He gave Sarah-Ann an apologetic smile.

"Yes, of course." Sarah-Ann shivered as she regained her senses. "Mary, would you put the kettle over the fire for me? I need to go upstairs."

As soon as they were alone, Mary turned to Mr Wetherby. "I knew the letter wouldn't arrive. We should have given her some warning. I don't suppose I'd be best pleased to have people turning up before I'd sorted myself out."

"She doesn't seem her usual self and I don't think it's because we're here," Mr Wetherby said.

"At least Mr Flemming isn't here."

Mr Wetherby grunted and picked up the newspaper as he took a seat by the fire.

Sarah-Ann rejoined them a few minutes later. "There, that's better. You caught me by surprise."

"I'm sorry," Mary said. "It was my fault. When I got your letter I didn't want to wait until later in the week to see you. We've been worried about you; will you tell us what's wrong?"

Sarah-Ann hesitated and stared at Mr Wetherby.

"I want to help." Mr Wetherby's voice was strong but calm. "I can't if I don't know what the problem is."

Sarah-Ann took a sip of the tea Mary offered her and walked to the window, seemingly choosing her words.

"It's Mr Flemming," she said. "I've heard some terrible things about him and I don't know what to do."

❧

Mr Wetherby stayed for longer than planned, but eventually he stood up to leave. He wasn't going to the workshop though. His pace was brisk as he walked towards the town centre and by the time he reached the pawnbroker's he was ready for a fight. He stopped outside the shop and when he was satisfied there were no customers inside, he went in and locked the door behind him.

Mr Flemming stood behind the counter. "What are you doing here?"

"I'm here to see you. Are you alone?"

Mr Flemming glanced into the back room. "Miss Houghton'll be here soon."

"I'll make it quick then." Mr Wetherby walked towards him so that only the counter separated them. "You once promised me you'd take good care of your wife, but you lied. I've just come from your house and Sarah-Ann's distraught … again."

"What the hell were you doing in my house?"

"Escorting my wife to see her friend. What in God's name are you playing at, messing about with young women?"

Mr Flemming's eyes flashed with anger. "What's it got to do with you?"

"It's got everything to do with me. I care about Sarah-Ann and I won't stand by and see her humiliated."

"Her … humiliated? Is that all you're concerned about? She was the one who humiliated me if you remember. She's no one but herself to blame."

Mr Wetherby banged his hand on the counter. "That's a lie and you know it."

"Why … because no one found out about her sordid little affair?"

"We've been through this a thousand times. There was nothing to find out."

"Then why did she turn against me so suddenly?" Mr Flemming poked Mr Wetherby in the shoulder. "I came home from work one night to find you and her together; she's not been interested in me since. There are only so many times you can force yourself on them before you tire of it. It's nice to be wanted again."

"You disgust me." Mr Wetherby stood up straight. "I've told you, she's like a sister to me."

"What I saw that afternoon wasn't the behaviour of a brother and sister. I should have kicked her out there and then."

"It would've been better if you had. I know what you

did to her and I'm sorry I didn't have you arrested for killing her baby."

"I couldn't be sure it was my baby though, could I?" Mr Flemming spat his words out. "It's a pity it was only the child who died."

Mr Wetherby recoiled before he grabbed Mr Flemming by the lapels of his jacket. "That's a despicable thing to say."

"At least that way I'd be a widower and not the husband of a whore." He threw Mr Wetherby's hands from him. "Now get out of my shop."

"Right, that does it. I'm taking Sarah-Ann back to Handsworth. You won't see her again until you show some remorse for what you've just said."

"You'll do no such thing. She's my wife. Besides, she'll be no good to you in Handsworth; you spend all your time in Birmingham."

"Well, perhaps I'll go home more often. I'll do what I have to, to stop you hurting her again. If a man can deliberately throw his wife downstairs and watch while she loses her baby, heaven knows what else he's capable of."

"You take her away and I'll make sure that everyone in town knows the sort of man you really are. You're nothing more than a common, lying cheat. Now get out. I've enough dirt on you to ruin your reputation and I won't hesitate to use it."

Mr Wetherby glared as he put his face to within an inch of Mr Flemming's. "You do anything of the sort and I'll sue you for every penny you have."

Chapter 48

Handsworth, Staffordshire.

S ARAH-ANN SAT IN THE BACK room of Wetherby House, some embroidery on her knee. William-Wetherby and Eleanor played on the floor in front of her, while Harriet sat to her right.

"I must say, I didn't expect you to stay in Handsworth for so long," Harriet said. "Doesn't Mr Flemming mind?"

"That's enough, Harriet," Mary said. "Aunt Sarah-Ann has her reasons for being here and they're not for general discussion."

Harriet took a deep breath and studied Sarah-Ann before she tried again. "How long have you been here? It must be over a month. Do you still go back to Birmingham?"

"Harriet, I said enough." Mary stood up to serve afternoon tea. "Will you slice the cake for me?"

Before Harriet could stand up, there was a knock on the front door. Moments later they heard the voice of Mr Flemming.

"It's Frederick." Sarah-Ann's eyes were wide as she threw her embroidery onto the chair next to her and turned to Mary. "What shall I do?"

"You'll have to see him. We can't pretend you and Elizabeth aren't here. Why don't you take him into the front room?"

"Charles is in there; please don't wake him," Harriet said.

Sarah-Ann glared at Harriet before she turned back to Mary. "What if he gets violent?"

"I'm sure he won't," Mary said.

"I'll talk to him in the hall." Sarah-Ann spoke to herself, but before she reached the door, the maid knocked and let herself in.

"A gentleman to see you, ma'am," she said to Sarah-Ann.

"A nice place you've got here, Mrs Wetherby." Mr Flemming pushed his way past the maid. "I hadn't realised you'd gone up so much in the world."

"What do you want, Frederick?" Sarah-Ann stepped in front of him to stop him sitting down.

"Well, that's a nice welcome when you haven't seen me for so long." Mr Flemming took hold of the top of her arms. "Over a month you've been gone."

Mary picked up her knitting. "Why don't we go into the morning room so you can talk in private. Harriet, bring the children."

With her widening girth as she carried her fourth child, Harriet was in no hurry to leave, but a withering glance from Sarah-Ann caused her to reach for the children and follow Mary from the room.

"What do you want?" Sarah-Ann said again when they were alone.

"Why haven't you come home?" Mr Flemming shook Sarah-Ann. "A wife should live under the same roof as her husband, not with her bit on the side. It's funny how you're so friendly with his wife. I bet she doesn't know."

Sarah-Ann pulled herself away. "He is not my bit on the side."

"Then why don't you come home? It's nearly Christmas after all."

"Why should I? There's nothing to come home for. You're out every night and when you do come home you reek of ale and do nothing but pass out on the bed."

"If that's the way you feel, you leave me with no choice. I'm going to file for a divorce."

The words hit Sarah-Ann like a punch to the stomach. "A divorce? You can't do that."

"There's no point us being married if you're going to live here. I was going to give you the option of coming home with me, plead with you even, but I've changed my mind. Looking at this house I reckon I could make a small fortune if I claim damages from Mr Wetherby."

Sarah-Ann sat down before she collapsed. "You can't do that."

"I think you'll find I can and if I cite Mr Wetherby as your lover, I could clean him out." Mr Flemming walked to the mantelpiece and picked up an ornate clock. "They've got a few expensive things here."

"You've no proof we were lovers. It's all in your head. The only reason I'm living here now is because of you. If you hadn't started carrying on with half the women in Birmingham I wouldn't be here."

Mr Flemming put the clock down and walked back over to her. "It's no business of yours what I do. You should be grateful I put a roof over your head."

"I've got my own money," Sarah-Ann said. "I'll get my own house."

"You have nothing." Mr Flemming snorted. "That money's mine and you can't touch it."

Sarah-Ann jumped from her seat. "That was my father's money; he left it for my own use."

"Is that what you think? I had you down as being brighter than that." Mr Flemming ran his hand down the side of her face. "You know everything passed to me when we got married and there's nothing you can do about it. Such a shame."

"You can't do this, Frederick."

"I wish you'd stop saying that, because clearly I can." His voice was sickeningly calm. "I'll take Elizabeth home with me this evening too. After all, she is mine."

"No, you can't do that. Not Elizabeth. Please … I'll come back with you." Sarah-Ann grabbed his arm but he shook her off.

"I don't want you back. You've made it perfectly clear you don't want me, but I want Elizabeth. She can look after me."

"Don't be ridiculous. She's seven years old."

He rubbed his hands together. "I'll get a housekeeper then. I'm going to do very nicely out of this. Why didn't I think of it sooner?"

❧

Mr Flemming had gone by the time Mr Wetherby arrived home. When he walked into the back room, Mary was sitting in her usual seat but Sarah-Ann had disappeared.

"No Sarah-Ann?" He walked to the table and sat down.

"Mr Flemming called this afternoon."

Mr Wetherby stood up again. "He came here? I hope you didn't let him in."

"We didn't have any choice. He was in here before we could stop him."

"He didn't take Sarah-Ann back with him, did he?" Mr Wetherby was at the door before Mary answered.

"No, but he took Elizabeth. I haven't seen Sarah-Ann since he left. As he was leaving she ran upstairs and locked her bedroom door."

"Haven't you been up to see her?"

"I wanted to give her some time to calm down."

Mr Wetherby let out a gasp. "I don't believe you sometimes. That man could have done anything to her."

A minute later, Mr Wetherby was upstairs knocking on Sarah-Ann's bedroom door.

"Sarah-Ann, please, let me in. We need to talk."

"What is there to talk about?"

Mr Wetherby struggled to understand her through her sobs. "Please, you have to let me in. I want to help, but I can't if you won't talk to me."

It took a couple of minutes but eventually Sarah-Ann opened the door and retreated to the window.

"Did he hurt you?" Mr Wetherby walked to her and put his hands on her shoulders.

Sarah-Ann shook her head. "It would have been easier if he had."

"What did he want?" Mr Wetherby turned her towards him and held her as she buried her head in his shoulder.

"He wants a divorce." She started crying again. "He's

taken Elizabeth and says he won't give me any of Pa's money back. He's going to sue you for damages as well."

Mr Wetherby pushed her away, holding her at arm's length. "He'll do nothing of the sort. He's gone too far this time. I don't know what he's playing at, but he's not treating you like that and he won't get a penny from me. He's the reason you're here and he's no proof you've committed adultery. Besides, he won't be able to afford it." He handed her a cloth from the washbasin. "Stop crying and wipe your face. He's not going to do any of those things. We have time and we're going to sort this out."

Chapter 49

SARAH-ANN LAY IN BED STARING at the ceiling. Not that she could see it, it was still too dark, but it didn't matter. Nothing mattered anymore. She was about to lose her home, her money, and most importantly, her daughter. It was over three months since she'd spoken to Elizabeth and she couldn't take much more. She hadn't seen her at Christmas and Mr Flemming had returned the present she had sent for her. She'd seen her every day since, from a distance, but that didn't count. Each morning she would walk to High Street to catch a glimpse of her as Mr Flemming took her to the shop, but he never let her out of his sight. Once, when Elizabeth had seen her, Mr Flemming had dragged her into the shop so viciously that Sarah-Ann daren't risk being seen again. What did she have to do to see her daughter alone?

As a glimmer of light forced its way through the curtains, there was a knock on the bedroom door and Mary walked in.

"A cup of tea for you," she said. "Did you sleep any better last night?"

Sarah-Ann sat up in bed. "How can I sleep knowing I may never see my daughter again?"

"It won't come to that. You have to trust Mr Wetherby. He said he'll sort something out."

"When though?" Tears filled her eyes. "It's been over three months and nothing's changed."

"He wasn't expecting to deal with a sudden campaign for a general election. Now Mr Disraeli's won he'll have more time. I'll speak to him again, but when he says he'll do something, he usually does. Drink your tea and follow me downstairs. Don't forget Martha's coming today. She should be here by mid-morning."

❦

Mary had said goodbye to Mr Wetherby and laid a place at the breakfast table for Sarah-Ann by the time she came downstairs.

"I'm not hungry." Sarah-Ann walked past the table and sat in a chair by the fire.

"You have to eat. You'll be no good to anyone if you make yourself ill. Here, I'll butter a slice of bread for you."

"You don't know what it's like. To have a child you can never see …"

Mary thought back to the time Mr Wetherby had taken William to Birmingham against her will. He'd probably been the same age as Elizabeth was now. He'd only been gone a week, but it had broken Mary's heart. It had almost ruined her relationship with Mr Wetherby. She had never told Sarah-Ann and decided that now wasn't the time.

"No, I don't suppose I do," she said. "It can't be easy."

When Martha arrived, Sarah-Ann was asleep by the fire. Mary stood up to go and meet her in the hallway but Sarah-Ann opened her eyes at the sound of her sister's voice.

"What time is it?" Sarah-Ann sat up and rubbed her eyes.

"Just gone half past ten," Martha said as she walked into the room. "Have you been asleep?"

"I've not been sleeping well. I must have dozed off."

"Still no word on Elizabeth?" Martha asked.

Sarah-Ann shook her head.

"I'm sorry. I'm sure something will be sorted out soon."

"I've told her that," Mary said. "She just won't believe me."

"Well, I've got some other news to take your mind off things," Martha said. "I had a visit from Jane Dainty yesterday. Apparently Aunt Rebecca's ill and Jane doesn't think she has long left."

"What a shame," Mary said. "Although probably no great surprise. She's well into her eighties."

"She'll be the last of that generation though. It's sad, isn't it?"

When Sarah-Ann made no comment, Mary turned to her. The colour had drained from her face. "What's up with you? I didn't think you were close to Aunt Rebecca."

"She can't die." Sarah-Ann's eyes were wide with horror. "Not yet, not until everything's sorted out."

"What are you talking about?" Mary said.

"She can't die. I need that inheritance. He'll take it all."

A wave of realisation crossed Mary's face. "We need to do something. If the divorce hasn't gone through by the time Aunt Rebecca dies, the money Aunt Lucy left will pass to Mr Flemming."

Sarah-Ann put her hands over her face, to hide her sobs.

"Can it be finalised that quickly?" Martha asked.

Mary shrugged. "I've no idea, but we need Mr Wetherby to do something. It's taking him too long. She can't lose Elizabeth and all her inheritance."

"I'll go and visit Aunt Rebecca, see how ill she really is," Martha said. "I'll go now and write as soon as I can."

The following day, the postman arrived as punctual as ever and handed Mary four letters. Three were addressed to her; the fourth looked like an official document for Mr Wetherby. It was probably something from the Conservative Association. She studied the envelopes addressed to her. One was from Alice, the second was in Mary-Ann's handwriting and the other came from Martha. Taking the letter opener from behind the clock on the mantelpiece, she opened the letter from Martha.

Dear Mary

I visited Aunt Rebecca yesterday but didn't speak to her. She sleeps now most of the time and it doesn't look like she'll last much longer.
Please ask Mr Wetherby to hurry.

Martha

Mary sat down and reread the letter, thankful that Sarah-Ann was out of the room. It was ten past two. Mr Wetherby wouldn't be home for hours yet. She needed to hide the letter before Sarah-Ann came back. She didn't want to worry her further. She was putting the letter into the top drawer of the sideboard when Sarah-Ann returned.

"What are you doing?" Sarah-Ann asked.

"Nothing … just looking for the letter opener."

"It's on the table."

Mary turned around and picked it up. "So it is, I can't see for looking. I've letters from Mary-Ann and Alice." Mary held them in the air before she took the letter opener and dramatically sliced the top of the envelope from Mary-Ann. As she read, she turned her back on Sarah-Ann to hide the smile on her face. Mary-Ann was expecting her second child later in the year and had written to say the family were moving to Handsworth. How wonderful to have all her grandchildren close by. Mary said a silent prayer of thanks, but had to straighten her face again. She couldn't tell Sarah-Ann, not in the state she was in. Putting the letter in her apron, she picked up the envelope from Alice and opened it quickly.

"Nothing to report, only the usual dull stuff," Mary said after she gave it a brief glance and tossed it onto the table.

"Do you see much of her now you live here?" Sarah-Ann asked.

"Who? Alice? Not really. I was going to Birmingham every few weeks until you moved in, but I haven't been for a while." Mary thought of Richard. She hadn't seen him for months and he'd be wondering where she was. "I'll go down for the day next time Martha visits you."

As soon as Mary heard Mr Wetherby arrive home, she jumped up and went into the hall. Putting her finger to her lips, she waved William Junior into the morning room and shut the door behind him. She then waited for Mr Wetherby to take off his hat and coat before she ushered him into the front room.

"What's going on?" Mr Wetherby said as she closed the door behind them.

"I don't want to wake Sarah-Ann, she's asleep by the fire, but I need to talk to you."

A puzzled expression crossed Mr Wetherby's face. "Go on."

"We've heard from Martha that Aunt Rebecca's ill. She went to see her yesterday and doesn't think she'll last much longer."

"What's wrong with that?"

"The thing is, Aunt Lucy left a lot of possessions to Aunt Rebecca. The will stipulated that when Aunt Rebecca died everything should be sold and divided between the family. Sarah-Ann's due to inherit a share of the money. As long as Aunt Rebecca's alive, everything's fine, but if she dies before the divorce is finalised, the money will go straight to Mr Flemming. We can't let that happen; she needs the money. Is there a chance the divorce can be speeded up?"

Mr Wetherby shook his head. "I'm trying to stop the divorce, not speed it up. If it goes through she can forget any chance of seeing Elizabeth until she comes of age."

"But that means she'll have to go back and live with him. We can't trust him."

"It's the only way." Mr Wetherby stroked his beard. "He's probably bluffing about the divorce anyway. He won't be able to afford it."

"I hope you're right, but you need to tell her. She's no idea what's going on."

Mr Wetherby followed Mary into the back room. As Sarah-Ann was still asleep he picked up the letter waiting for him on the table.

"It came this morning," Mary said absently. "It looks official."

"It does indeed." Mr Wetherby frowned as he turned it over in his hands before picking up the letter opener. Mary watched as he slit open the top of the envelope and pulled out the heavy cream paper. When he remained silent, she put some water over the fire to boil.

"I need to go and see Susannah after tea," she said, ignoring Mr Wetherby's silence. "Alice isn't well and I want to see if Susannah knows any more about it. Are you listening to me?"

"Sorry, yes, of course, off you go."

"I'm not going yet, after tea. It will give you time to talk as well." She nodded at Sarah-Ann.

Mr Wetherby took his handkerchief from his pocket and wiped his forehead as he reread the letter. Once he had finished, he glanced at his pocket watch. "That can wait. I need to go out. Something's cropped up."

৵৵

Mr Wetherby folded the letter and put it in the inside pocket of his coat before he reached for his hat and stepped outside. The cool air felt good on his face, and he took several deep breaths before he walked around to the back of the house. The horses were stabled, and the driver had gone for the night, but he didn't care. He would harness them and drive the carriage himself. Once he'd quietened the dogs down again. The only thing that mattered was stopping that scoundrel Flemming. He'd only gone and served the divorce papers and was claiming damages from him. Well, he'd gone too far. Mr Flemming had no proof that he and Sarah-Ann had committed adultery, and unless he put a stop to the proceedings the whole town would hear of his shameful secret. *You might treat Sarah-Ann any way you like, but you will not threaten me and get away with it.*

Chapter 50

THE PREVIOUS WEEK WHEN MARY had told Sarah-Ann about the letter from Martha, she had locked herself in her bedroom and refused to come out. Now she had to tell her Aunt Rebecca was dead. Her stomach churned as she reread the most recent letter from Martha. How she wished Mr Wetherby was here. He'd know what to say, but he wouldn't be home until this afternoon and Mary wouldn't be able to keep the news to herself until then.

Sarah-Ann stayed downstairs long enough for Mary to show her the letter before she fled back to her room. Mary stood in the middle of the room, her arms hanging limply by her sides. When Sarah-Ann slammed her bedroom door the sound jolted Mary to her senses and a moment later she moved to pick up her writing case. She needed help. Mr Wetherby hadn't told Sarah-Ann of his plans and didn't have any sense of urgency. She needed Martha to come to Handsworth to help her work out what they needed to do next.

Sarah-Ann had not returned to the living room by the time Mr Wetherby came home. Mary had tried to talk to her, but the bedroom door was locked and when Mary realised she was talking to herself she returned downstairs.

Fortunately, with it being Easter Saturday, Mr Wetherby wasn't late arriving home. Once he had sat down, Mary handed him the letter. "Aunt Rebecca died on Tuesday. Sarah-Ann's taken it badly."

Mr Wetherby said nothing while he buttered himself a piece of bread.

Mary put her hand on his arm. "Is there anything you can do to help her?"

"Perhaps," he said after some thought. "I'm working on something at the moment, but I need to speak to her. Whatever we may think, I believe her best option is to go back to him. I need to tell her and make sure she's willing to go."

"It won't be easy after everything that's been said."

"You might be right, but the alternatives will be worse."

∾∾

After he'd eaten, Mr Wetherby went upstairs and knocked on Sarah-Ann's bedroom door.

"We need to talk," he said. "Please let me in."

A moment later, the door opened and Sarah-Ann returned to the chair she'd been sitting on.

"He's won, hasn't he?" Sarah-Ann's voice was calm. "He's got my house, my money and my daughter. Now he wants me on the streets."

Mr Wetherby sat on the bed opposite her and reached for her hand.

"There is another way."

Sarah-Ann's brow furrowed.

"You need to go back to him."

"Go back!" Sarah-Ann choked on her words. "How can

I do that? Even if I wanted to, he wouldn't have me. He's more interested in getting his hands on your money."

"He has no proof, whatsoever, that you committed adultery. Without it, he can shout all he likes, but it won't help him."

"He saw us."

"He saw me look at you and he jumped to his own conclusions. That isn't proof. Besides, I've found a way to prove his adultery. We can use it to make sure he drops the proceedings and takes you back with a smile on his face. If I do that, are you happy to go?"

Sarah-Ann closed her eyes and put her hands to her head.

"It would mean being with Elizabeth again," Mr Wetherby said.

"I don't have much choice, do I? I either have both of them or neither."

"You know it makes sense. Leave it with me, and you'll be back home before the end of the month."

❦

Mary had no idea what Mr Wetherby had said to Sarah-Ann, but it had certainly had an effect. She was still subdued, but when the invitation came to go to Aunt Rebecca's funeral, she accepted. Mary hadn't bothered to ask Mr Wetherby if she could go and sat by the fire waiting for Sarah-Ann to come back.

"How was it?" Mary asked as soon as Sarah-Ann walked in.

"I wasn't left any more money if that's what you mean."

"So who got Aunt Rebecca's possessions? She had quite a number of houses in her own name didn't she?"

"They were split amongst a few of her friends, and the Daintys got most of her houses."

"Even Charles?"

"Even Charles. They ended up with more than anyone else. We worked out the only ones left out were your two, Elizabeth and Catherine. Martha wasn't happy that her daughter got nothing but her son did."

"What happened to supporting all the women in the family?"

Sarah-Ann shrugged. "Seems they didn't trust us so much after all."

❧

Birmingham, Warwickshire.

Two weeks later Mr Wetherby had all the information he needed to confront Mr Flemming. Once he was satisfied everything was in place he headed to the pawnshop. There were two customers looking at the rings when he went in and he took the opportunity to view some pocket watches while he waited. As soon as the customers left he followed them to the door and locked it behind them.

"Get out of my shop. I don't want you here and you've no right to stop my customers from coming in." Mr Flemming walked to the door, intent on opening it again.

"Suit yourself. Let them in if you want them to hear what a scoundrel you are."

Mr Flemming stopped and glared at him. "What do you want?"

"I want you to stop the divorce proceedings." Mr Wetherby's voice was calm and commanding.

"I'll do no such thing."

"I think you will. Not only that, I'm taking Elizabeth home with me today. I presume she's in the back."

Mr Flemming moved to close the door to the back room. "You're not laying a finger on my daughter."

"Sarah-Ann will bring her home once she knows the proceedings have been dropped and once you've put all her father's money into a separate bank account in her name."

"Who the hell do you think you are coming in here and telling me what to do?"

Mr Wetherby put a pile of papers onto the counter. "I am the man who now has a full dossier on all the women you've been carrying on with over the last six months. They weren't hard to track down and with a bit of cajoling they were all prepared to sign a statement to say you'd forced your way onto them."

"That's not true, I didn't force anyone."

"I've got signed documents from thirteen women saying you did. It will be your word against theirs."

"Thirteen? What do you take me for? You're lying."

"The evidence doesn't lie."

"Nobody will believe women like that over me."

"I did think of that." Mr Wetherby flicked through the papers. "That's why I've got statements from six men who are prepared to swear that these women are telling the truth. Men who saw you with them before you dragged them away to commit adultery."

Mr Flemming grabbed the papers from the desk and glanced through them. "These are nothing but forgeries. They're not signed."

"You don't think I'm going to give you all the names,

do you, so you can go and intimidate everyone. Those are copies. I've got another set, with names and signatures, stored away for safekeeping."

Mr Flemming's eyebrow twitched as he stared at Mr Wetherby.

"Don't forget as well," Mr Wetherby said. "Sarah-Ann is prepared to stand up in court should I decide to accuse you of assault and the murder of your unborn son."

"That would be your word against mine."

Mr Wetherby gave him a crooked smile. "And who's going to believe you when we have nineteen people testifying against you? Let's see how long your business survives once the allegations become public knowledge."

Mr Flemming threw the papers to one side and jumped over the counter. "You blackguard, I always knew you were despicable."

Mr Wetherby backed away, once again putting the counter between the two of them. "That's rich coming from the biggest scoundrel in Birmingham. All I'm doing is stopping you from ruining Sarah-Ann." He moved to the door and called into the back room. "Elizabeth, get your coat, you're going to see your mother."

"You stay where you are," Mr Flemming shouted.

Mr Wetherby grabbed him by the collar. "She's coming home with me, and Sarah-Ann will write and tell you when she's coming back. You'd better make her welcome or the ruination of your business will be the least of your troubles."

Chapter 51

Handsworth, Staffordshire.

SARAH-ANN GRIPPED ELIZABETH'S HAND WHEN the doorbell rang, her stomach churning at the thought of seeing her husband again. Ten past six. He must have shut up the shop early. It had been a week since Mr Wetherby had told her she was going home, but she wasn't ready for it. Would she ever be ready?

"Are you all right?" Mary asked. "You've gone white."

Sarah-Ann gave her a weak smile. "I'll be fine. Let's just get this over with."

A moment later the maid knocked on the door and showed Mr Flemming in.

"Good afternoon, Mr Flemming," Mary said.

"Mrs Wetherby." He inclined his head towards her before he turned to Elizabeth. "Let's take you home. I've missed you these last few weeks."

Elizabeth giggled as her father picked her up and pulled her into a hug. "I've missed you too."

"Our things are in the hall," Sarah-Ann said when he continued to ignore her. "We'd better put them in the carriage."

Mr Flemming put Elizabeth down and stared at Sarah-

Ann. "What are you waiting for? You brought everything here; you can take it out again. I'd hoped Mrs Wetherby might have a pot of tea waiting for me."

Mary let out a small cough. "Yes, I think there'll be enough left from earlier. Why don't you help Sarah-Ann while I pour another cup?"

Reluctantly, Mr Flemming followed Sarah-Ann out into the hall and picked up two of her bags. "Don't think I'm going to be running around after you once you're back. The only reason we're going to be playing happy families again is because of Elizabeth. Is that clear? I don't want you home any more than you want to come, but Elizabeth's the important one."

"Can we at least be civil to each other?" Sarah-Ann said. "It will make life a lot more bearable for both of us."

Mr Flemming grunted. "If we must, but if I go out of an evening, I don't want you nagging me about it for the next week."

"I won't as long as you're sober. If you come home at eleven o'clock every night, reeking of ale, I'll be back here. We both know that wouldn't be in your best interests."

"What's Wetherby been saying?"

"He's told me everything. I know what you've been up to and I know he'll ruin you if needs be. As long as we're both aware of the facts, it might help us get along a little better."

"Bloody man," Mr Flemming said under his breath.

Sarah-Ann lifted a small bag into the carriage. "I heard that, and I don't want to hear any more about Mr Wetherby. He's been very generous to me and I won't have a word said against him."

Mr Flemming was about to object when Mr Wetherby's carriage turned in to the driveway, the chestnut horses standing out against the dullness of the day.

"Mr Flemming," Mr Wetherby said as he jumped down from the carriage.

"Come to keep an eye on me, have you?"

"If you must know, I hadn't expected you to be here yet, but yes, that's precisely why I've come home. I'm also here to remind you that if I hear you're still having illicit interactions with the women of the town, I will not hesitate to expose you for the scoundrel you are."

Mr Flemming glared at Mr Wetherby before he headed for the door. "I'm going to get Elizabeth. For some reason, I've gone off that cup of tea."

৵৵

With Sarah-Ann gone, Mary was keen to go to Birmingham. She'd only managed to visit once since Christmas, almost five months ago, and had an overwhelming urge to see Richard. It was all she could think of, but with Harriet due to give birth to her fourth child at any time, and with Mary-Ann about to move house, she could hardly go rushing off to Birmingham. As Mary-Ann was also expecting another baby, Mary had offered her and little Rose a room at Wetherby House, while Mr Diver arranged the move.

With Mary-Ann not due to arrive for another week, Mary walked around to Church Hill Road. She knocked on the door and was surprised when William opened it for her.

"What are you doing here?" Mary said. "I came to keep Harriet company."

"She's a bit preoccupied at the moment." William

closed the door and took Mary's cloak. "The baby's on its way. The doctor's upstairs now."

Mary clapped her hands under her chin. "How exciting. How long's he been here?"

"A couple of hours. Hopefully it won't be too long this time."

"Where are the children?"

"Out in the back garden. Charles should be asleep in his pram and the other two were playing last time I checked. Don't disturb them; it's easier with them outside for now."

Mary peeped out the window at William-Wetherby and Eleanor before she made a cup of tea for her and William.

"I got a letter from Mary-Ann yesterday," Mary said. "They're almost ready for the move."

"I don't know why they're moving to Havelock Road. Even though it's in Handsworth, it's not close by and the place is still like a building site."

"It doesn't matter. It's closer than Saltley and once it's finished the houses will be lovely."

"Perhaps." William knew the houses were going to be large and impressive, but as he sat down he imagined Harriet pleading with him to move there as well. Where she thought they'd find the money from, he'd no idea.

Mary had just sat down opposite him when they heard the sound of crying from upstairs.

"That doesn't sound like Charles," William said with a smile. "I suppose that means everything went smoothly."

Mary shook her head. "You really have no idea."

Twenty minutes later the doctor called and the two of them went upstairs to the bedroom.

"Another girl, Mr Jackson," the doctor said. "She's

healthy enough and your wife is fine. Don't stay with her too long; she needs her rest. I'll let myself out."

William smiled when he saw Harriet and followed Mary into the room.

"Let me see her," Mary said. "What a beauty. A healthy size too."

"A bit too big if you ask me, but we won't go into that. What are you doing here?"

"I called to keep you company for the afternoon, but I clearly wasn't needed."

Harriet smiled. "You're always welcome. While you're here would you mind helping out with the children? I've left some food in the pantry; it just needs serving."

"It's about time you had some help around the house," Mary said. "Shall I send one of my maids round for a couple of weeks? With Sarah-Ann gone, they don't have as much to do."

"Mother, I've now got four children. Mr Wetherby doesn't pay me enough for a maid as well."

Mary frowned. "It's about time he did. You shouldn't be living like a poor relation."

"We're not poor; we just have other priorities."

"I'd say we need a bigger house before we find a maid," Harriet said. "It's all well and good putting the children in one room while they're little, but before long, the boys will need their own room."

William rolled his eyes. "We haven't got the money at the moment."

"If Mr Diver can afford a new house, then we should be able to as well," Harriet said. "It would be wonderful if we could move there too."

"Shall I have a word with Mr Wetherby?" Mary asked. "I'm sure he'd say it was a good investment."

"No, we're fine … thank you." William said. "William-Wetherby's only six. He's not going to need his own room for years yet."

Harriet sighed. "I hope I'm not going to have the same trouble getting you to move from this house as I did from my uncle's. You're going to have to get used to the idea that we need to move to a bigger house."

๛

Harriet spent most of her confinement reading and thinking. Their new daughter, Margaret, was a contented child, which gave her plenty of time. It hadn't been a casual remark when she'd said they needed to move house, and if Mary-Ann could move, they could too. Admittedly, William didn't earn enough money to move anywhere at the moment, but she would work on that.

Once her confinement was over, she broached the subject again.

"Do you remember the day Margaret was born?" she started.

"Hmm," William said as he turned over the page of the newspaper.

"We spoke of getting a bigger house."

"You spoke of getting a bigger house." William put the paper on his knee. "I said there was no hurry."

"You also said you didn't earn enough money to afford a higher rent."

"I'm glad you were listening."

"Have you noticed that the men in the family who earn

the most money are the ones who have their own businesses? Mr Wetherby obviously, but Mr Diver too. My uncle was never poor either."

"We're not poor."

"Maybe not, but if you ran your own business, we'd be able to have the bigger house we need."

"Have you forgotten I'm a partner with Mr Wetherby? Half the business is mine."

"In theory it is, but he takes more out of it than you do. Don't you think it would be better if you had your half back and ran it yourself?"

"Split Mr Wetherby's business in half?"

"Don't look so frightened. It shouldn't all be his in the first place. I could do the books for you, so you could concentrate on bringing in the business and the manufacturing."

"Bringing in the business is the part of the job I've never done. Mr Wetherby has all the contacts and keeps them to himself. He's also unlikely to agree to me setting up a competing business."

Harriet thought for a moment. "All right, let's say you can't start your own business right away, but what about learning everything you need to, so that in a year or two, you'll be ready?"

"If I say yes, does that mean you'll stop going on about it?"

"Only if you promise to find out everything from Mr Wetherby. Promise?"

"If it makes you happy, I promise."

Chapter 52

MARY TOOK A SIP OF tea as she read her letters. Sarah-Ann's was mostly reassuring. Despite the tensions between her and Mr Flemming, it seemed they had survived Christmas and were managing to live in the same house without arguing. Probably in no small part thanks to Elizabeth.

Alice's letter was more concerning. It had started off in her usual bland way, but as Mary was about to put it down and pour another cup of tea, a phrase caught her eye. Alice was off work. That wasn't like her. She'd never been frightened of hard work and she needed the money. Mary read a little further and became more concerned when she turned over the page to read that Alice didn't think she'd be able to make it to the wedding of their niece, Clara, the following month.

Clara was Susannah's daughter and Mary put on her hat and coat and walked the short distance to her house. Susannah was kneeling on the front doorstep, scrubbing it with a hard brush, when Mary arrived.

"Have I come at a bad time?" Mary said.

"Of course not; I'm about finished. What brings you here?"

"Can't I visit my sister without a reason?"

"Of course you can, but you generally do have a reason."

Mary smiled. "Well, maybe I do, but I'd rather not talk out here. Can we go inside?"

Susannah led the way into the small back room and put the kettle over the fire. The house always reminded Mary of the one she lived in before she married Mr Wetherby. It was small but perfectly adequate for Susannah and Clara.

"Have you heard from Alice?" she said once Susannah poured the tea.

"I got a letter from her the other day but she didn't say much. Why?"

"I've received this." Mary held the letter in front of her. "I'm worried about her. She doesn't sound well and said she might not make the wedding."

"She hasn't told me. What's the matter with her?"

"She has a pain in her back and can't go to work."

"It'll be her age. She's too old to be doing so much manual work."

Mary choked on her tea. "It's not much different from the work you were just doing, except she's younger than you and gets paid for it."

"She's not much younger," Susannah said, pushing her fingers into her hair.

"That's beside the point. I'm worried about her. She wouldn't miss work unless there was something wrong."

"You're right. When did you last see her?"

"I've not been to Birmingham for a few weeks, but she was fine last time I went. In fact I thought she'd put a bit of weight on and I teased her she was earning too much money if she was eating so well. I'm happy to go down to Birmingham every few weeks and keep an eye on her."

"I thought you hated Birmingham?"

"I do." Mary focussed on the tea leaves in the bottom of her cup. "But we can't leave her on her own."

"We need to persuade her to move up here. You've got plenty of room at Wetherby House."

"She doesn't want to live with us."

Susannah frowned. "Are you sure? Well, I suppose she can come here. Once Clara moves out, I'll be on my own."

Mary took a deep breath. "I'll see what she says, but knowing her she probably won't want to come."

Birmingham, Warwickshire.

Mary accepted Mr Wetherby's hand as she climbed down from the carriage, a bunch of flowers clutched in her other hand.

"I won't come in." Mr Wetherby put her bag by her feet and knocked on the door. "Too much to do."

"That's all right. I'll probably have to walk into town later. I bet she's got no food in."

"Do you want me to take you?"

"Not at all." Mary waved her hand at him. "It's only a five-minute walk. Once I've been in the house for half an hour I'll be glad of some air, even if it is full of smoke."

Mr Wetherby kissed her on the forehead. "I'm sure it's not that bad. I'll pick you up tomorrow."

Mary waited for the carriage to turn onto Summer Lane before she pushed the door and let herself in. Alice sat by the fire with a blanket over her knee and several shawls draped over her shoulders.

"I thought I saw the horses. They're such a lovely colour, so distinctive," she said. "I presume Mr Wetherby brought you?"

"He did and he'll be back for me late tomorrow. I don't like leaving Mary-Ann alone for too long now she has those two little girls."

"She has other help, doesn't she?"

Mary sighed. "She does, but the baby isn't sleeping well at the moment. If I call in the afternoon, at least she can have a lie down before Mr Diver gets home. Now, let me put these flowers in some water before I do anything else."

"You don't need to bring fresh flowers every time you come."

"I like to bring them. They brighten up the room and they're pretty in the window." Mary scanned the room. "Where did you put the vase I bought you?"

"It's in the cupboard. I'm not likely to buy flowers for myself."

Mary smiled. *Exactly.*

"You didn't need to come," Alice said. "I spoke to the doctor when he visited the house I work at. He thinks I've caught a chill and told me to keep warm. It should pass."

"Well that's something. How long have you been sat there like that for though? I bet you've not been out to buy any food."

"My neighbour brings me some bread each morning and I've enough butter for a few days yet."

"You'll need more than that." Mary studied the inside of the cupboards. "Let me have a cup of tea and then I'll go and get you some things in."

It was still only nine o'clock when Mary reached the

costermonger's. She took her time looking at each of the stalls before making her purchases. Once she'd bought what she needed she made her way to St Martin's church. Months ago she'd worked out it was an area of Birmingham Mr Wetherby was unlikely to visit and she could sit on the wall and wait.

She hadn't been waiting long before Richard's familiar figure rounded the corner and walked straight towards her. She smiled at him but kept her distance. There were still plenty of folks around here who knew Mr Wetherby.

"You saw the flowers."

"I've been driving down Frankfort Street every day for the last fortnight looking for them. Why've you been away so long?"

"I've not had any reason to call. Fortunately Alice is ill at the moment, which gave me an excuse to visit her."

Richard smiled at her. "I take it it's nothing serious then."

Mary chortled. "No, only a chill. I've just been to do her shopping."

"You must be cold sitting there. Why don't we go to the market and I can buy you a cup of soup? I could do with some too."

With the crowds surrounding them, Mary let Richard take her hand as they searched for somewhere secluded to stop.

"Is Mr Wetherby still neglecting you?" Richard asked when they stopped walking.

"I don't see any more of him than I did, if that's what you mean."

"Do you mind?"

"Why should I mind?" Mary gazed into Richard's eyes.

"The other week I overheard some folk saying he'd left home and he's living down here."

The words sounded familiar to Mary. "Aunt Lucy told me before she died." Mary paused while she thought. "Be honest with me. Do you think he's seeing anyone else?"

Richard let out a whistle. "That's a big question. How would I know?"

"Because you deliver coal around half of Birmingham."

"I don't go near Summer Lane … unless I'm looking for you."

"You're still bound to hear things."

Richard reached up and stroked her cheek. "If I thought he was doing anything to upset you or ruin your reputation, do you think I'd let him get away with it?"

"You would tell me?"

"What about if I start delivering around Handsworth. How many deliveries a week do you think you'd need?"

Mary blushed, causing Richard to laugh at her.

"I haven't seen you turn that colour for years."

"It might not be funny soon. Susannah wants me to ask Alice if she'll move to Handsworth. I'm not going to encourage her at the moment, but if she doesn't get any better …"

"We'll find a way. If Mr Wetherby keeps leaving you alone, he's no one but himself to blame."

Chapter 53

Handsworth, Staffordshire.

It was only half past eight in the morning but Harriet felt as if she had done a full day's work. It was a similar pattern most days, but with Clara's wedding later that morning, everything needed to be rushed. As usual, Charles was the cause of all the problems. Since their fourth child, Margaret, had been born a year ago, Charles constantly wanted all of Harriet's attention. To keep him calm, Harriet often ignored her other children while he was in the room, but this morning he had walked in when she was feeding Margaret. As soon as he saw them, he let out a shriek and ran across the room. At first he hit the baby before he tried to pull her from Harriet's arms. Within seconds Margaret was crying and, when Harriet clung to her, Charles screamed louder. In frustration, Harriet smacked Charles firmly across the back of his legs and put him out of the room. She finished feeding Margaret with tears running down her cheeks, listening to screams that were interspersed with the sound of tiny fists beating on the door.

Once Margaret was settled, Harriet returned to Charles.

Eleanor had disappeared and so it was just the two of them, but he wouldn't be pacified. In sheer frustration, Harriet locked him in his room and went downstairs, shutting the door behind her to block out his screams.

By the time William came home half an hour later, Charles had cried himself to sleep.

"Aren't you ready to go?" William said. "I thought you'd be waiting for me."

"Please don't start, I've had enough of today already. We need to do something about Charles; I can't cope with him anymore."

"Where is he now?"

"In his room, asleep, I suppose, but please don't go and check, you might wake him up."

"We'll have to wake him up to take him next door. Just be thankful he isn't coming to the wedding with us."

"Give me five more minutes and then you can go to him. Maybe when he's out of my sight he'll behave himself."

The marriage of Miss Clara Whitley to Mr John Brown was held in Handsworth Parish Church. Clara looked delightful as she walked down the aisle on the arm of her brother, the train of her cream silk gown behind her. The service was short and as the bride and groom left to sign the wedding register, Mary marvelled at how well Susannah had managed since the death of her husband all those years ago. In fact, she wasn't sure how she did manage. She'd been present at the reading of the will, more to keep her sister company than out of expectation, and she'd been shocked at how little money Mr Whitley had left. Despite that, her sister hadn't needed to work since and she was doing her daughter proud today. She once asked Susannah how she managed but she didn't get an answer.

Alice leaned over and broke into her thoughts. "She's done all right for herself, hasn't she, our Susannah? Where does she get her money from? I wonder."

"I don't know, perhaps we should ask her."

"We couldn't possibly … could we?" Alice's eyes widened.

Mary studied her sister closely. To the casual observer, she was the same as ever, but Mary suspected she hadn't recovered from her recent illness.

"You don't think I'm getting any better, do you?" Alice said.

Mary cocked her head. "Are you?"

"I've been better, I'm just tired all the time and I have a constant ache in my back, nothing too painful, but you know it's there. I thought it might be better not to come today, but to tell you the truth, I wanted to be here."

"Have you seen the doctor again?"

Alice shook her head.

"Sitting in these pews won't help," Mary added. "The sooner they start the work on this church the better; I wonder if it's safe to sit here some days."

"Don't say that." Alice studied the rafters overhead. "I can't move fast if anything falls."

"If you're so bad, why don't you stay with us for a few days? Mr Wetherby will call the doctor out."

Alice pulled a face.

"Don't look at me like that. If you're not going to work, you might as well stay here. If you don't want to stay at

Wetherby House, Susannah has said you can stay there. She'll be on her own now Clara's moving out."

"Maybe for a day or two but I need to go back to work on Monday. Will you tell her for me?"

At that moment, the wedding party returned from signing the register and Clara, with her new husband, walked down the aisle to the sound of Mendelssohn's "Wedding March". Mary stayed to listen to the music but as the last of the guests filed past her, she stood up in a panic. The wedding breakfast was being held at Wetherby House and she had to be at the house before the guests.

"I need to go," she said to Alice. "I've left Cook and Emily at home preparing the food, but I should be there to greet the guests. Are you coming?"

Mary hurried out but by the time she approached the door Alice had fallen behind. She started to go back but Alice waved her on.

"You go; I'll follow with the others. I'm fine, honestly."

Mary wasn't convinced and searched for William. He was making his way to the door with Harriet and Margaret, although Harriet looked as if she was trying to hide behind him. Mary wondered what the problem was until she spotted the rector. He was bound to mention the baptism.

"William," she said when she was close enough to be heard, "Aunt Alice isn't well and I have to get back to the house. Will you wait for her?"

"Yes, of course, but …" He turned to Harriet.

"Please, no buts. Harriet, you come with me." She took Harriet's arm and pushed her towards the door. "I'm sorry, Rector, I'm in a dreadful hurry." With that they walked into the churchyard without a pause.

"I'll apologise to him on Sunday," Mary said with a grin. "I needed William to take care of Alice."

Harriet smiled back before her face fell into a frown. "Is she all right? She doesn't seem her usual self."

Mary checked over her shoulder to make sure no one could hear them. "To tell you the truth, I don't think she is. I just pray she gets better. She doesn't want to move to Handsworth and it's quite convenient for me to go to Birmingham every few weeks."

Chapter 54

TWO DAYS LATER, MARY KNOCKED on the front door and let herself in to Susannah's living room. She expected Alice to be waiting for her but when the room was empty, she shouted up the stairs. Within a minute Susannah came down.

"She's nearly ready. I still don't think she should be going back to Birmingham, but I can't do anything to talk her out of it."

Mary glanced at the clock. "If she's not ready soon, she won't be going anywhere. Mr Wetherby was getting impatient when I left. It's not like her to be late."

"She's constantly tired. She couldn't get out of bed this morning."

"At least I'm travelling with her. Mr Wetherby will make sure she sees the doctor when she's home."

It was another two minutes before Alice arrived, by which time Mr Wetherby had ordered the carriage to the front of the house. As soon as they were settled, the driver flicked the reins and the horses moved forward.

"Are you sure you don't want me to stay with you?" Mary asked Alice.

"I'm sure. As long as the doctor can give me something for the tiredness I'll be fine."

"Well, if he doesn't, you must let me know."

৵৵

Harriet dropped two one-shilling coins into her tin and smiled as she placed it in the back of the cupboard. It was such a nice feeling to save a bit of money at the end of each week. It was a straightforward affair to balance the books and she wished she could do them for the business as well. Whenever she asked William about it, he dismissed her questions and she was beginning to think he'd gone back on his promise to learn everything about the company. When they sat by the fire on Sunday afternoon, she decided it was a good time to ask him.

"William, do you remember last year when you promised to find out everything about the business? I haven't seen much of it happening."

"Well, you won't when you're at home, but I am learning more."

"Are you sure? From what I can see, he doesn't treat you much like a partner. You're always getting pushed out. I didn't say anything at the time, but did you see him with William Junior at Clara's wedding?"

"What about it?"

"They're as thick as thieves. I overheard them talking and he treats him more as a business partner than you. Does he ever consult you about decision-making?"

William shifted in his chair. "Occasionally. He hasn't lately but I don't suppose there's been much to discuss."

"What do you mean, 'I don't suppose'? You should know. You should talk to him every week about the orders, find out where the business is coming from, whether the number of employees is right, that sort of thing. He's supposed to be teaching you. Do you ever talk to him about that?"

William studied his hands. "Sometimes."

"That's what I thought. Mr Wetherby spends most of his time in Birmingham with William Junior, while you're left up here, more like a foreman."

"Your uncle was based in Handsworth and I've taken on his role. It's right that Mr Wetherby works mainly with his business and I stay with mine."

"But the other week when he laid off those men in Handsworth, did you know anything about it beforehand or was the first you heard of it when he told you to sack them?"

"That was different." William stood up and paced the room. "We had an order cancelled and we didn't need them. It all happened quickly, there was no time to ask my opinion."

"But it should have been your decision to make, not his. You should have been the first to hear about the cancellation not him. How did he know you didn't have something else for them to do?"

William opened his mouth to speak, but was distracted when a thought occurred to him. "How did you know we laid off those men? I didn't tell you."

"I heard them talking about it at the wedding ... amongst other things. They were discussing the future of the business and the direction they should be taking. I got the distinct impression it was William Junior who said you should do the firing. The pompous little ..."

"Harriet, stop. He is my brother and like it or not he's Mr Wetherby's son. Unfortunately, I'm not."

Harriet sighed. "That's not the point. The point is, half the business is yours by rights and they're taking it from you. You need to remind him of that."

"I'll speak to Mr Wetherby next time I see him, ask him if there's anything I need to know."

"You need to be more forceful. Tell him you want a meeting with him once a week."

William flinched. "Once a week? There's no need for that. Leave it with me. I'll speak to him on Sunday when we go to Wetherby House for dinner."

"Make sure that you do." Harriet's eyes twinkled as she spoke. "Don't forget I'll be watching and listening to everything that goes on."

William kissed the top of her head. "No surprise there then."

Chapter 55

ALTHOUGH CHRISTMAS WAS APPROACHING, THE winter was harsh for the time of year and Mary pulled her coat tight around her as she walked the short distance to Susannah's house. Since Alice had agreed to move to Handsworth it had become a daily ritual. When she arrived, the door was unlocked and she went straight to the back room where Susannah sat knitting.

"All on your own?" She took off her coat and draped it over the back of a chair. "Where's Alice?"

"In bed. She's been bad today; she could barely move when she tried to get out of bed this morning."

"Did you call the doctor?"

"I don't think there's any point. What can he do for her now? He was here the other day and told me not to give her too much meat and told her to stay off the gin. As you can imagine, it didn't go down well. She said that if she were in pain, she'd rather do it with a cup of gin by her side. At least then it would be bearable."

"I don't like this," Mary said. "She's got worse over the last few days, and she's so swollen. Let me go and see her and if she's no better I'm calling the doctor whether she likes it or not."

Once upstairs, Mary knocked on the door. When she got no reply she pushed the door and found Alice lying on the bed groaning and dripping with perspiration.

Mary hurried to the side of the bed and crouched down, taking hold of Alice's hand. "Oh my, you look terrible. What's the matter?" Alice didn't answer for a long while but after several minutes she gave Mary a faint smile.

"Thank you, you know how to make someone feel better. Fortunately, I think the worst of it's passed. I've been feeling terrible all day. The pain in my back was excruciating, but suddenly it's gone. The sharp pain has anyway; it still feels like I've been punched repeatedly in the back. I'm just exhausted. Can you help me sit up?"

Mary put some pillows behind her back and soaked a cloth in the water basin to wipe her face. Gradually the colour returned to her cheeks and she stopped perspiring.

"I've no idea what that was, but I hope I never have to go through it again. It was like being stabbed in the back and the knife twisted. I couldn't even face my gin, although I could manage a bit now if you wouldn't mind pouring it."

"Susannah told me the doctor said no more gin. It might be what's making you ill."

"What do doctors know? It's the only pleasure I have in life and he wants to take it away. I might listen if I stopped swelling up like this, but it makes no difference."

Mary stood up and poured gin into two glasses. "All I can say is it's a good job you moved to Handsworth. When you're not ill it's company for Susannah too."

"Aren't you lonely in that house of yours with Mr Wetherby away for most of the week?"

"Not really." Mary thought about it. "You and Susannah are here, and I see a lot of Mary-Ann and Harriet. Emily and Cook look after me and I have visitors in the afternoons as well."

"Do you see much of Sarah-Ann nowadays?"

"No, but she writes about three times a week. There seems to be a truce between her and Mr Flemming."

"Is she happy, do you think?"

Mary sighed. "I like to think so, but I don't know. Mr Flemming won't let me visit and he stops her going further than the local shops."

"How can he do that when he's at work all day?"

"He has people watching out for her. If they see her leave the street, they tell him."

"How terrible. To think I was so envious of her when she came to Birmingham and found a husband straight away. Do you think the courtship was too quick?"

Mary shrugged. "Things changed when she lost the baby. Neither of them will admit it, but they blame each other. At least they have Elizabeth."

As Mary was talking, tears started to roll down Alice's face. "What's the matter? Are you in pain again?"

"No, but look at the state of me; I'm like an old woman. Sarah-Ann's only a couple of years younger than us, yet she's still so beautiful with those dusky eyes and skin like porcelain."

"You can't compare yourself to Sarah-Ann when you're ill."

"But look at you as well. You're so elegant and stylish; no one would think we're twins."

"Nobody will see you as you are except me and Susannah. Once you're well again …"

"I'm not going to get well again." Alice was sobbing now. "My whole life will have been a total waste."

"Come on now, don't be silly."

"I'm not being silly. When I think of all the trouble I've caused I think it would have been better if I hadn't been born."

Mary thought of the trouble Alice had caused her, as well as their brother and sister, years earlier. "Are you talking about John and Katharine?"

Alice nodded. "And you. I'm sorry."

ço√

Harriet set down her pen and turned back to the previous pages in her ledger. William hadn't been paid as much as usual, which meant they had spent all but their last penny this week. She wanted to buy William-Wetherby and Eleanor new winter coats but she wasn't going to have enough. William might not like talking about money. She would have to ask him about it.

As soon as he arrived home he walked to the fire to warm his hands.

"It's getting cold out there," he said. "It wouldn't surprise me if there's a frost tonight."

"I hope you're wrong; we're not ready for cold weather yet."

"What do you mean we're not ready?" William went and sat with her at the table.

"William-Wetherby and Eleanor need new coats but we haven't got enough money."

"Why not? What have you been buying?"

"Nothing I shouldn't but Mr Wetherby hasn't paid you as much money this week."

"Are you sure?" William raised his eyebrow at her.

"Yes, I double-checked." Harriet turned back through the pages of the ledger to show him the entries. "I'm wondering if the business is in trouble. I read in the paper the other week about how prices are dropping and businesses are struggling."

"He hasn't said anything if he is," William said.

"That's what bothers me. If he's having problems, you should know about it. He has no right to take significant decisions without talking to you first."

"To be fair, he's always in Birmingham and I haven't seen him for a few weeks."

"Stop making excuses for him." Harriet stood up and paced the room. "You can't let him get away with this type of behaviour. He should treat you with more respect. Besides, he comes to Handsworth every Saturday and Sunday. He should have the decency to come and see you if he needs to."

"What can I add to the discussion? He's been running a business for thirty years."

"You'll never learn if he doesn't speak to you. It was part of the deal that he'd teach you. Since he's got his hands on my uncle's business he's conveniently forgotten his side of the bargain."

William sighed. "He's busy."

"I bet William Junior knew about it," Harriet added with a flourish. "In fact it was probably him who suggested the pay cut in the first place. I don't suppose for one minute it applies to him though. I've never known anyone spend money like he does. You will speak to Mr Wetherby, won't you?"

"I suppose so. I'll call around on Saturday once he's home."

"And remember, it's so I can buy coats for the children. Ask him if he'd like to see them walking the streets like paupers?"

Chapter 56

As Mr Wetherby was home so infrequently, Mary liked to change into her finer clothes, re-powder her face and apply a little rose water before he arrived. Whether he noticed, she had no idea, but it made her feel better. With it being Saturday she had gone upstairs early to get herself ready, but as she was fastening her necklace she heard the dogs barking and the front door bang. She reached for her earrings and clasped them to her ears before she hurried downstairs.

As she reached the bottom of the stairs, the maid was leaving the back room. "Is Mr Wetherby home?"

"No, it's Mr Jackson. He's waiting for you."

Relieved she hadn't misjudged the time, Mary checked her reflection in the hall mirror before she went in to see her son.

"William, what a lovely surprise. I wasn't expecting you."

"I want a word with Mr Wetherby and so I thought I'd call and see you first. I presume he isn't back yet?"

"Not yet, but he shouldn't be long. Is there a problem?"

"I just need to ask him about the business. I don't have many opportunities to meet with him these days."

"No, I'd noticed. You'd think he had enough to do at work without sitting on all these council committees."

"Does William Junior go to the council meetings with him?"

"I don't think so. From what I can tell, he's not the slightest bit interested. He's more bothered about finding a wife. He goes to great expense to be at the right places. I don't know where he gets his money from."

"He does live the good life. I must have done something wrong."

"Things are different for you, you have a wife and four children; he only has himself to think of. I'm sure his days of prudence will come."

"You're right, but it's hard when you can't provide winter coats for your children."

Mary cocked her head and frowned at him. "Things can't be that bad."

"Harriet's gone over the figures and …"

"Harriet's done the figures? She must have made a mistake."

"No, I don't think … look, can you forget I mentioned Harriet. I know the figures as well as she does and they're right. In fact, can we forget we had this conversation? I'll call back and see Mr Wetherby some other time."

He was about to leave when Mr Wetherby and William Junior arrived home.

"They're here now," Mary said. "You might as well stay."

"Please, Mother, no mention of Harriet and I'd like to talk to Mr Wetherby in private if I can."

Mr Wetherby walked over to the fire and rubbed his

hands. "I didn't expect to see you here," he said to William. "Have you got a problem?"

"I wondered if we could have a word … in private?"

"You can say what you like here. We're all family and I'd like to have a cup of tea by the fire. It's jolly cold travelling from Birmingham at this time of year."

"With respect, I'd like to talk about our business and I don't think it's a conversation we should burden Mother with."

"Well, if we go into the other room, you'll have to make it quick. The fire won't be made up. William Junior, are you coming?"

"Please, don't trouble William Junior." William turned to his brother for support.

"It's no trouble," William Junior said, smiling at William's discomfort.

William had never been angry with Mr Wetherby before, but watching William Junior saunter to the door provoked something within him.

"No, please. Can't I talk to Mr Wetherby on my own without William Junior always being present? We're supposed to be partners in a business but I don't remember the last time we sat down together. It's like I don't exist, being kept up here while the two of you make all the decisions in Birmingham. Has William Junior become a partner in the business without my knowledge?" William looked around the room, shocked by his own outburst, before his eyes settled on his mother.

"William Junior, come into the other room with me so Father can stay by the fire and talk to William." Mary stood up and took William Junior by the elbow. He was about to object when Mr Wetherby spoke.

"That would be helpful." He gave William Junior a look that left him in no doubt he should do as his mother suggested.

"That was quite an outburst," Mr Wetherby said when the two of them were alone. "I didn't think you had it in you. It's reassuring to see you have some passion. Now, what can I do for you?"

"I'm concerned I'm nothing more in this business than your local foreman in Handsworth. When Mr Watkins passed his business to me, I thought the agreement was for the two firms to merge and for us to work as partners, but it's not working like that. I rarely see you alone and I'm not aware of a lot of decisions being taken."

"As I recall you didn't want to be bothered with the business. I thought the only reason you accepted the company was because I'd run it."

"I wanted you to take charge because I had no experience of the office side of things, but I wanted to learn. Now I'm pushed out of everything by William Junior. I expect he knows more about what's going on than I do."

"If only that were true." Mr Wetherby let out a long sigh. "I try to teach him, obviously. He's my son and one day I hope all this will be his, but he's only interested in spending my money. I have to say I've been disappointed in both of you, thinking neither of you were interested."

"I didn't mean to give you that impression. Will you teach me?"

"I'll have to think about how to do it. It will be difficult with you in Handsworth and me in Birmingham and I can't leave William Junior on his own for too long. You'll have to come to Birmingham for one or two days a week, but that means we'll have to work out how we manage here. I'll get back to you." Mr Wetherby took out his pocket watch. "Do you want to tell your mother she can come back in?"

"Before I go, there was something else. It might be a mistake, but I didn't receive my usual wages this week. Do you know anything about it?"

"Ah, that. I wondered if you'd notice."

"Of course I noticed. Harriet was hoping to buy new coats for the children, but there isn't enough money left."

"Surely you don't spend all your money every week? You should have some tucked away for bigger items. I used to manage on much less when I was your age."

"We do have four children to look after. Is the business in difficulty?"

Mr Wetherby paused before speaking. "I didn't want to worry you. It should only be temporary."

A look of concern crossed William's face. "How long's temporary? We should have spoken about this. Have you reduced everyone else's wages?"

"I don't know how long, but these things generally work themselves out."

"I'd like to see the books. I need to understand what's going on. Have the orders dried up?"

"No, we still have orders, but I've had to reduce the prices to compete. It's affecting everyone, not only us. I'll tell you what, how much do new coats cost? I'll buy them for you; that way it'll make up for the wages. I'll try and sort something out for next week."

"Don't you need to reduce the costs of production rather than cutting wages?"

"Cutting wages does reduce the cost of production."

William took a deep breath. "I didn't mean that. What I meant was, shouldn't you be looking to reduce your costs on raw materials and processes to make the business more efficient. It might mean you need fewer workers, but at least those you let go will be able to find other jobs."

"There might not be any other jobs. Haven't you noticed businesses closing? Another two have folded this year; there are only about a dozen of us making hooks and eyes now."

"But less competition must be good."

"It would be under normal circumstances, but not at the moment."

William was out of his depth. He needed to be briefed before he spoke to Mr Wetherby but Harriet hadn't mentioned anything about this.

"Look at the time," William said as he glanced at the grandfather clock. "I must be going. Will you let me know when we can have a proper discussion about the business?"

Mr Wetherby nodded as William opened the door to the hall and almost bumped into his mother.

"Sorry I've been so long, but I'm going now." He bent down to kiss her on the cheek. "I'll see you soon."

"Did Mr Wetherby give you any money for the coats?" she asked. William looked at her in surprise. "I thought not." Mary walked into the back room and stood in front of Mr Wetherby. "Were you going to give William some money?"

Mr Wetherby was about to speak, but a look from Mary made him stop and put his hand in his pocket. "Will this be enough?" he said as he gave William two crown coins.

Chapter 57

HARRIET POUNDED THE PASTRY SHE was making as if it was dough. She would have been better making bread but she was behind in her schedule and needed to make more mince pies for Christmas. How she'd kept her temper with Charles she didn't know. She had walked into the living room at precisely the moment Charles tried to wash his young sister in boiling water. He was now locked in his room and Harriet wondered how long she could keep him there.

As she rolled out the pastry, there was a knock on the front door and Mary let herself in.

Harriet stopped her rolling. "What brings you here?"

"I wanted a word," Mary said. "I'm afraid we won't be able to host the party on Christmas night."

"Why not?"

"It's Alice. She's looking worse by the day. She's in a lot of pain and swollen up to such an extent she can barely walk. Susannah thinks that by Christmas she'll be completely bedbound and we can't leave her on her own. Susannah's asked us to join them for the day."

Creases formed on Harriet's forehead. "What a shame."

"The thing is," Mary continued, "if I'm out for dinner,

I won't have time to get home and do the evening. Would you mind hosting everyone?"

Harriet hesitated. "I don't mind, but … how many will there be?"

"Well, all the family in Handsworth, so myself with Mr Wetherby, William Junior and Charlotte; Susannah with Clara and her husband; Amelia and her family; and Mary-Ann and Mr Diver with little Rose and Daisy." Mary counted them on her fingers. "About twenty-one. Is that a problem?"

"Will Mary-Ann and Mr Diver join us, given she's so close to giving birth again?"

"She wants to. It will depend on how she feels on the day, but we can't exclude them."

Harriet's brow creased. "I'd like to say yes, but this house is so small compared to yours."

Mary looked around. "I suppose it is, but nearly half of those coming will be small children."

"It's not only the space." Harriet wiped her hands on her apron to delay answering. "William hasn't been bringing home as much money as he used to and we're finding it difficult to make ends meet. I'm trying to cut back as much as I can, but I won't have enough money to put on a decent spread for that number of people."

"Oh my dear, don't worry about that," Mary said. "I'll provide the food, but what's this about William? How long's it been going on?"

"Several weeks now. William's spoken to Mr Wetherby, but nothing's changed. He got some money to buy coats for the children, but his wage hasn't increased."

"Leave it with me," Mary said. "I'll talk to Mr Wetherby

and find out what's going on. I'm not going to stand by and have my son disgraced."

Harriet stood and smiled at all the food laid out before her. She had had deliveries from the butcher and grocer in the last hour and was struggling to find places to put everything. William arrived home from work as she was clearing a space in the pantry.

"Good grief, where did all this come from?" He placed his hat on the table and took off his coat.

Harriet flashed him a broad grin. "Your mother. She said she'd provide the food for Christmas night, and this is what's arrived so far. I'm expecting the baker tomorrow morning as well. Goodness knows how much she's spent."

"She's been up to something." William took a handful of crown coins from his pocket.

"Where did you get that from?" Harriet's eyes were wide with disbelief.

"It's the money I should have been paid. Mr Wetherby said my pay cut was a mistake."

"A mistake? The only mistake was that your mother found out about it, I shouldn't wonder. What a relief though. It's been horrible these last few weeks." She went to the cupboard and brought out her tin. It was empty. "You can put it in here. The bills are paid for this week but we need to keep some aside in case he tries any tricks again. We can't trust him."

William dropped the coins into the tin. "Of course we can trust him. He won't do it again."

"We'll see," Harriet said. "Now, go and sit down, I need

to get on. I've still got to find somewhere to put all this food."

As Christmas Day dawned, Charles was in a particularly good mood and Harriet allowed herself a couple of glasses of sherry once they returned from church. The Christmas dinner of goose with roasted vegetables had been cooking for most of the morning and there was just time to hand out the presents before she needed to tidy up and prepare for the evening.

At five o'clock with everything ready, Harriet poured herself a glass of mulled wine and sat down to wait for her guests.

"I don't know how everyone's going to fit in here," she said as William sat down opposite her. "Trust it to be the last of the moon too. We can't even send the children outside."

"Stop worrying. The children are happy enough upstairs at the moment and their cousins can join them when they arrive."

"They can't eat upstairs. I'm going to have to do three sittings for tea. In the New Year, we need to find a bigger house."

"Now you're being ridiculous. Only yesterday we had no money. Where do you think we'd get the money to rent anywhere bigger?"

Harriet shrugged. "We need to work on your mother. I'm sure Mr Wetherby gives William Junior a lot more than he gives you."

"You don't know that."

"Not for certain, but look at the clothes he wears. He has his suits made in London. You couldn't do that."

"He doesn't have a wife and four children to take care of."

"That's beside the point. If we can persuade your mother that he earns more than you, she won't let it pass. She likes you a lot more than she likes him."

William shook his head. "Where do you get these ideas from?"

"I can tell these things." Harriet gave William a look to suggest it was as well not arguing. "And you know I'm right."

By ten o'clock with the guests gone and the children in bed, Harriet sat by the fire again, this time with a glass of port.

"You were wonderful today," William said as he came down the stairs. "I wish we could entertain more often."

"We'll definitely need a bigger house if we do."

William shook his head. "I spoke to Mr Wetherby while he was here. It's all confirmed, in the New Year I'm going to work in Birmingham for a couple of days a week. He said he's going to give me a large pay rise too. I didn't need to ask."

"Praise the Lord." Harriet raised her glass. "Your mother's wonderful. I don't know what she said, but she's about the only person Mr Wetherby listens to. Heaven help us if anything happens to her."

"Don't talk like that." William's face grew stern. "I know you didn't mean anything by it, but I thought she looked tired today."

"She's probably just worried about your Aunt Alice."

"Maybe, but they are the same age. What if she's ill?"

"If she's ill, Mr Wetherby will make sure she gets the best treatment possible. She's in a lot better position than your Aunt Alice."

William nodded. "You're right of course, but I can't bear the thought of anything happening to her."

Harriet chose her next words carefully. "As much as it pains you to talk about it, you do need to think about the time when she might not be around. Mr Wetherby might be different without her to keep him under control."

William rested his head on the back of the chair and closed his eyes. "Do we have to talk about this now? It's Christmas night."

"I don't want to be morbid, but you need to think about the future." Harriet took a deep breath. "Your mother won't live forever. You need to be prepared in case she dies before Mr Wetherby and he starts his tricks again … or even worse, William Junior does."

William opened his eyes. "He wouldn't do that."

"I'd hope not, but you never know. Wouldn't it be better if you were running your own company by then rather than relying on him? After everything he's done these last few weeks, I don't trust him, and I certainly wouldn't trust William Junior if he were in charge."

"You worry too much. We're in the middle of an economic downturn; that's why things have been hard. He wouldn't have cut my wages otherwise."

"But how can you be sure something like this won't happen again? You've no idea what will happen in five or ten years' time." Harriet finished her glass of port. "If you set up your own business and your mother lives for another twenty years, you won't have lost anything … but if she doesn't, at least we'll be able to take care of ourselves."

Chapter 58

MARY CAME DOWNSTAIRS AND LOOKED at the clock in the back room. Not yet half past nine, too early for church. She sat by the fire to wait for the rest of the family, but immediately stood up again and went for her coat. She needed to see Susannah. She didn't know why; she'd seen her every day for the last fortnight, and she wouldn't be expected.

When she reached her sister's house, Susannah opened the door before she had a chance to knock.

"I'm glad you're here," she said. "I was about to come for you. Alice is in a bad way. I don't think she's got long left."

Mary pushed past her sister and ran up the stairs, only slowing as she reached the bedroom door. She knocked and went in. With the curtains drawn, the light in the room was dim but Mary could see the shape of Alice lying on the bed.

"Alice," she said as she went over to her.

Alice's eyes flickered open and she squeezed the hand Mary offered her.

"Thank you for coming."

"Don't speak; save your energy," Mary said. "I'll sit with you before I go to church."

Alice wiped the side of her face on the pillow as tears trickled from her eyes.

"Are you in pain?" Mary asked.

Alice shook her head.

"What's the matter then?"

Alice remained silent and Mary waited as she squeezed her eyes together as if trying to hold back the tears. After a moment Alice took a deep breath.

"I have to tell you this ... I'm sorry, I should have told you years ago." A sob left Alice's lips. "I never meant to hurt you. I need your forgiveness before I die."

Mary pulled her hand away and stood up as Alice shook her head again.

"I'm sorry. So, so sorry." Alice repeated the words again and again as she sobbed into the pillow.

Mary straightened up and stared at her sister. "You told Father, didn't you?"

"Please say you'll forgive me. I never meant for you to be banished, really I didn't."

Mary walked from the bed as a chill ran through her body. Why was she surprised? It was what she'd suspected, but Alice had always denied it. What now? How did she respond? Her mind was numb, fixed on the scene over thirty-five years ago when her father had found her lying with Charles.

"I only wanted Father to stop you seeing Charles," Alice continued. "You were my best friend and he'd stolen you from me."

Mary turned back to face her sister. "He'd stolen me? You didn't want him for yourself?"

"No." Alice reached out her hand to Mary. "I wanted

you. I didn't want him to take you from me. I ended up losing everything the day you left. Please say you'll forgive me."

The hatred in Mary's eyes was unmistakable. "You lost everything. You ruined my life because you didn't want me to be with Charles. You even smiled as Father threw me out."

"I didn't smile … honestly I didn't. I just thought it would make you change your mind." Alice closed her eyes to avoid Mary's glare. "I didn't think you'd go."

Mary couldn't speak. Her whole life had been shaped by that one act of treachery. Charles's arrest and imprisonment may even have been what killed him. Looking back, he'd never recovered from it.

"You killed him," Mary's voice hissed as she walked back to the bed.

Alice opened her eyes wide. "I didn't … you know I didn't. It was consumption. I couldn't help that."

"If it hadn't been for you he might still be alive today."

Alice put her hands to her face. "You can't say that … please don't think it. I didn't mean to upset you. I just want your forgiveness before it's too late."

Mary studied the pitiful face of her sister, her heart pounding. Why had she ever believed her? Why had she accepted her back into her life, when deep down she'd known what she'd done? It was a long time before she spoke. "You disgust me. Not only did you ruin my life, but you've lied about it ever since. You want forgiveness? Well, may God forgive you, because as sure as I'm standing here, I never will." Mary turned and looked at Susannah who was standing unnoticed by the door. "I need to go. I'll let myself out."

☙❧

It was turned four o'clock when Emily opened the front door to Susannah. She showed her into the back room where Mary sat with Mr Wetherby.

"She's gone," Susannah said when Mary glanced up.

Mary gestured for Susannah to sit down but said nothing.

"I can't stay long. I've asked one of the local boys to fetch the doctor. He won't be long."

Mr Wetherby put his newspaper on his knee and looked at Mary. "Aren't you going to say anything?"

"What is there to say?" Mary continued with her embroidery.

"Your twin sister has just died. I'd have thought you might show a little emotion. What's up with you? You've been in a strange mood all day."

Mary shrugged. "She's been ill for months. It's not a surprise."

"Maybe not, but I'd expect a bit more of a response. Don't you want to go and see her? It's the least you should do."

"We'll see her before the funeral. There's no rush."

Mr Wetherby looked at Susannah and then back to Mary before he stood up. "You can't leave Susannah to do everything. I know you're upset, but let me get your coat. I'll come with you."

When they reached the bedroom, it was dark except for the light of a small candle situated near the top of the bed. Susannah went into the room, while Mary and Mr Wetherby remained by the door. Staring in disgust at the disfigured shape of her sister, Mary didn't move when Mr Wetherby put his arm around her shoulders.

"I wish she'd had a better life," Susannah said, wiping her eyes with a handkerchief. "All she ever wanted was a husband and a family."

"She got the life she deserved," Mary said.

Mr Wetherby removed his arm and turned to her. "You can't mean that?"

Mary said nothing as her stare remained fixed on her sister.

"The least we can do is make sure she isn't on her own any longer," he continued. "I think she should take the first place in the family grave."

"No." Mary's voice was a higher pitch than it should have been. "I mean … we won't all fit in it as it is. I want my children with me."

"William will need his own plot the number of children he has, Mr Diver too. We won't all fit into this one. I'd have thought you'd be pleased."

Mary bowed her head. What could she say? Mr Wetherby must never know what happened all those years ago. Not now. Not ever.

～

Four days later, William squeezed his mother's hand before he stood up and fell into line behind his aunt's coffin as it left the church. The men made their way up the hill to a plot alongside the north wall of the churchyard. The gathering was pitiful. Besides himself, there was only his mother's brother John; Mr Wetherby and William Junior. With the birth of Mary-Ann's baby imminent, even Mr Diver had stayed away. Several neighbours stood behind them, but they were present for Mr Wetherby's benefit rather than Alice's. It was a bitterly cold day and William stood by the grave with his head bowed and hands clasped in front of him, in much the same way as everyone else. The rector read the words committing the body to the ground and quickly brought the proceedings to a close.

"We'll all be here one day," Mr Wetherby said as they made their way back to the church. "You might want to consider buying a plot for your family, William."

"I'm sure we don't need to do it yet."

"If you don't do it soon, all the best positions will be taken. My plot holds seven. You'll need one about the same size, although I don't suppose that wife of yours will want to be buried here."

"Is she a dissenter?" John asked, raising his eyebrow.

"It's a long story," William said. "At the moment, Harriet insists we go to the Congregational Church, but I wouldn't go so far as to say she wouldn't want to be buried here. I'd like her to be buried here, but whether she'd agree to buy a plot I'm not sure. She'd like a bigger house first."

"You need to do both. What is it with you that you take so much notice of what she thinks," Mr Wetherby said. "You should just tell her what you're doing."

"There are ways of dealing with Harriet and that is not one of them. I'll speak to her, but at least when we come to organise her funeral, she won't be able to argue with me."

৵৵

Harriet was waiting by the church door when William returned; her cloak pulled tightly around her.

"Where's Mother?" William asked. "I thought she'd be with you."

"Aunt Susannah's just told me she wanted to get back to Charlotte," Harriet said.

"Isn't she going to the wake?" William turned to Mr Wetherby as he joined their group. "Do you know why Mother would have gone home?"

"Don't ask me. I've no idea what she's doing. I've not had a sensible word from her since Sunday."

Harriet thought for a moment. "Actually, Mr Wetherby, didn't I hear you say earlier that Charlotte had gone to stay with one of your sisters for the day?"

"Yes, I took her to Amelia's earlier. Why?"

Harriet looked back to William. "There's something wrong here. She wouldn't have walked all the way there on her own. Did she leave in a carriage?"

William walked to the edge of the churchyard and peered over the wall. "The carriages we came in are still here."

"What's going on?" Mr Wetherby said. "Who wouldn't have walked where?"

"Mother," William said. "She's either gone home to an empty house, walked to Aunt Amelia's or she was lying to Aunt Susannah."

"Why on earth would she do that?" Mr Wetherby grasped the significance of the conversation. "William, you take my carriage and go to Amelia's. I'll walk back to Wetherby House and see if she's there. If you find her, take her to the wake. I'll meet you there. Harriet you go directly to the tavern and pray she's with her sisters. If she is, make sure you keep her there until I arrive."

When Harriet arrived at the Grove Tavern, William Junior was the only member of the funeral party who was not a Chadwick.

"Where've you been?" he asked Harriet.

"Your mother's gone off by herself and we don't know where she is. Mr Wetherby and William have gone to find her."

"How did that happen?" William Junior glared across the table to his mother's sisters. When none of them spoke, he stood up and went to the bar.

It was another half an hour before William arrived at the tavern and sat next to Harriet. Several minutes later, Mr Wetherby joined them but there was no sign of Mary.

"What do we do now?" William said. "Where else can we look?"

Mr Wetherby took the glass of ale Mary's brother John offered him. "I was beginning to think you weren't coming," John said. "It's a poor send-off as it is, without you all going missing."

"Have you seen Mary since we came back from the grave?"

"No, I was with you."

"What about Susannah, Katharine or your wife? They must have seen her." Mr Wetherby stared at the women sitting around the adjacent table.

"Do any of you know where my wife is?" he asked as he leaned across the table. Susannah's cheeks coloured when Mr Wetherby looked directly at her.

"Where is she?" Mr Wetherby's voice was getting louder.

Susannah put her napkin to her mouth. "I don't know. She was upset and said she couldn't stay in church. I thought she'd just stepped outside for some air."

"She's spent a lot of time with you recently. You must have some idea where she might have gone?"

Susannah sighed. "Why don't you have something to eat? We shouldn't let the food go to waste. I'm sure she'll be back when she's ready."

Mr Wetherby glared at William Junior as he bit into another pie. "How can we eat at a time like this? Your mother's not been herself for days, and now she's disappeared. Don't you want to know where she is?"

"Of course." William Junior spoke with his mouth full. "But Aunt Susannah's right ..."

"Mr Wetherby, please, calm down," Susannah said. "I'm sure Mary's fine but she wanted to be alone. I have an idea where she might be, but give her some time. Once we've finished here, I'll tell you where I think she is."

Chapter 59

Birmingham, Warwickshire.

MARY STARED OUT OF THE window of the carriage as it turned into Bull Street. Not far to go now. She took a half-crown coin from her bag, and wrapped it in a small slip of paper, ready to pass to the driver.

As the carriage came to a stop, the driver jumped down from his seat and held the door open for her.

"Speak to no one else about this," Mary said as she passed him the small package. "And please be as quick as you can."

Once the carriage pulled away, Mary glanced up and down the street before she walked into the burial ground. She knew where she was going and was relieved there was nobody around to offer her directions.

She saw no one as she walked to the grave and as soon as she found the spot, she knelt down and bowed her head. She hadn't cried since Alice's death, but now years of emotion poured from her. Tears for the life she had lost, tears for the deception Alice had hidden for so long and, for the first time, tears of guilt. Had it not been for her, Charles may well still be alive. Had she not succumbed to his charms, to his touch, to those eyes. If she hadn't told Alice of her hopes for the future, none of this would have happened. As the sobbing consumed her energy, she let herself fall to the ground, her right arm reaching out to caress the grave.

Whether she lay there for minutes or hours, she had no idea, but she was shaken from her grief by a hand pulling on her shoulder.

"Mary, what on earth's the matter?" Richard knelt beside her and lifted her up to cradle her in his arms. "Why are you wearing mourning clothes? What's happened?"

Mary shook her head as she clung to him, her tears still falling. "It's Alice."

A frown crossed Richard's face. "I'm sorry. I guess you cared for her more than you realised. Why did you come here though?"

"If he'd never met me, he might still be alive." She accepted the handkerchief Richard offered her. "I wouldn't have made Alice jealous."

"I think we're going to have to take this more slowly. I've no idea what you're talking about."

He allowed Mary to regain her composure before he coaxed the information from her.

"So what will you do now?"

"Did you ask the coach driver to wait for us?"

Richard nodded.

"I want to go to Frankfort Street. I need to remove every trace of her from this earth."

"Are you sure? You're not thinking rationally. Why don't you wait?"

"I need to do it. I don't want it hanging over me. Will you come with me?"

"Of course I will. I'm not letting you go alone. Take some deep breaths and calm down, then we'll go."

It took several minutes before she was ready to move, and once they were inside the carriage, Richard lifted Mary's hand to his lips and kissed it tenderly. "You can't blame yourself. Falling in love isn't a crime. Jealousy's the sin here and Alice is the guilty one. Not you."

Mary smiled. "Thank you for always being here for me. I don't know what I'd do without you."

Richard's face hardened. "I'd have been around more if we'd been allowed to marry each other. Please don't think it was easy for me to walk away from you. I wanted you so much."

"Really? I thought you'd been happy enough with Mrs Richard."

"Happy enough, but not as happy as I would have been with you."

Mary shook her head as a tingle ran through her body. "I can only say that Alice got what she deserved."

Five minutes later, the carriage pulled up outside Alice's house on Frankfort Street.

"I won't be able to call and put flowers in the window anymore." Mary gave Richard a sad smile.

"We'll find a way. With Mr Wetherby in Birmingham so often, I'm sure I could find my way to Handsworth once or twice a week."

The sadness disappeared from Mary's eyes. "I'd like that. Not to the house of course. I'll have to find somewhere more suitable for us to meet."

"We've got time to think about it. Come on; let's get into the house before we have everyone looking at us. I'll let the carriage go. We can find another one later."

While Richard paid the driver, Mary opened the front door with the key she'd taken from Alice's room in Handsworth. A moment later he followed her into the house. Once they knew they were alone, he took her in his arms. Mary melted into his embrace as he kissed her in a way she hadn't been kissed for years.

"Thank you for meeting me today," she said. "I was worried you might be out or that Mrs Richard would have opened the door to the driver."

Richard smiled. "I'll always be here for you."

He kissed her again before he took her hand and led her up the stairs to Alice's room. Mary offered no resistance as he shut the door behind them, unaware that a carriage, pulled by two chestnut horses, had just arrived outside the house.

The Next Instalment...

Part 3: *When Time Runs Out*

As tensions within the family grow, Harriet's refusal to be silenced could be the undoing of them all...

Harriet won't stand by while her family's inheritance slips through their fingers. Her uncle worked hard to build a stable business before he passed it to her husband William. But when her stepfather-in-law, Mr. Wetherby, presumes ownership of the company, Harriet fights to stand her ground...

William longs for a quiet life, but with a growing family and Harriet's determination to succeed, he stretches himself beyond his means. When Mr. Wetherby refuses to help, only the intervention of William's mother Mary keeps their dream of a better future in reach...

After a tragic twist of fate, collaborating with Mr. Wetherby becomes impossible, and Harriet and William must somehow carve out a living without him. But as tensions in the family business escalate, Harriet may have far more to worry about than pursuing her own ambitions...

When Time Runs Out is the third book in The *Ambition & Destiny* Series. If you like family sagas and accurate historical depictions, you'll love the third book in this captivating series.

GOLD Quality Mark
"This is a beautifully written and edited book ... a continuation of a series that has been a delight throughout."
BooksGoSocial

To read *When Time Runs Out* visit:
http://mybook.to/WTRO

Further Books
The *Ambition & Destiny* Series

Part 4: *Only One Winner*
A prosperous father. A headstrong son. One woman
caught in the middle.

ৎ৵৶

Part 5: *Different World*
As William-Wetherby seeks a new life, revenge is the
only thing on his mind...

ৎ৵৶

To find details of availability visit
http://Author.to/VLMcBeath

Thank you for reading
Less Than Equals.
I hope you enjoyed it.

If you did, I'd be delighted if you'd share your
thoughts and leave a review here.
myBook.to/LTEAMZ

It will be much appreciated.

I'd love to keep in touch with you!

I send out regular monthly newsletters with
details of new releases and special offers.

By signing up for the newsletter you'll also
get a FREE digital copy of *Condemned by
Fate*.

To get your copy and keep in touch,
visit: **vlmcbeath.com**

Author's Note and Acknowledgements

Writing *Less Than Equals* has taken me on quite an unexpected journey. In the recesses of our minds, I imagine most of us realise that Victorian women had lives that were much more difficult than ours, but in telling Harriet's story, it brought the understanding to a whole new level.

As mentioned in the Legal Notes, all characterisation in the series is fictitious, but a lot of the events in this book (and in Part 3: *When Time Runs Out*) relating to Harriet did actually happen. Why they happened is the part of the story I will never know for certain. My gut feeling, from snippets I've picked up while researching the story, is that Harriet was an intelligent woman. I imagine, however, that in the mid-1800's this was more of a hindrance than a help to her general well-being, and something she paid the price for. Many times while writing the book, it crossed my mind that had I been born then, I don't know how I would have survived. In my opinion, it goes to show that even though full equality between men and women is still a way off, if we look back in time, we can see how far we've come. Probably a lot further than most people imagine.

As with all the other books in the series, I couldn't have

finished this work on my own, and I would like to thank my family and friends for the support they have provided along the way. In particular, I would like to thank my daughters Emma and Sarah; my mum and dad, Marg and Terry; brother-in-law Dave, and friends Marie and Rachel for taking the time to read various drafts of the book and either give me words of encouragement or valuable insights into how it could be improved.

I must also thank Wendy Janes and Susan Buchanan for their wonderful editorial feedback and proofreading. I am continuing to learn and hope that with each book that appears, life will get a little easier for all of us.

Once again I must give special mention to my husband, Stuart. He now seems to have embraced the role of chief reviewer, even on occasions turning off the TV so he can read the books! With the release of *Less Than Equals* he can now go back to his films, but not for too long. I'm hoping Part 3 of the series, *When Time Runs Out*, will be available before the end of the year.

I hope you'll join me and continue the journey.

About the Author

Val started researching her family tree back in 2008. At that time, she had no idea what she would find or where it would lead. By 2010, she had discovered a story so compelling, she was inspired to turn it into a novel. Initially writing for herself, the story grew beyond anything she ever imagined and she is now in the process of publishing The *Ambition & Destiny* Series.

Prior to writing, Val trained as a scientist and has worked for the pharmaceutical industry for many years. In 2012, she set up her own consultancy business, and currently splits her time between business and writing.

Born and raised in Liverpool (UK), Val now lives in Cheshire with her husband, youngest daughter and a cat. In addition to family history, her interests include rock music and Liverpool Football Club.

For further information about The *Ambition & Destiny* Series, Victorian History or Val's experiences as she wrote the book, visit her website at: vlmcbeath.com

Follow Me at:
Website: https://valmcbeath.com

Twitter: https://twitter.com/valmcbeath

Facebook: https://www.facebook.com/VLMcBeath

Pinterest: https://uk.pinterest.com/valmcbeath

Amazon: https://www.amazon.com/
VL-McBeath/e/B01N2TJWEX/

BookBub: https://www.bookbub.com/
authors/vl-mcbeath

Goodreads: https://www.goodreads.com/
author/show/16104358.V_L_McBeath